Souvenirs

ERIN SPINETO

SEA PEPTIDE PUBLISHING

To Tony.
For enduring one of the worst first dates on record. And for not cutting bait right there.

CONTENT NOTES

This book is light and beachy. But just like in life, we all have stuff we've been through. Emerson and Finn are no different. And when we finally learn what they've been through, everything else makes much more sense.

But just like it's a good idea to check out the warning flags lifeguards throw up on the beach before you end up being sucked out into huge surf at Waimea, I've put up a few flags below to guide you.

If you're a just-jump-in-and-see kind of person, then skip the flags. They will spoil the thrill of finding out at exactly the right moment in the story and they give away a lot.

If you want to know if you might stumble into the deep end when you were looking for a lounge chair in the shallows, then read on.

BEACH HAZARD FLAGS
There is no cheating in this story. I promise. Just trust me.

This book does contain some scenes that discuss an ectopic pregnancy. It is only discussed in Chapters 24 and 36 as an event that occurs before the start of the story's timeline. In Chapter 24, Finn recounts the story to the reader. In Chapter 36, Finn tells the story to Em.

If you are sensitive to this topic and aren't ready to be exposed to it, you may want to skip Chapters 24 and 36 or skip this book entirely until you are ready to deal with this difficult topic.

This story also mentions the untimely death of a spouse, a side character, in the gap between the two timelines. Em recounts the story to Finn in Chapter 21 and to the reader in Chapter 23.

If you are sensitive to this topic and aren't ready to be exposed to it, you may want to skip Chapters 21 and 23 or skip this book entirely until you are ready to deal with this difficult topic.

An undiagnosed thyroid condition shows up in multiple chapters along with the wacky symptoms of this disease. In a way, it is a first-hand account, as I have been through it myself.

Chapter 1

EMERSON
PRESENT DAY

*J*ust because you begin the next season of life, does not guarantee life won't turn around and taunt you with echoes from a bygone fall.

When my friend, Indigo, invited me on her spur-of-the-moment trip to visit Charlie in Maui, I thought it would be the perfect kickstart to this new season. Two years is long enough to spend in winter. It's time for spring and there's no better place to coerce spring's appearance than Maui.

As this spring rolls around, I will focus on strengthening my weaknesses just like Tim taught me. Build community and friendships which I never had time to do after dropping out of Stanford and getting swept up in Tim. I let way too many friendships languish, and it's about time I start investing in them again.

After all, when your world goes to hell, your friends are the ones who will pick you up and bring you back to life and if you haven't invested in those relationships, there won't be anyone there to help you recover.

Back in college, I used to dream of leaving it all behind and running away to Maui. I can't believe people have actually done that. They live here, in this summery wonderland, and never have to leave.

Indigo and I turn off the road and pull into a long gravel driveway lined with baby palm trees on each side. Those are new. I was here last year when we filmed Indigo's short film, *Promises*, but it looks like they have made plenty of improvements. When we make it to the end of the driveway, Charlie nearly sprints out of the main house to meet us.

"Indigo! Emerson!" She waves furiously at us as she approaches from the house. It's a two-story, aqua, plantation-style home. Huge windows, large overhangs, and an enormous porch wrapping around the whole thing.

Indigo and I hop out of the car and in what has become our typical greeting, Charlie lifts her *Pinky and the Brain* t-shirt to show off the Expression Med patch surrounding her Dexcom Continuous Glucose Monitor. It's a giant gecko.

I lower the edge of my skirt to reveal mine on the upper part of my bum. I chose a sunset behind palm trees just for this trip, trying to use anything I can to force myself into a sunny mood.

"Ooh. I love that one. Perfect for today," she squeals. Charlie was never a squealer back home, but I think the Maui joy has sunk deep into her bones and has to come out somewhere. She wraps me in a fierce hug. "Now, grab your bags, and let me show you to your palace."

I shoulder my blue backpack stuffed with bikinis and shorts and my way bigger gear bag packed with diabetes supplies as I follow Charlie and Indigo through the orchard to the cutest little aqua shack that resembles a mini-sized version of the main house.

It has a raised wrap-around porch that looks like it might eventually get a railing, but for now is a perfect sunbathing platform. I hope we will have time to lounge out there in the next two weeks.

Although we spent a whirlwind three days here a while back, I never got to see inside the Ohana. It's in the middle of a remodel, with exposed pipes and interior walls down to the studs, but you can see how amazing it will be once it's finished. With a kitchen in the back that is open to the sleeping quarters, a bathroom tucked into another corner that thankfully has walls—well, if you consider sheets nailed to the studs walls—and an entire back wall of windows looking out over the slope of the property that runs towards to the sea, it is going to be the perfect vacation villa.

It has everything a person could need to stay here forever. Much more than the tent I was willing to live in just to be here as a kid.

Greyson, Charlie's husband, pops his head in the front door. "Hey, ladies. Glad you're here. I'm gonna hit the store for Game Night refreshments. You want anything?"

"Do you guys take anything special in your coffee?" Charlie asks.

"Grass-fed butter if you have it," Indigo says. "And maybe a bit of vanilla extract?"

Charlie's grossed-out face matches mine as we both say, "Butter in your coffee?"

"So good. And seriously good for you." Indigo has been experimenting with some weird combos for nutrition, but I can't fault her. I have been embarking on my own journey of food as medicine over the last few years.

"Butter, check." Greyson says. "And, Charlie, is that vanilla extract science experiment of yours just about done?"

"Yeah, it should be just about ready." Charlie looks to Indigo. "I'll decant some into a jar and throw it in the cupboard."

"I'll be back soon, Babe." He gives Charlie a quick kiss before disappearing.

"You make your own vanilla extract?" I practically yell. I have been meaning to try that one for a while but haven't found the motivation to actually do it. "I'd love to see how it turned out."

"You'll be the first to try it." She swings open the fridge door. "I stocked the fridge with little snacks and drinks and, of course, sugars, but you're more than welcome to use the main kitchen. We'll probably do some family-style meals in there this week."

"You are so sweet. Thanks, Charlie," I say.

"You care which bed I take?" Indigo asks after she dumps her bags on the one closest to the wall of windows.

"I'm good wherever."

"So, do you guys want to get settled in and freshen up before Game Night or we could hit the ocean?" Charlie asks.

"Game Night?" Indigo and I both ask at the same time.

Charlie plops on my bed as I drop my backpack next to it and join her. "It's kind of a tradition around here. I don't know how long they've all been doing it, but every Friday we all get together and play a game. I know it sounds sort of kooky, but it's so cool to have everyone together every single week. It's getting harder and harder to find time to see friends now that we're full-grown adults. With everyone's weird work schedule and real-life responsibilities, it's hard not to drift apart."

I know all too well how easy it is to lose touch with once inseparable friends. I don't care how lame their games are, I want in. "So, are we playing like Chutes and Ladders and hopscotch?"

"Nooo," Charlie practically sings. "Billie's our Game Master and she concocts the craziest games ever. She combines games we've played before but adds a whole new layer to make them really fun and, honestly, amazing at making all of us open up. I had to play Game Master for a couple of months when she was gone and I sucked compared to her. She is a Game Wizard."

"What's the game for tonight?" Indigo asks.

"Who knows? She never tells us ahead of time, except to request certain food and decoration supplies that go along with the theme. Greyson and I have so much fun trying to guess the game from the supply list. I don't think we've gotten it right once."

"I'm in," I say.

"Me too," Indigo says.

"We've got a little over an hour? Thoughts?" Charlie asks again.

"No better way to freshen up than a little salt water." I hope they agree.

"We should do it. I could barely keep Sonny from jumping out of the car when she saw the ocean on our drive up. I think she is in some serious need of getting in the water."

After a quick dip in an ocean that has no business being that warm and a brief rinse in the outdoor shower on the backside of the garage, I slip into a loose skirt and tank top, loving that there's no need to bring a sweater, even though it's only March.

I make my way along the path through what I can only call an orchard, stopping to try to identify all of the fruit growing. There are golden oranges on my left, gigantic mangoes and fragrant guava to my right, and neon yellow lemons and deep green limes throughout. I'm stumped by some weird yellow fruit that looks like a bunch of pointy fingers reaching up from the stem. I'll have to ask about that one later.

By the time my fruit inspection is concluded, the fire pit is blazing and people have already taken seats around it. Behind them, a folding table is set up with potato chips in plastic neon green bowls, solo cups in bright yellow, and Nerds and Jolly Ranchers in a bowl labeled Sugars. Stickers in yellow gingham that say, "Ugh, As If" and others that say in blue sparkly script, "Rollin' with the Homies" are scattered about the table in front of a pink cassette player that is blaring Nirvana. I'm getting the feeling that this might be a 90s kind of thing.

I join Charlie next to the fire who introduces me around. Billie, our Game Master, is dressed in a crop top that hangs off her shoulder and short jean shorts with a flannel tied around her waist. I guess she even dresses for the theme.

Ryder, her boyfriend, is wearing the hell out of a pair of four-color neon banded Quiksilver trunks and a tight-fitting black shirt. Amazing what love will make you do.

Charlie checks her watch. "One last bathroom break. I don't want to miss a thing."

"Billie, this place looks amazing. Any hints to tonight's game?" I ask.

"I hope you're okay with getting personal. I probably should have picked a less revealing game with new people, but there's no better way to get to know someone than to jump right in. But, no hints until it's time to start. Wouldn't want anyone to have time to figure out how to get out of the game if it's too revealing." Sounds like she has a particular someone in mind.

Ryder laughs. "He would, too. Anything to avoid feelings."

"Who's that?" I ask, feeling a bit out of the loop.

A deep voice distracts them before they have a chance to answer. "The party's here. Can we get this thing started?"

"Sonny, this is JJ who thinks he's the life of the party, I guess," Charlie says.

"You get to come sit right next to me," he says playfully as he takes my hand and leads us to the low wooden chairs surrounding the fire pit.

"Guess it's time to start, guys," Billie calls out and people fill in the remaining chairs.

Ryder takes the chair next to Billie, with Charlie and Greyson on the other side of them.

By the time the sunlight wanes, we are well into our game for the night. I look around the fire as I take the last sip of my drink. I have only been here in this new place for a few hours and already I'm awash in community, surrounded by people who are embracing life, moving toward their goals, and enjoying every minute of it.

I, on the other hand, have spent the last two years stuck. Stuck in the past. Stuck in my own anguish. Stuck in a permanent state of dormancy.

But that stops here.

New season, new me. Or maybe I'm finally getting back to the old me—the free-spirited, daydreaming, lighthearted me. The old flower bulbs that have been tucked underground to survive the winter are now ready to burst forth again for a new spring of neon color, vibrant beauty, and unrestrained joy.

It's hard to contain the triumph that surges from that decision, so I use the momentum to go get another beer from the fridge inside. "Anyone else need another?" I ask, holding up my empty bottle.

JJ twists his bottle toward me. "IPNA, please," he says emphasizing the N. "It looks so much like the regular IPA. But it's nothing like it."

"Got it. One IPA coming up."

"IPNA," he says, all stressed.

I just laugh. That was too easy.

I bound up the steps to the main house, rounding the corner

toward the fridge. Tugging the heavy stainless steel door open, I'm greeted by a fridge that is clearly divided into sections for different people. The top shelf is a jumble of plastic produce bags filled with veggies at various stages of decay, a few take-out containers, and an uncovered bowl of what must be week-old mac-and-cheese. It must be JJ's, the few IPNA bottles in a half-empty cardboard carrier a dead giveaway.

The middle shelf is a stack of color-coordinated containers that hold what looks to be a week's worth of prepped meals. Maybe Charlie and Grey's shelf. With her whole making-her-own-vanilla-extract kick, I think she may be into making things from scratch.

The bottom shelf has a few packages of steak on the left, chicken lined up in the middle, and beer on the right. I think the beer's up for grabs, so I pluck one from the bottom shelf for myself and one of JJ's precious IPNAs from the top shelf.

I spin to return to the party and jump a little at the man who somehow snuck up on me. He stands between the counters and kitchen island, leaving no room for retreat. His massive shoulders fill the entire space.

I try to look for another way out as if I could just turn and run to avoid the intensity of this moment.

He remains silent, his thick chocolate hair gleaming in the light. The imposing way he stands there tells me he is the owner of this place, the King of this particular Jungle, the mysterious owner of the bottom shelf of meat and beer.

I wait for him to break this wordless standoff, to introduce himself or to yell at me to get out of his fridge. He does neither, only lifts his hand to scratch his grizzled beard like he's struggling to find words, too.

And under that thick, well-cut beard, it feels familiar. Like I might have known him in a previous life. He actually looks a little like Fi—

My right hand relaxes just enough for the bottle to start slipping.

It's Finn.

My Finn.

The bottle slides a little further.

Finnegan Ruth MacGregor. With the blue-green eyes. With the infectious smile. With the piece of my heart that he smashed to bits and kept as a souvenir.

He seems to smile at the fact that I recognize him.

My hand wilts a little more, and the bottle fully lurches out of it.

Instinctively, I try to catch it with my left hand, forgetting that it, too, has a bottle in it.

After an embarrassing display of clumsiness, I'm surrounded by hops and bubbles and a million tiny sharp shards of glass.

But I can't take my eyes off of Finnegan Ruth MacGregor, standing in the flesh in front of me.

Chapter 2

EMERSON
FIRST DAY OF FRESHMAN YEAR

The sketchy waiter slams two bottles and one tall glass of water on the grimy tabletop without a word. The two complete strangers that the administration at the University of California at San Diego thought would be my perfect roommates snatch their beers, clinking them before I even have a chance to lift my water.

In the tiny, wood-paneled bar in a town the girls called PB, a microphone and barstool sit empty on a corner stage. The crowd is a mix of students and beach bums who decided never to leave a good thing.

I mutter an unnecessarily quiet, "Cheers," and try to distract myself from the disconnect coming from my roommates by studying the backdrop for this next phase of my life. Not that a dingy college bar is my life, but rather it is the first encounter of four years of new experiences completely different than any I have ever been exposed to before.

After my delayed arrival at the graduate apartment, Claire and Morgan invited me out, but I'm sure they're already regretting that impulsive offer. I'm not the girl they were envisioning living with and I am nothing like Suzie, their BFF since sophomore year, who had to move home last minute.

You see, I missed the deadline to turn in my freshman housing application, not because I was irresponsible, but because it is a bit hard to predict when one might find an outgoing international post office in the jungles of Bali and even harder to know how long it would take to get from that small village back to the States.

I wasn't the usual kid who pushed hard their entire high school career, pursuing perfect grades and all the right sports and service projects and extracurriculars, and then went off to four years of college to do it all over again.

When I finished high school at sixteen, I postponed my admission to UCSD. Because I grew up surrounded by such a narrow experience of the world, I wanted to go experience the world in a way that would show me something different than the upper-class neighborhood ripe with parents making money hand over fist so they could push their kids to have an identical life in another upper-class neighborhood, repeating the cycle all over again.

I wanted to see the world that I read about in books. The aboriginal tribes of Papua New Guinea who killed missionaries and inspired their wives to go back and continue their work there. The favelas of Brazil that shaped the minds of future writers. The entire continent of Antarctica that inspired so many to race to the very bottom of the world.

So, I delayed my college admission and went on a year-long mission trip. After a quick training, we spent five months in the Australian Outback and five in Papua New Guinea. And, in an attempt to provide us with the space to process all that we had seen and to prepare for the transition back to the hectic, overpopulated life at home, we spent one month on the beaches of Bali.

Even God rested on the seventh day.

An unintended side-effect of that one decision put me in the only open campus housing available, the graduate apartments. Not the fresh start I was hoping for. For the first time in my life, I should have been on a level playing field with my peers. I'd get to live with kids who were starting out in a new town, at a new school, discovering everything for the first time. The best pizza place. The least crowded surf breaks. The professors to avoid if you don't want to be called out in front of a lecture hall of your peers.

Instead, I'm stuck with girls who have grown desensitized and bored with every new thrill. Girls who view me like I have always been seen, an under-aged interloper whose sole purpose is to ruin their good time.

My inability to engage with them or even pretend to be a normal college kid is only reinforcing that impression. Transitioning from a year in forsaken lands to this crowded bar has me gasping for air. The cacophony of chatter and bodies pressed in close proximity to get a good view of the stage are screaming at me to leave, but bailing on my designated driver responsibilities would be just one more thing driving a wedge between me and my roommates.

A scruffy guy hops on stage and lifts a guitar from the stand, sliding the strap over his broad shoulders. Claire and Morgan vanish into the throng now pulsating at the foot of the stage and I'm grateful for the space.

"Uhh, hi." He tugs the bill of his cap a little lower and grasps his guitar. "This is 'Change My Name.'" He adjusts the strap over his shoulder. "Yeah. Okay."

At the sound of the first measure of his acoustic guitar, my entire body relaxes. The tension in my back and shoulders that I hadn't noticed releases and I'm able to take my first full breath since I got back from my trip.

He layers on grainy vocals in a song that I've never heard but hits me like I have known it my whole life. It sounds like a combination of Tom Petty and Kurt Cobain if he grew up in Kentucky.

His voice brings me to a place in my mind I've never been before, filled with a stillness that has me convinced I could sit here listening to him sing for the remainder of time and be perfectly content.

His songs are folksy and full of Americana and even though in spots they would sound amazing with a steel guitar or a fiddle backing him, they are simply perfection with only his voice and the soft strumming of his guitar.

After a defiantly free-wheeling song that lauds his desire to live a big, big life, he lays his guitar back on the stand and the void his silence leaves behind is palpable. He turns back to the audience and the thought that flashes across his face lights up a smile that has every girl instantly falling in love. He has that sort of charm; one look, one smile, and girls are forever lost.

He nods as if answering himself in an internal dialog I would pay anything to be privy to, then reaches for a faded blue, mid-depth guitar with a smattering of acoustic openings toward the fretboard. You can tell by the way he grasps the instrument that it holds special meaning to him.

He strums a chord and is a bit apologetic when he says, "Uhh, this is a bit of a Buffett cover."

I sure hope it is one of Buffett's more obscure songs. I'm not sure I could handle the disappointment of watching this guy belt out Margaritaville right now.

From the very first chord, I recognize the song—after all, the soundtrack to my childhood was every single Jimmy Buffet album ever produced—but it is nearly impossible to pin down which song it is.

Once he starts singing with his gruff, infinitely compassionate tone, I instantly recognize the lyrics to "Someday I Will" that I've heard a thousand times before. I used them to make sense of myself so many times while I was growing up.

The first time I heard the song, I was eight and in the midst of the first of many dark times drowned in what I would eventually come to christen as the Pit of Despair. All the pressure adults put on me to know exactly who I was and what I would do with the curse they called 'my gift' drove me crazy. I had enough of a mind to fully understand all the horrors of this world—famine, war, pain, separation—but didn't have the emotional maturity to deal with it. And I felt all the responsibility to rectify every wrong. After all, I had spent my entire childhood hearing how lucky I was and how I would grow up to do something remarkable with my mind.

When I heard Jimmy sing that I didn't have to have it all figured out, that I could just say, "Someday I will," all that pressure evaporated. I can remember feeling light for the first time in my young life.

Hearing the verses again for what feels like the first time pins down something I have been feeling for a while. After coming home from my mission trip, I had once again been feeling those same nebulous feelings. Hearing the lyrics this time, with the soothing melody and the man's voice craggy like whiskey in the morning, I once again found the words.

I was lost and floundering, but I didn't have to think it all through. Didn't have to know where to start, I would just say, Someday I Will. And all the stress of knowing what my life had to be, what major to declare, what career to pursue, and how to explain myself to people who had such different life paths, simply evaporated. Once again, I could live in the present.

***

The next morning, on the way to my first-ever college class, I'm still singing his version of "Someday I Will" in my head and out loud in the shower and the car.

Stepping out of the elevator on the third floor of the Freshman dorm building that I should be living in, I make my way down the dark hallway looking for room 315.

When I swing open the door, the musician from last night is the only thing I can see. He completely dominates the room, all cocky, with his legs up on the table.

I pause in the doorway, unable to convince myself to find a seat. And it shouldn't be hard. Every seat at the long conference table is empty except for the one he is leaning back on as a smile spreads across his face.

I can't sit here in the doorway forever. I can't leave; it's the first day of my first college class. So, I force myself to take the closest seat I find, which I now realize is directly across from him.

I stare out the window, trying not to act like a total freak while replaying his voice in my head like I've been doing on repeat for the last twelve hours.

His voice haunted my dreams all night and was my alarm in the morning. I even tried to play Jimmy's version of it to clear my mind, but it no longer held the same power. It was flat and uninspired.

The way this guy in front of me sang it with such passion and the freakin' joy that emanated from him when he'd sing the line, "So whatever thrills you, anything you love to do, Just say someday I will." There was no way a studio recording of a great storyteller with only average musical talent could ever hold a candle to this man's voice.

And now, I have to be in the same classroom with him four hours a week as he teaches Analytical Writing 101.

It's no wonder he's teaching my writing class. I could tell last night that he was a writer by the way he felt those lines. If I didn't know any better, I would have sworn he wrote "Someday I Will" himself.

I don't know how I'm going to be able to look at him and process what he's saying while he shares amazing things about literature and writing so I don't fail this class, when the only thing I want to do is study him while he sings.

When he catches me gazing at him, I have to say something, to explain why I'm staring other than I need to hear his voice again even if it's only to hear him teach.

So, I go with the only thing that could be construed as normal for the start of a class. "Do you have a sign-in sheet for us?"

He fiddles around in his bag looking for it and I realize I am well on my way to earning the first F of my life.

Chapter 3

FINN
PRESENT DAY

Stepping out of the shower after a crap day at work, I dig through my dresser looking for a shirt that could somehow pass for 90s style. Billie always asks us to dress for the theme of Game Night and if I can do it without having to think too much, I'll appease her.

Growing up on the beaches of North Carolina, my style has always been a bit of 90s beach style—Vans, bright trunks, and whatever t-shirt I could find—as long as you don't count my brief stint in Nashville. But even then, I didn't go full ten-gallon hat and boots.

I choose an old shirt with a pink Billabong logo and a pair of slip-on Vans and hope it does the trick.

Now, if I can get my hands on the leftover pizza I stashed away in the fridge, I might be able to muster up enough enthusiasm to avoid raining on everyone's Game Night vibe. As long as Grey or JJ didn't ignore the Sharpie marks all over the box proclaiming its contents as mine, I will be in heaven.

I round the kitchen island to see a great bum sticking out of the fridge. Charlie didn't say anything about her friend having such a nice body. Maybe I don't totally hate her for inviting friends to stay.

She stands and turns to me and I can feel her eyes study me

from my legs over my abs, up my chest, and I don't hate the heat that follows her glance.

When her eyes settle on my face, they shout that she recognizes me. What's even more shocking is that she's somehow able to smile about that realization. Not the usual reaction I get from people who knew me once.

It only takes me a split second to place her. She has a few more years on her and a heap more confidence radiating from that beautiful face.

Emerson Malone is smiling at me.

It's not the reunion I expect. Not the one I played out in my head a million different ways a million different times. It's not the one where she ignites in anger and beats me up. Or the one where she simply turns and walks away without ever saying a word.

She manages to smile. Like the memory of me is actually good.

My eyes are fixed on her face, a little older and somehow prettier until a crash draws my eyes away.

Shards of glass skitter across the floor and my only thought is to protect her bare feet from every single one.

Without a word, I lay my hands on her hips and lift her onto the counter, then walk to the broom closet. With the door open I take a deep breath, before returning to the instrument of my demise whose eyes have not left me since that flash of recognition appeared on her face.

I sweep the glass into the dustpan and stand, the smell of hops filling me with hope.

Em is here.

I dump the glass in the bin and return the broom to the closet, but I know in my shocked stupor, I missed some glass. There's no way I can risk her bare feet finding any of them.

I move her way, crossing my hands and taking hers in mine before spinning and draping her arms over my shoulders. I let go and run my hands under her legs. She lets out a tiny gasp when I hoist her up on my back.

I carry her outside, setting her down on the porch boards that are too rough for her delicate feet. When I spin to face her, she is still gazing at me just as unable as I am to find words that feel big enough to capture this moment.

"The beers," she mutters.

I run back in and nab two fresh bottles. I pop the tops on the bottle opener I nailed to the front post of the porch and hand them to her. I finally form words just about as inadequate as her first words to me after four years of silence, "Welcome to Maui."

Em ends our standoff, slipping off to join the others around the fire. My feet are plastered to the faded blue porch boards. Em, my little Em, is here. She's in my yard. With my friends.

For the last four years, I have been living in an Em-less world and it is only now that I realize I have been wandering this earth as a zombie. In four short years, I have forgotten what it is to be alive.

Drawn in by an irresistible force, I follow her to the yard and drop into an empty chair to take her in, firelight dancing across her face, making her eyes flint as the light passes in and out of them.

"You want to jump in for this round," I hear Greyson's deep voice as if it's underwater.

I can only nod, not willing to take my eyes off Em for a second lest she evaporate like a mist.

"It's First Time, Last Time," Charlie interrupts my marveling. "You remember how to play it?"

"Yeah. Yeah. Everyone tells their story about the first time or the last time they did whatever is on the card. Then we vote on the best one. Most points wins."

"Worst first day of work," Charlie calls out.

Em steals a quick glance my way and I try to school my face, to hide this feeling of wonder.

"Earth to Finn," I think it's Billie's voice, but I can't drag my eyes off Em to verify. "Worst first day of work?"

My whole world just exploded and they expect me to tell some random story? "I dunno. First day of working at Burger King."

I go back to studying Em.

"What happened?"

I draw my gaze from Em long enough to glower at Billie. "I was working at Burger King."

"Okay. What is going on here?" JJ asks, waving his hand between me and Em. "I'm getting a total Grey's Anatomy vibe."

"What the hell does that mean?" I snarl. Okay, maybe I'm not doing as good of a job schooling my emotions as I thought.

"You know. The chick bangs some Rando from the bar and the next day she starts her job and Rando is her new boss. The whole, I never thought I'd have to see you again after we did all sorts of tawdry stuff with our naked bodies. So, you two hook up in a past life?"

I look to Em, hoping she'll be able to explain. If I give them the real story it would be worse than admitting she's some past hook-up.

"We didn't hook up," Em goes with the obviously simple answer. It's not enough to appease the hungry faces before us.

"We knew each other?" I look to Em to see if that sounds right.

"We were friends in college." She sighs deeply before continuing. "And then we weren't," she declares.

"Friends with benefits?" Indigo asks, refilling her glass with more red.

"No!" we both shout in unison.

"Best friends," I clarify.

Em flinches at the word like it pricks the old scab of pain.

Charlie, always the expert at pulling conversations out of an awkward tailspin, reads the next card. "Last time you left the country."

After a few more rounds, my head slowly rights itself from this horrendous tailspin enough for me to attempt to play.

Indigo draws another card. "Last time you cried at a movie."

At the sound of this Em smiles and lowers her head. Looks like she's got a good one.

Her smile draws one from me, the muscles feeling like they haven't had to work in this manner in years.

While Greyson launches into his story, Em gives him her complete attention, allowing me another look her way. She's the same Em I remember, long straight blond hair halfway down her back, rocking a tank top and a loose skirt, but she's different somehow. More relaxed, maybe. More comfortable with herself.

"You're up, Finn," Gamemaster Charlie declares.

"Three years back. I saw *Walk Hard*. It got me." It's enough to move on to the next person, everyone so accustomed to my complete lack of ability to open up at these Game Nights.

"Em? You got something more than a two-word answer?"

"This is really embarrassing, but it was September, four years ago, I think. I was on a first date with this guy and we were going to see some romcom, but it had sold out. And the only other thing that was playing was a revival of Titanic." Charlie shakes her head at the embarrassment of it all.

"Ooooh, when Jack lets go of Rose's hand. That was just..." Indigo starts.

"Perfect," Charlie finishes.

"I have no idea. We didn't make it that far," Em says.

I expect that's the end of her story. Em has always held her emotions close to the vest. But she takes a long deep breath and as her cheeks wash over with pink, to my amazement, she continues.

"They hit the iceberg and everyone is panicking that the boat's going down. They don't have enough life rafts. They're loading women and children into the boats. One guy has to rip this four-year-old out of his dad's hands and shove him into a raft."

She stares into the fire for a moment drawing strength from the jumping flames.

"And the band, you know, the band is still playing. Their hands are glued to their instruments as their eyes dart around at the total chaos erupting around them, but it's like they have no idea what to do so they just keep playing because it makes them feel like they are somehow taking action. Doing something, you know?"

I look around the fire. She has every last one of them enraptured, hanging on every word. They all look like I must have looked this whole night, hungry to be in the presence of this woman as she shares who she is.

"And the camera slowly pushes in on the guitar player, his eyes start to slow, and you can tell he's moving from taking in all the outside world to the stream of his thoughts growing louder and louder. And then his eyes stop, and he grasps the neck of his guitar with his left hand and lowers it to the deck as his right hand slips down to..." she fades off, her eyes growing glossy as her right hand moves to her hip.

This is not the Em I once knew. My Em, who sliced her foot wide open, the fin of her surfboard coming all the way through the other side of her foot, without shedding one tear, who took a serious medical diagnosis like it was nothing. She would never show emotion and here she is getting teary-eyed at the *memory* of a time she cried.

How does that happen? How could she have changed so much in so little time? Or was she always this way, and somehow I didn't know it? I didn't know her.

"He...," she tries again, the power of the memory too heavy to lift.

"Draws his weapon?" I say, trying to help.

She shakes her head. "And he.."

She jerks her hand up in the shape of a gun, but a few inches up and she can't lift it anymore. She, instead, lifts her fist up to cover her mouth, the first tear threatening to drop.

"Finishes things." I do the heavy lifting.

"And I lose it. This is not some pretty girl crying where one tear drops and she cutely wipes it away with her ring finger and then does the wave thing."

She lifts her hand, waving her fingers up and down in an attempt to dry the imaginary tears of a pretty cryer.

Indigo and Charlie join in the mocking, wiping their fingers under their eyes and waving both hands wildly in front of their faces.

"This isn't even an ugly cry. This is an all-out forget where you are, unstoppable, Niagara Falls type of crying."

"Really? All from that?" JJ teases.

"I think it ripped open a wound that hadn't healed yet. That guy. With his guitar. And the look of despair. It felt like I was getting to see something on screen that I maybe missed in real life," she looks to me for confirmation.

I drop my eyes to the fire, still wearing the mask that I've smoothed void of all the guilt and longing churning beneath.

"In that moment, I think I finally let myself grieve for it," she finishes.

That guy.

His guitar.

I wore that look of despair for a good long time after she left four years ago. Still do most of the time.

I never, not even for a second, suspected that she was grieving, too.

"We have to leave the theater, I'm bawling so bad. So this guy helps me up and honestly, I have no idea where I'm going or what's happening, until the crying process finally begins to reverse itself."

Em takes a long draw from her beer.

"I feel like a total idiot, losing it like this on a first date. He must have thought I was a total lunatic and, clearly, I was not hot enough to warrant putting up with that kind of crazy."

She is and always was hot enough to make up for any kind of crazy.

"He didn't cut bait and run right there?" Greyson asks.

"Nope. The date lasted another two days. I recover well." She smiles at herself. "When I finally open my eyes, we're in his car in front of the water at Scripps Pier. He's sitting silently next to me, his hand on my back. So, I wipe my eyes," she draws the back of her hand across her eyes, "and he turns to me, leaning down to look me in the eye, and he says, "If ever you're ready to share that story, I'd love to hear it.""

And, now, all three girls are getting misty-eyed. Greyson rubs Charlie's knee, reassuring her.

And I just feel, I don't know... angry? Like I want to beat the crap out of someone, but I don't know who. Maybe the director of Titanic for producing the garbage that made her cry like that. Or that guy for some reason I can't quite nail down.

Or, maybe I want to beat the crap out of myself for not being there. Four years ago would have been just two months after I let her go to Stanford.

Alone.

I should have been there for her, to be the one who sat by

her when she cried. If she ever gives me the chance to be in her life again, there's no way I'll ever let a single tear fall without being there.

"So what happened to the guy? You get a second date?" Ryder asks.

"I married the guy," she says with a huge grin.

I see people's mouths move as they talk, but my ears have stopped allowing sound in. Like they went on strike the moment they had to endure hearing that word come out of Em's mouth.

Married.

I scratch the side of my beard, twisting at the edges of my mustache.

Em is married.

I uncross my left leg and lean forward, my elbows on my knees.

My Em. Married.

I lean back again. Lift my right leg onto my left knee.

How?

I cover my mouth with my hand letting my fingers scratch the side of my beard up and down.

"Finn. Earth to Finn," JJ shakes the blue arm of my beach chair. "What's your vote?"

I look up to find five pairs of eyes staring at me from the mini whiteboards that came with the game. They all have "Sonny" written on them.

"Sonny?" I ask.

Who the hell is Sonny? And why are we writing his name on whiteboards?

No one answers me. They only lower their boards and wipe them off.

"So, I have Ryder with eight, Billie with twelve, JJ nine, Indigo fourteen, Sonny with nineteen, Grey six, I have four, and Finn with zero," Charlie shares.

I look around the fire counting off people as I go.

Greyson, Ryder, JJ, Indigo, Billie, Charlie, me. What about Em? Sonny? Em is Sonny?

Apparently, she *did* change that much in four short years. She changed so much that I don't even know her name anymore.

I let us get so far apart that I didn't know she got married. I didn't know she become a woman who is so sure of herself, so comfortable, that she can share a deeply personal and profoundly sad story with total strangers without any sense of unease.

I let my total inability to express myself deprive me of four years with this woman.

And she shared those years, and she'll share all the years she has left, with another guy.

Chapter 4

FINN
SEPTEMBER, FRESHMAN YEAR

I'm sitting at the table in my Freshman writing class a good ten minutes early, leaning back in my wooden chair, legs up on the table.

I'm feeling pretty cocky at finally getting myself to where I always knew I should be, when in comes the most beautiful woman I have ever laid eyes on. She's dressed in a cut-off jean skirt hanging low on her hips, with a flowing white tank top not long enough to cover her tight midriff.

I sit up in my chair, causing the front legs to come crashing back to the ground, catching my legs up on the table.

I settle my feet on the ground, trying to recover smoothly. I rub the back of my neck while I lean back in my chair, fully in charge of my swagger once again.

She stands with the light from the wall of windows behind me lighting up the smattering of freckles brushed across her round nose and pink cheeks, pausing in the doorway like she knows I need more time to soak in this angel in front of me.

She sits down awkwardly and pulls out her notebook with a picture of the whole cartoon gang from the 80s T&C shirts emblazoned on the front cover and one lime green and one turquoise pen. She pretends to look out the wall of windows behind me, but I catch her stealing a few glances my way.

Finally, after five minutes of awkward silence during which I'm desperately trying to come up with something clever to say, she asks me, "So, do you have like a sign-in sheet or something?"

And I realize she thinks I'm the professor.

I don't want to embarrass her and I figure I can use it to my advantage, so I say, "Yeah. Thanks for reminding me. Now, where did I put that sign-in sheet?"

I fumble through my bag. "Damn. I think I left it in my office. I must have gotten caught up in my lesson planning and research. I'll just have to make one now."

I rip out a sheet of notebook paper and draw three columns on it. At the top of each, I write, Name, Phone Number, and Signature, and slide it her way with a pen on top.

She pushes aside my plain blue pen and, with her own bright lime green one, she writes her name, Emerson Malone, her pen pausing briefly when she gets to the phone number column. I think I've been made, but she shrugs and fills it out, signs it, and slides the paper back to me.

I check out her number. "562 area code. Where's that from?"

"Seal Beach." She eyes me suspiciously.

"No way. I spent a couple of summers there in middle school," I say, grateful to have found a connection.

"Then, why don't you know the area code?" She laughs at my poor attempts to connect.

Wow. This woman is questioning her professor, or the man she thinks is her professor, a mere five minutes after meeting him. I'm in for a wild ride this semester.

"I never paid much attention I guess. My phone remembers all that stuff for me."

"Prove it," she says lifting her head defiantly. She has her B.S. meter on high alert.

"What?" I ask, stalling for more time.

She leans her elbows on the table, quite satisfied that she has caught me in a lie. "Prove that you lived in Seal." Her long blond hair falls forward over her shoulder as she leans even farther toward me like she's hungry to be proven wrong about me.

I'm happy to comply. "How am I supposed to do that?" I need to know the rules of the game before I win it.

"You lived there, you figure it out." She gathers her hair from in front of both shoulders and twirls it around her finger, laying the spun gold over her left shoulder.

I pretend to be thinking deeply to buy me time to take a closer look at her. Her skin is glowing bronze, not only across her beautiful face but across her chest and bare shoulders. She has a joy and energy that can be felt instantly and it looks like they can be stoked by a good battle of wits. It's gonna take my absolute best effort to impress this woman.

"On a good north-west swell, the north side of the pier will actually have a semi-decent wave as it bounces off the break wall next to the pier." I scrub my hand through my thick brown hair, knowing it will get mussed in a way that all the girls tend to love. "Nick's has the best breakfast burritos in town."

She tries to stifle her smile, but I can see it growing by the minute.

I throw in one last comment to cement my name in the winners column of this game. "And halfway down the pier is the only place in Southern California that you can watch the sunset over land since Seal Beach technically points to the south, and after a full day of the Santa Ana winds blowing the pollution from LA out to sea, the sight is one to nearly bring a man to tears."

She's hypnotized. I definitely earned points on that one. And right when I think I see the hearts begin to form in her eyes, the professor walks in and slams his briefcase on the table, muttering, "Damned freshmen can never find this classroom. It's on the third floor of their dorms for Pete's sake. How hard could it be?"

Her eyes flit to me and I can see the expletives streaming through her head. All I can do is offer an innocent shrug.

I spend the rest of class trying to impress her with my deep answers, quoting Decante and Locke. But every answer I give, she questions and then eviscerates.

The professor catches me zoned out thinking about what it might take to convince this woman that I'm the man for her and asks, "Do you agree with Jim's assessment of the accuracy of the portrayal of women in the film?"

Damn. It really would have helped if I heard any of Jim's comments over the thrumming of my heart. "I think that..."

Em props her chin up with the back of her hand giving me her full attention, which totally scrambles my brain.

"...for us to, like, think we know what women in the fifties wanted or needed is impossible. It's like..."

She smiles and I lose all ability to think, to remember the name of a scientist I studied for two solid years.

"...the scientist who said that thing about the cat and the box and you will never know until you open the box. You know the one I'm talking about."

I look around at a roomful of kids who don't have the slightest clue who I'm talking about and a flirtatious Em who is trying to hide her haughty grin because she has already laid out her plan to complete the academic castration she has been performing on me for the better part of an hour.

She barely waits a second after I finish to start in.

"You expect me to believe that people are so incredibly different a mere seventy years ago, that it's impossible for you to speculate that a woman might feel trapped or undervalued by a society that thought her greatest and only contribution could be to raise a little man who could grow up to do the real work for society?"

I don't dare open my mouth again for the remainder of the hour, which is fine by me. I'd rather sit and listen to the insight this woman displays any day of the week.

The moment class ends, before she even walks out the door, I text her.

FINN:

> **You want to continue your evisceration of my literary theories over a meal? How about lunch in the caf?**

I have to have more of this girl, even if all she does is destroy any sense of pride I have left.

She just stares at her screen. I give her a few minutes to make a decision before I realize she has no idea who texted her.

FINN:

This is Finn.

FINN:

From class.

Her head spins around to find me. And her gaze lights up parts of me that shouldn't be up in a classroom. I lift my brows hoping for a response.

She texts back.

EM:

If you can name the theorist that you tried so hard to quote as you fumbled through your 'you'll never know until you open the box' defense of the 50s view on women in Rebel Without a Cause, I'd consider it. But since I'm one of the few girls around here who actually consumes calories on a regular basis, I really can't wait for you to figure it out.

And she leaves.

I hate to admit, I follow her out, not wanting to miss a second of being in her brilliant presence. I hang back as she walks up to her beat-up, silver Honda Civic. I watch her retrieve a surfboard from the front seat, strap it to her roof rack, and take off.

I show up to class the next week early, hoping for another private sparring match, but Em shows up five minutes late, hair still dripping saltwater. She takes a seat toward the back of the table, pulls out a sandwich, and opens a diet Dr Pepper.

The teacher gives her an approving nod like they have some sort of secret agreement. Another kid tries to bring out a bag of chips and he shoots that kid a glare that I'm sure he will cry to mommy about during their nightly phone calls.

Halfway through class, after thirty minutes of silence from her, she finally looks up from her sandwich and starts in on a diatribe on music choices in 90s movies.

I take this opportunity to scribble on a piece of notebook paper and hold it up to her. Erwin Schrödinger.

She continues her explanation, not missing a beat. If anything, she starts arguing her point more forcibly and directs it more toward me.

I lower my message and write under it, The Campus Pour, and hold it up again.

She scrunches her face in confusion but finishes her speech without a hitch.

When she's done with her argument, I add "8 p.m. tonight?" and flash the question her way.

She laughs, then looks at her paper and bounces her pen up and down in her hand like she's considering my offer. Then she grins and swiftly writes on her pale blue paper before holding it up for me.

"Idk. Is the cat alive?"

I guess I'll have to show up to find out.

When we get to The Campus Pour, our banter is just as strong, the tension just as palpable. Until our waitress comes to take our order.

"Can I get a pulled pork sandwich, and, what kind of beer do you have on tap?" I'm going to need something to slow down my heart. It hasn't stopped racing since I saw her cryptic reply to my invite earlier today.

The waitress lists off their beers.

"How about a Stone?"

"Sure. Can I see some ID?" I take out my wallet and hand her my license.

"Great." She hands it back. "And for you, miss."

"Could I get the Hawaiian Chicken Sandwich and fries, please?" Em asks.

"And a beer for you, too?"

"Just a diet Dr Pepper for me. Thanks." She shoots the waitress a grateful smile..

"You didn't want a drink? Is that because you're afraid I'll take advantage of you if you drink? Because, I promise," I hold up my cub scout salute, "I'll be a total gentleman."

"It's not that." She lowers her head. "I don't have a fake ID," she says, pointing to my ID.

I laugh. "Mine's not fake."

Once again, that BS meter of hers is on high alert. "Let me see."

I hand over my license.

She runs her fingers over the words like she's treasuring a photo of her long-lost soldier boy.

"Finnegan Ruth MacGregor." She looks from the license to me. "Ruth? Really? What kind of hell did you get for that in middle school?"

"None. I never let anyone know."

I haven't told anyone since middle school, either. All of my friends believe my parents were too poor to afford the lettering on my birth certificate so they never gave me a middle name. I'm not sure why it isn't bothering me that a girl I barely know now has that ammo against me, but I don't foresee hating the torture she intends to inflict upon me with it anyway.

"Smart kid." She looks back to the license. "And your birthday is?" She's still not convinced it's real.

"One. Twenty-three," I count off without hesitation.

She suddenly looks very intimidated. "Why are you in a freshman class if you're twenty-one?"

"You don't have to be eighteen to be a freshman, babe." I should know. Not only was I a late-start kid, but was unfairly held back in third grade. I was way too energetic to sit still for eight hours a day and had parents who didn't believe in medicating their kid. Add to that my one-year stint foolishly trying to make it big in Nashville and you have a freshman who can legally drink.

She mutters under her breath, "Tell me about it."

Just as I suspected, she is older than all of those troglodytes that have been vying for her attention in class just as much as I have been. "So, you're 20?"

She laughs. "Not quite."

"Nineteen?"

"Nope."

She smiles because once again I'm playing catch up to her.

I start running through the other possibilities.

She's under 21.

Not 20...

Or 19...

Or 18...

Crap.

My face drops.

I'm out on a date with a seventeen-year-old.

SEVENTEEN!

I scrub my hand across my face. Completely reckless.

There's no way this girl, who could run circles around every freshman in that class and probably half the professors on that campus could only be seventeen. She has so much wisdom. So much empathy for people who have nothing. So many firsthand accounts of kids in slums.

When did she have the time to acquire all of that in seventeen short years? And what the hell have I been wasting my time with during my twenty-one years on this earth?

Oh, yeah. That's right. I thought the best use of my time was partying and playing music. This little girl has been running laps around my sorry carcass.

After my fear of the cops coming to drag me away for planning a date with a minor has subsided, and I shelve all of my lascivious thoughts far, far away, never to be seen again, we have a great time discussing literature and science and, my favorite, music.

"So, since you know so much about music theory before you've even set foot in your music theory classes, who is your favorite musician?" she asks as she twirls her hair around her hand and lays it over her shoulder. I'm quickly realizing it's one of her nervous habits.

After hearing her go on and on in class about writers and

philosophers I hadn't even heard about, let alone read, I'm going to have to try really hard to impress this kid.

"Probably Johann Sebastian Bach. Western tonal harmony would not exist in its current form if it weren't for him."

"Huh."

After I put my absolute best into a well-thought-out and highbrow argument, I get only a 'huh'? "Then, who's your favorite musician?" I wait for her to school me once again.

"You know 'The Brandenburg Concertos' were pretty decent, but my favorite, without hesitation, is Jimmy Buffett."

Jimmy Buffett.

Jimmy Buffett?

After all her intellectual talk, deep down she was just a Parrot Head.

"Jimmy Buffett? Jimmy, four chords and a whole lot of liquor, Buffett. Really? 'Why Don't We Get Drunk and Screw' outweighs Bach's 'Concerto for Two Violins in D Minor'?"

"You didn't ask who I thought the most influential musician was or the most talented or even the most original. You said favorite. And for my money, 'Death of an Unpopular Poet' or 'Souvenirs' or 'California Promises' really can't be beat." She raises her soda to take a winning sip.

"'Souvenirs'? Did Buffett even sing that?" I challenge.

"It was a cover, but he recorded it on his *Cafe Margaritaville* album, so I'm gonna count it."

She knows her Buffett.

After closing down the place, I slowly walk her to her car, hoping to savor every last minute in this girl's presence. I start to hum the tune to 'California Promises', partly to tease her and partly to use the one thing I know impresses the ladies the most, my voice.

Instead of being dazzled by my talent, she performs the most beautiful and heartfelt version of the song that I've ever heard.

My gaze whips her way, barely able to keep up my humming. The dark sky hides most of her face from me, but her voice makes it seem like she feels every single word of it, like she wrote it or lived it herself.

I know she had me beat in most admirable life experiences, but when did she find the time to love and get her heart broken in a way that could let her sing like this?

When she gets to the chorus, I can't stop myself from jumping in and singing harmony with her. "I will never love another. Wait for me till I return."

A broad grin spreads across that cute little face of hers when she hears my voice join hers. "But she never will. He waits for her beside the water. Faithful still, to California promises."

From that moment on, Emerson Malone became my favorite musician.

Chapter 5

EMERSON
PRESENT DAY

*O*kay. That was not the reunion I was expecting.

I used to have this recurring dream. I'm at Lake Arrowhead in the mountains walking around the village up there. I pop into a curio shop, round a display of little glass animals, and run into Finn. We just stand there, staring at each other, smiling. We don't say a thing, just look at each other, and, in that moment, we know that everything is forgiven.

I wake up grinning, like everything is right in the world again.

I know it was just a pipe dream. It could never actually play out like that. But, after four years of trying to imagine what it would be like if I ever saw Finn again, I at least thought it would be... more. More angry or more happy or more hurt. More something.

That was just a big ol' pile of nothing. With the exception of him welcoming me to Maui, he didn't even talk to me. Didn't look at me. After thirty minutes of pretending to participate in Game Night, he simply got up and disappeared. He saw me and went about his business as if it didn't completely shatter him to see me.

Because it *didn't* shatter him.

But it shattered me.

And I guess that makes sense. I was always more invested in

our relationship—or, I guess, friendship as he demanded we call it—than he was. And it goes to show after all that time, it was no big deal for him to run into me.

Not wanting to sit with that thought too long, I push myself up from bed to lean against the wall behind me. "Indigo? You up?" I peer across the expansive room to find her floral-print bedspread already made up neatly.

Over the music of the birds, the distant sound of laughter drifts in the room. Looks like it's time to face reality. I slip on a swimsuit and a pair of loose shorts, and head for the door, before stopping short. I spin around and head back for my nightstand to fill up on the meds that keep me running.

I pop a thyroid pill and a few supplements for the fatigue, then shoot up with some long-acting insulin. I check my pump to make sure I have enough short-acting insulin to get through the day. I know it's a little unconventional to do it this way, using insulin shots and an insulin pump, but I'm so forgetful I have to have redundancies in my insulin plan.

Once I'm covered for the day, I make my way to the main house.

"One more try. Just one more. There's no way they're all the same," Indigo begs before closing her eyes.

JJ digs his hand into a box of Froot Loops and places a green one in her hand.

Indigo chews carefully like she's eating a fancy piece of chocolate. I know she doesn't eat junk food a lot, but there's no way she hasn't tasted Froot Loops before.

Finn has his back turned to me, fussing with something on the opposite counter giving me a few brief moments to take in his old wrinkled tee hanging loosely over his broad shoulders.

"Raspberry," Indigo exclaims, and everyone starts busting up.

I'm totally lost. "Looks like I'm late to the party," I say awkwardly.

Charlie turns to me, wiping tears from her eyes. "Sonny!"

Finn practically twitches at the sound of my name. So, maybe we've passed from indifference to slight irritation.

Charlie hands me a few pieces of cereal. "Did you know that all Froot Loops are the same flavor?"

"They are not!" Indigo practically yells.

"You haven't gotten one right, Indigo," Greyson says. "Give it up. They're all the same."

The toaster pops. Finn brings a plate of toast to the island, butters two pieces and slides them my way without a word, but with a smile that says it might be a peace offering.

"Thanks." I reach to pick up a piece and realize it's cinnamon bread. The kind with icing on the crust that you have to pick up fresh from a bakery.

My hand freezes just shy of the slice.

You won't cry. You can't cry. You have endured much worse.

But in this moment, it feels insurmountable.

Soon after meeting Finn, we had fallen into the habits and rituals that form with friends. He began watching the sunrise from the beach on Saturday mornings. On his way back, he would stop by Gino's Bakery to buy a loaf of fresh baked cinnamon bread and we would greet the morning with cinnamon toast and our choice of morning caffeine.

For four whole years, every weekend in my life began with cinnamon toast and Finn. Until they didn't.

I haven't been able to have cinnamon bread since.

But here he is, Saturday morning, laughing and talking and sharing our ritual with just anyone nearby. Which means one of two things.

One, our ritual, the one I thought was just for me and Finn, wasn't. He just did it for himself and it had nothing to do with me. I built up this time to be something that it wasn't, special and sweet and intimate. Instead, it was boring and pedestrian and meaningless.

Or even worse, maybe it was special, but it wasn't all that hard for Finn to go on doing it because my leaving didn't affect him at all. Because *I* didn't affect him at all.

Charlie dusts her hands off on her shorts. "We were thinking of driving over to Ryder's and getting in a little surf. You up for it, Sonny?"

"I can drive." Finn's offer stops everyone in their tracks.

JJ cups his ear and leans toward Finn. "Can you say that

again in my good ear? It sounded like you just said you'd come surf with us instead of working another twenty-five hour day."

"Shut up, JJ. Go grab whatever board you want from the board rack and throw it in the back of the truck. I'm gonna grab some trunks." And just like that, Finn disappears, but the stunned looks he leaves remain.

"Wow," Greyson exclaims. "Maybe I should go into the fire station because I think the apocalypse may have just started."

This draws laughs from everyone. I'm still clueless.

"Go get changed and I'll show you where the board rack is," Charlie says.

We drive between the two volcanic mountains that make up this island until a little sliver of deep blue appears ahead. When the road veers to the right, we're greeted with a view of the entire Pacific to the right and the other half of this amazing peanut-shaped island lounging in that vast sea to the left.

Indigo rolls down her window and hoots. Soon all the windows are down, hands flying in the wind like little surfboards riding the waves. We tuck in and out of shady tunnels made of trees covering the highway, until they give way to a sandy bay.

"That would be such a great place to swim," I mutter under my breath.

"You sound like Ryder and Billie," JJ says. "Those two are always scouting the best new places to swim. Maybe they'll take you out while you're here."

This, at least, draws a reaction from Finn, if you can count half-second eye contact through the rearview mirror as a reaction.

We meet Ryder and Billie a little further down the road in a dirt patch beside the crystal-clear water. I wouldn't have even known this place was surfable if it weren't for the two old-timers already out in the lineup.

It doesn't take long to get ready. No wetsuits, no leashes, no paying for parking. Just a handful of friends and longboards going out to waste some time drawing all the joy out of this day.

Two quick steps down the sand and I launch myself into the water, landing on my board, surrounded by the shallow turquoise water. It is only then that I realize, I haven't been on a board in nearly two years.

There was a time when I was shocked if I went two days without getting in the ocean. Times when I would go days without letting my hair fully dry. And now it has been over seven hundred days without even once thinking about going surfing.

"Over here, Sonny," Charlie instructs. "It gets too shallow over there."

I follow her out, avoiding the underwater coral landmines. Billie is up and riding a wave before I even make it out to the lineup. She may have retired from professional surfing years ago, but you'd never know it.

My arms are aching before I'm even halfway out. I am so dreadfully out of shape. I wonder if I'll even be able to take off. They say it's like riding a bike, but could you realistically get back on your bike and ride down a mountain if you haven't moved at all in the last two years?

Not that it's even that big out here today. Nothing but a couple of tiny rollers, but it still makes me question myself. And so goes another bullet point on my list of things to focus on this year. Get into shape. And that starts with a run tomorrow morning.

Billie splashes me as she paddles by, slowing enough to match my speed. "Make sure you fall flat out here. Not much water between you and the reef."

Great. So, I don't even know if I can stand up anymore and, if I fall, I'm gonna crash into the reef. If it weren't so gorgeous and warm out here, I might paddle back in. That, and I simply can't let any more days go by without actually surfing. Three more and it would make a full two years. No way I can let that happen.

I spot a small wave heading my way. I slide back on my board and eggbeater my legs to spin around. Laying down, I paddle as fast as my weak arms will carry me until I feel the wave pick up my board. I pop up like I have done a million times before and, thankfully, I don't look like a jellyfish on land.

I cross-step toward the nose to a chorus of shouts and howls from my friends, and every moment of my time spent on a board comes back to me. The feeling of gliding across the water, the wave barely breaking, is the ultimate freedom. The only thoughts in my head are of the here and now. The yellows and greens of the reef below me as I go whizzing by. The wind blows my hair off my shoulders. The sun's rays peek through the trees on shore as it rises into the sky. If I could only grab ahold of this peace and take it with me back on land.

When the wave peters out, I lay back down on my board and turn out to sea, knowing that all is right with the world again.

The lulls between sets seem to stretch out unto eternity. But, out here, they aren't just something to be endured. It's just one more amazing part of this experience.

When the next set shows up on the horizon, JJ cries, "Party wave."

We all spin around and paddle for the same wave. JJ and I nearly collide as I'm getting up. Charlie hops onto Billie's board. Ryder leaps onto JJ's. And soon we're figuring out just how many people can fit on one board before it turns over and spills us all out onto the reef.

On our paddle back out, a whole pod of spinner dolphins swim by just beyond the lineup. Indigo, leading the pack, paddles right past the lineup, close enough to see them, but giving the creatures plenty of space. Charlie, Billie, and I follow behind. I guess dolphins aren't as enchanting to the guys who stay inside catching more waves.

Soon, the dolphins are gone and we are left simply floating on our boards in the afternoon sunshine. Indigo rolls off her board into the water, nearly knocking Charlie over. She stays in the water, hanging her arms on her board and mine. Billie stands on her board and jumps into the water before connecting her board and Charlie's board to our little makeshift flotilla.

I lay down on my board, resting my chin on my folded hands. Finn is paddling back out from another wave. He catches me watching him and immediately drops his eyes to the water. That boy is allergic to looking at me.

I turn back to my girls. "Hey, why was everyone so shocked that Finn came today?"

"He's a workaholic." Charlie adjusts the top of her black and white checked bikini. "I swear, that boy is a vampire. Grey and I don't see him unless it's before dawn or after dark."

"Does he go into the studio all day? Or is he playing live every day?"

"He's in the office or at one of his properties. Even when he comes home, he's drawing up plans or ordering stuff. He doesn't know how to turn it off. The only time we get him to stop working is for Game Night."

Office? Properties? What the heck is he doing with his life? How is he not writing and playing and performing? I can't imagine Finn doing anything but music. "He's not a musician?"

"Musician? Finn? Can you imagine Finn as the center of attention? I think he'd burst into flames immediately," Charlie laughs.

"I would pay money to see that," Billie adds. "He'd get up to the mic and grunt. Then play a song while glaring at the audience."

"He does know his music, though. Remember the Jeopardy Game Night? He ran the whole music category before you even finished the clues."

"And did you hear him in the truck on the way over?" Charlie asks. "Jumping in with a history of that song and when it was made and who wrote it and produced it and played every instrument. That was wild."

"And he used actual whole sentences. Not just, Bell Bottom Blues. Dominoes."

"I think he used up his daily ten-word quota for the whole next month," Billie adds.

"What?" I ask.

"Finn's got a ten-word limit per day. Even getting a 'Hi' out of him is a win."

These girls seem to know a completely different Finn than I knew. Working all the time. Not talking. He is different, that's for sure. Sadder, maybe. Definitely quieter.

When did he get like this? He used to be so gregarious and outgoing. And he was the center of all his friends. Everyone wanted to be around him at all times. We used to talk for hours and hours, well into the night.

At some of his gigs, he would stop playing and get so distracted telling the story of how a song came to be that his bandmates had to start playing the lead in to get him back on track. Now, all he does is grunt and grimace.

And avoid me.

"Maybe he hasn't had anyone to push him in cold water lately," I let slip.

"What?" Charlie asks.

"It was just something I used to do when he'd get in a funk."

Finn had his moods back then. When I first met him, he would slip into days of darkness. Eventually, I could recognize the first signs of it and took to pushing him into the nearest body of water to snap him out of it. In trunks or fully dressed. In the middle of a surf session or in the middle of a wedding. Even if it was fifty degrees in the middle of January. There was something about the shock of the cold water that blasted him out of his head.

"So, you gonna give us the deets on that one?" Charlie asks.

"Pushing him in water?" I ask.

"No. You and Finn! How'd that happen?" Billie presses.

Indigo gives me a quick look checking to make sure I'm ready to go there. Ready to talk about anything closely related to romance and feelings. She knows all about Timmy. I even gave her permission to let the girls know so they would give me some space if I needed it, but I don't know if she actually did.

"There's no real deets. We were just friends in college. Nothing big." That should be obvious from Finn's reaction to my presence here.

"And now?" Charlie waggles her eyebrows.

"Still friends. If that." There's no hope of ever being more. He knows my old freakish ways. My cringey naivety. My embarrassing awkwardness. There's no way I'm humiliating myself again that way for him just to have him turn me down. I learned my lesson on that one. "Let's go get some more waves."

I paddle back in, not waiting to see if they'll follow.

Trying to push those thoughts far from my head, I focus on catching as many waves as possible with my spaghetti arms.

When everyone decides to paddle in, I'm in no hurry to get back on land where avoiding my dark thoughts is so much harder.

Charlie and Greyson take a wave in together while he holds onto her waist the whole way in. Those two are pukingly sweet. JJ, Indigo, Ryder, and Billie aren't far behind.

Soon, it's only Finn and me and the old-timer couple who paddled out well before we did. When I'm that age, I hope to God that I'm in that good of shape, to stay in the water for hours and look all the more spritely for it.

She paddles her board closer to him, reaching out to hold the edge of his board, and says, "Surf kisses?" He leans over and gives her a salty kiss right there.

And I realize, I may be able to get in good enough shape to paddle into the surf at eighty, but I'm never going to have that again. I got my chance. My one great love. My Timmy. And it's over.

My list flashes in my mind. My list of goals for this year. The year that starts in three short days. The goal right above the newly penned Get In Shape comes into focus. Invest in friendships so you'll have a network of support to catch you when the next big storm hits.

I tried to weather the last storm alone. And, I can tell you, it makes things a hundred times worse. I neglected my friendships in the years prior, so when it came time to turn to them, they were too far away to reach. I thank God that Indigo reached out to me because I was so far gone, I couldn't figure out who to ask for help.

It's probably best I paddle in and keep investing in these friendships. Waves aren't going to help me like friends will for that future storm.

The shower water is cool as it pours over my face. Much cooler than the balmy ocean. Everyone else has moved on to the trucks, changing into dry clothes, hopefully in preparation to go get some plate lunch. My stomach growls.

"Hey," Finn mumbles as he flips on the shower opposite me. Is a 'Hey' worth even more than a 'Hi' from him? I mean, it is a whole extra letter.

"Hey." My arms throb as I try to wring the water from my hair, drawing out a laugh. "I am so out of shape."

Finn laughs. "Now that you're married, you let yourself go?"

I never got the time to let myself go.

I don't have the heart to correct him and I sure don't want to delve into that conversation after having such a great day in the water again. It might be the first day in forever that I've just had fun. Not struggling to pretend like I'm having fun, or forcing myself to do the things that I used to have fun doing. But simple, unadulterated, uncomplicated fun, goofing off, being silly, and enjoying the moment. I'm in no rush to complicate that.

"You know there is only one way to get in shape, right?" Finn tries to distract me from the depths I'm currently considering plunging into. He leans up against the shower pole that separates us, making his shoulders flex. "You want to go with me on my morning run?"

Knowing Finn, that's probably a forty-mile run right up the side of the Haleakala crater.

But, I guess we've established that I don't really know Finn anymore. "You promise to go easy on me? You won't leave me behind?"

"Never."

If only that was true...

Chapter 6

EMERSON
FALL, FRESHMAN YEAR

Forming a band must be like shooting fish in a barrel when you're in a music program. Finn instantly had a whole group of friends within weeks of school starting. And, of course, with bandmates come girls.

I, on the other hand, haven't been so lucky in the finding friends game, not that it was ever my strength in life. Living with a bunch of grad students hasn't made it any easier.

Finn was gracious enough to include me with his group, but they are so different from me, that it's hard not to get completely up in my head when I'm around them.

I glance down at the stamp on my hand that screams everything that's been running through my head. Under 21. It might as well say, "Too young and naive."

Cash slides a pitcher onto the table and picks a stool between Cassidy and Rhett before filling up pint glasses for the table. He fills one and slides it across the table toward me. "You gonna be a big girl tonight?" he sneers.

Finn intercepts the drink and takes a long draw. "Thanks, man. I needed that." He slides a little closer to me, giving my knee a reassuring squeeze under the table.

Cassidy leans forward, her elbows on the table. "So, are you two hooking up or something?"

I've only known Finn for two weeks. I don't know why she would think we'd be doing that. But, this is college, and two weeks may be much longer than she'd wait. "We're not sleeping together," I say quietly.

The whole table laughs as if I should have known it was a complete impossibility.

"Nice, Cassidy," Finn snarls.

She breaks into an overly friendly smile before leaning forward just a hint more.

Finn turns to me, easing into a smile. "Anyway, she's much too good for me. I'd wreck a sweet girl like her."

The band on stage begins their set just in time. It's a bit too hardcore for my taste, but at least it means the end of that awful discussion.

So, not only am I way too young to be in here—really, too young to be hanging out with Finn and his rowdy friends at all—and totally outgunned when it comes to musical knowledge compared to this group of music majors, now I am just a clueless little girl.

Sitting around Rhett and Cash's tiny living room after the show, Cassidy seems to have moved her target from Finn to Rhett. They are all wrapped up in one another on the futon. Finn is leaning against the doorway to the kitchen as Cash tosses him the last of the twelve-pack he brought with him.

I don't know why no one else has noticed that Finn doesn't actually drink. Oh, he'll accept a beer when one's passed his way or if everyone else is drinking at the table, but he just takes a sip or two and then holds onto it for the next hour before setting it down somewhere and forgetting about it.

"Hey, what do we owe you for the tickets, Rhett?" Finn asks.

Rhett tears himself from Cassidy's mouth long enough to answer. "It was one seventy, forty-two for everyone."

"So, how much is that each?" Cassidy asks.

I pick up the empty cans and take them to the kitchen as all four of them take out their phones.

"Thirty-four oh eight and four-tenths each," I say before rounding the corner to the kitchen.

Crap.

I really should have kept my mouth shut. I swear I can hear their phones hit their laps and their jaws hit the floor. Grabbing two more beers for the boys, I hurry back to try to sweep that under the rug.

"I think she had that before any of you even turned on your phones," Finn teases.

"You did that in your head?" Cassidy asks.

"It's division by five. Double it and kill a zero," I say like it should be common knowledge. But knowing where this conversation is headed, I drop the beers on the table and run back to the kitchen to hide.

"Dude! Your little sis is a freakin' genius," Rhett says. Finn must have introduced me that way, and he certainly doesn't correct him for it now.

"I know, it's crazy. You have to see it. It's like she's a human calculator. Hey, Em," he calls my way. "Come here and show them that thing."

I whip around the corner, grab him by the shirt, and drag him outside, absolutely livid.

I muster my harshest voice. "Finnegan Ruth MacGregor, don't ever put me on display like that again."

He laughs off my serious tone. "Why? It's incredible what you can do."

"You are the only person who doesn't think I'm a total freak. Which is why I may have told you some stuff, but that doesn't mean—"

His face grows concerned. "Some stuff? There's more?"

I may have shared with him a few horror stories from elementary and middle school, but I haven't told him everything. I left out most of the torture that was high school.

Like the first day of my freshman year.

I was twelve and trying to handle walking the halls with

eighteen-year-old men. Three of my brother's friends promised him they'd take me under their wing because we had a few classes together. So, before PE, they told me about the long-standing tradition of the varsity football team repainting the genders on the locker rooms. But the teachers had figured it out by now and were ready with paper signs to correct it.

They walked me into the girl's locker room only to stop at the door, shove me in, and shut the doors behind me. I looked up to find grown men standing there naked, full manly parts just hanging in the breeze, and there was no retreat.

The rest of high school was an ever-worsening parade of moments like that. I learned quickly not to trust what anyone said to me from then on.

I look up at him and try to stop the tears from exiting my eyes. Somehow, once they run down my face, I'm really crying. Anything before that doesn't count.

"In grade school, you can't hide the fact that you've skipped too many grades to count. Here, I can and I've worked really hard to do so. I'm not sure I could take it if you turned into another one of those people who finds out my secret and uses it to torture me."

I can see the moment he understands when his whole countenance changes. He's broken. He wraps his arms around me and whispers in my ear, "You can trust me with your secrets, Em. Please don't stop sharing them with me. I wouldn't survive that."

He pulls away from the hug and lifts my chin to look at him.

"I swear to Clapton that I will always protect you from anyone who doesn't realize that your mind coupled with that amazing heart of yours is one of the sweetest of God's creations."

Chapter 7

FINN
PRESENT DAY

I'm doing this all wrong. I saw the look on Em's face this morning when we were eating the cinnamon toast. I thought she would recognize the gesture and smile, but, instead, she looked crushed.

Four years ago, when things ended, that first Saturday I couldn't bear not to buy a loaf after sunrise. I deluded myself into thinking that somehow it would magically make her appear. Like she could smell it toasting wherever she was, and it would draw her back to me.

And in a way it did. Every Saturday, when that smell hits me, for just a second, she is there with me again. I can pretend she will come bounding through the door and share our Saturday morning ritual and that I didn't, in fact, ruin everything we had.

It isn't the only thing I have done over the years to send up smoke signals—ones she never sees.

Or maybe she did see them and that's why she's back.

Maybe I didn't completely destroy absolutely everything about my relationship with Em. Maybe she can find a way to forgive me.

I'm laid out flat on my stomach, half-buried under my bed, digging around for the box that contains all I have left of Em. I have to look back through it to make sure I'm not remembering it differently, how she always seemed to be smiling around me.

When we'd meet for lunch, she'd be scowling over her Neurobiology textbook and the moment she'd see me approaching, her whole face would light up. This was one of the only times in my life that I felt like I did something good. If I could just keep putting that smile on her face, if I never did anything else in life, just that one thing, I would be proud.

I shove aside a few empty beer cans and a pile of socks covered in dust, and grasp the dinged-up, locking wooden box, sliding it out.

Sitting up, I lean back against the bed frame, trying to steady myself for proof that I haven't built up our story to be way more than it really was.

I lift the lid and find a pic of Em in her cut-off jean skirt and crop tank on our surf trip to Ventura. Em busted through my front door late on a Thursday night like she was a beautiful version of Kramer. She was just as energetic that night.

She lifts a paper, nearly shoving it in my face, and says, "I passed, Finn. I actually passed my History mid-term." She didn't just pass, she got an A+. "Grab a board and your wetsuit, we're going surfing."

"Em, it's nearly ten."

"I know. If we leave now, we'll miss all the LA traffic and be at Rincon in a couple hours. I want to be the first one out in the lineup tomorrow, watching the sun rise from the water."

Rincon in the morning meant camping out in my van that night. She was eighteen by then, so at least I didn't have to worry about being woken up by some cop tapping on the glass with his flashlight before being carted away to jail. But it did mean sleeping next to Em all night. "That's a long drive for a sunrise we could just as well see here."

"Come on, Finny, we have to. It's on the dream list." I was useless when she called me Finny.

I took this pic in the dark the next morning before she slid on her wetsuit, nearly sprinting to the water's edge. The gigantic, satisfied smile on her face made the drive more than worth it.

I lift a whole stack of photos and flip through them. In every single one, Em is grinning. Unless she is pretending to give me her scary look, which is simply adorable.

"Finn! Greyson! The Ohana!" Indigo shouts.

I shove the mementos off of my lap and jump to my feet. Greyson flies down the stairs from his room at the top of the stairs. We all run out to the Ohana and fly through the open door.

I survey the scene. Indigo is flitting about screaming about towels. While Em stands there with both hands on a pipe in the kitchen that is spewing out water. She has positioned her body to take the entire brunt of the water, diverting it from flowing all over the sound equipment I store out here.

I come up behind her, placing my hand on the pipe above hers. With my other arm, I slowly move her out of the way so I'm taking the force of the water. She stays right beside me trying to divert more water from taking out thousands of dollars in equipment.

"Go get the main water line. It's on the far side of the garage, next to the side door," I command. Indigo and Grey sprint out the door.

I turn my head trying to avoid the backsplash coming from water jetting out in full force against my chest. My right foot slips in the pool forming around my feet, and it takes out Em's left leg. Plucking my hand from the pipe, I steady her with an arm around her waist, which allows a surge of water to fully drench my face.

We both move to block the flow, causing her hand to land on top of mine. She doesn't pull hers away. We glance at each other and bust out laughing.

"Was this just an elaborate plan to douse me in cold water?" I ask when our laughing dies down.

"It worked, didn't it?" She says haughtily like a cartoon villain. Her feet slip around beneath her making her look like she's running in place, reinforcing the cartoon appearance.

The flow finally begins to ease up, until it is only a pipe dripping more work onto my ever-growing To-do list of projects on this property.

Em leans against the soaking counter, relaxing. I lean up next to her, taking in her body. "You're actually wearing that?"

She looks down at her gray crop top and neon pink boyshorts. "Whatever. It was hot."

"That's not hot, that's freakin' sexy as hell," I let slip before I can control my mouth.

She looks up at me with a look I'm totally unfamiliar with coming from Em. From other girls sure, but never from Em, that is if you don't count the last night I saw her.

Greyson hustles in with Indigo close behind. "Did we get it?"

I drag my eyes from Em, not willing yet to move away from her. "Yeah. It's off. Towels are in the bathroom. Tall closet."

Indigo and Grey run to find them.

"Did it ruin your recording equipment?" Em is the only one who would know that under those wooden covers on a table against the wall is where I've hidden all of my now untouched equipment. No one has ever even bothered to ask.

I force myself from Em's side to check, lifting one cover after the next. "You saved it all. Thank you, Em."

Em goes to her open suitcase, all its contents now soaked along with nearly everything else within an eight-foot radius.

"Is your insulin ruined?" I couldn't bear to think that my unfinished project put her in any real danger.

"Nah. I keep it in a different bag up there by the bed."

Greyson tosses the stack of towels onto the lake now covering the whole place. "Well, you can't sleep in here. Come crash inside the main house and we'll clean up this mess in the morning," he says, looking to me for confirmation.

I shrug and head outside.

Once inside, I retrieve a few dry towels from the shelves next to the dryer tucked into the laundry room just beyond the dining room. I toss one each to Indigo and Em as they pull up a seat at the kitchen island. Indigo breaks the silence. "Did that really just happen?"

At the sound of the girls laughing, JJ staggers out of his room. "Someone forget to invite me to the midnight party?"

"A pipe burst in the Ohana. Literally burst. Water everywhere." Em swings her hands wildly trying to completely capture the scope of the event.

JJ rakes his eyes along Indigo's body. "I can see. You're soaked." He looks over at me. "They sleeping in here tonight?"

I nod.

"You can have my bed Indigo. I'll take the couch," JJ offers, probably trying to earn points.

"We're both adults. I think we can share a bed without it being weird," she says with more than a little suggestion in her voice.

Nervously, Em tucks her dripping hair behind her ear and begins to wipe at the drops of water on the island, not daring to meet my gaze.

JJ purrs as he takes Indigo's hand lifting her from her seat, "Come on, let's get you out of those wet clothes."

Grey laughs. "I'm going to try to sleep."

And then we're left alone, in my kitchen, in the middle of the night. Both adults.

Em sizes up my reaction. No matter how much I try to school my face, she's always been able to read my thoughts, and I'm terrified that what I'm thinking will be completely visible. Her eyes ask if we could share a bed without it being weird. I don't know about it not being weird, but I can at least get her some dry clothes. "I have something you can wear if you want."

Em wanders through my room, picking up a piece of coral I keep on my bookshelf.

I slide open my top drawer to grab a clean pair of boxer shorts, then two drawers lower to find a shirt. I can hear her continue to inspect my room until I hear her settle in by my nightstand.

"How do you open this?" she asks.

Crap.

Without even seeing it, I know what she is holding. I toss the shorts into the drawer and jump to her, hoping to distract her. "Why do you want to open it?"

She holds up a small frame displaying a card with hundreds of hand-painted fish swimming in one direction, creating a current of fish.

God, please don't let her open it.

I step even closer and can feel the heat off her body. Her hair is no longer dripping, but it's wet and hangs around her freckled cheeks like seaweed sticking to your body. The towel hangs over her shoulders, giving those hot pink boy shorts some coverage, but she is still way too exposed for me to be standing this close.

She flips the frame over, looking for a place to pry it open. "I want to see what I wrote."

There's no way I'm going to let her read what she wrote. It's not like I don't know exactly what is written there.

She looks up at me, pleading, "Please, Finny."

I'm useless to stop her when she calls me that. Without looking away from the lightest brown eyes ever, I put my hands on hers and help her flip it to the front. Then I push on the right side of the frame, sliding out the glass protecting that precious card.

Standing in front of Em, with my most treasured object open in her hands, I feel as bare as that card. Maybe for the first time ever, I have let her into my depths, and I don't know if it's because she has changed so much over the years, or if it's because I have.

She lowers her eyes to the frame and runs her fingers along the two solitary fish swimming against the current. She breathes deep like she's inhaling the past.

Then she lifts the front of the card, the motion dropping the towel from where it was perched on her shoulders. She glances to the ground where the blue terry cloth lays in a heap around her feet, but doesn't make a move toward it. Instead, she stares at those words written in tiny letters in the middle of a nearly blank card, 'i miss you.'

She runs her finger along the path that mine have traveled so often as if touching the depressions her pen made so many years ago would allow her to touch that time. To touch the girl she was then. To touch the old me.

She lets her eyes drift down to the only other words on the card at the far right bottom; Love, Em, the 'm' washed into a circle of wavy ink.

Her face scrunches up like she's trying to bring up the day she painted the card, but it only appears as a hazy image. Touching the damaged 'm', she lifts her eyes to mine. "Is it yours or mine?"

Since seeing her tell the story of her crying at that damned movie, how much that time period hurt her, I can't be sure whose tear it was that marred that perfect card, but I am sure that I never even want to doubt that I have caused her enough pain to let her tears fall. I won't do it again.

I let my gaze wash down her neck, over her collarbone. I would only have to move an inch and I could...

Husband.

Em is married. You cannot do that.

"It's been so long, it's hard to tell," I respond, if only to bring my thoughts back to where they should be.

I've been vulnerable in front of her long enough. I move back to find her clothes to cover herself with. Alone in my room, with her in only that top and panties, I am sure I can't keep myself from destroying her marriage.

I toss a few shirts aside. I have the bad habit of tossing already-worn shirts back into the drawer and cannot risk handing her a stinking shirt. My hand is on an inside-out maroon tee when I hear her feet shuffle on the bare wood floor, knocking into the box I had out earlier.

I gather the tee and shorts and rush over to her, stuffing them into her hands before she has a chance to inspect the box. It is one thing to have one of her cards framed on my nightstand. It is quite another to have a box of everything she has ever written to me and for me to be going through it the day after she shows up in my life again. That is just pathetic.

With my foot, I tap the box under the bed and realize I'm standing centimeters from her, my bare leg brushing hers. I let my gaze drop to her lips and my tongue instinctively swipes across my own lips.

She draws her lower lip under her teeth and slowly lets it glide back out. Her eyes flit from my mouth to my eyes and back. I can feel her breath on my face and smell her coconut shampoo. I glance down toward the bed we are standing next to and picture all we could be doing there.

I hear my brain growl out two distinct syllables.

Hus.

Band.

I point to the bathroom door. "You can change in there."

When the door closes behind Em, I bend down, shoving the pics and collection of drink coasters deep inside the box, and wedge it behind the guitar case and scattered empty beer bottles. I collapse onto the edge of the bed, breathing fully for the first time since hearing Indigo sound the alarm earlier.

I twist the frame back to its original position and lay back, struggling to come up with a plan for surviving an entire night of lying next to a married Em.

The image of the smile on Em's face after I told her how sexy she was flashes in my mind. It was like she had never been told that before or at least not for a while. I wonder if her husband ever tells her that. He'd have to be an ungrateful scumbag not to tell her every single day.

God, he could be a scumbag.

A scumbag who deprives her of affection.

Of love.

Chapter 8

FINN
SEPTEMBER, SENIOR YEAR

*I*t was just that simple; after that first definitely-not-a-date, we became friends. One day, I didn't know this world was inhabited with the beautiful creature named Em. The next, she was just there. Everywhere. In class. At my gigs. In my room. And when she wasn't actually present in my room, she was still there in my thoughts. My dreams. My soul.

I couldn't get her out.

I tried.

Even though I couldn't eradicate her from my life or my mind, I made sure she kept her distance, so that she knew, down to her very core, that there was no chance, no hope, no way in hell that we would ever be more than friends.

I'm not that guy.

Not for her.

Not for anyone.

At the beginning of the year, I helped Em move into her new duplex. She helped me pick out a new bedspread. We went grocery shopping together. The stuff that you usually do with your girlfriend. But she was not my girlfriend.

She may have been the woman in my life, but I knew better than to go there.

If only I had been strong enough to keep *her* from going there.

Em has convinced me to throw myself a housewarming party now that I had rented a small house just a few blocks from the beach. Royalties from a few songs I had written had been coming in strong the past year and I was ready to enjoy the fruit of my labors.

She said she'd take care of everything and, boy, has she. From the subtle decorations to the matching cupcakes, this is a barbecue for the books. I'm enjoying an iced tea as I take in the slice of ocean view visible from my backyard.

Our friends begin filtering into the backyard. I'm sure Em has already given them the dime tour of my new place. She's so comfortable here, I almost feel like I should say *our* new place.

She's wearing a bright yellow sundress with the thinnest of straps, which lights up against her deep tan skin from a summer full of time in the sun. A stripped-down acoustic version of 'Cowboy Take Me Away' comes on the Bluetooth speaker she set up and she begins to sway with the music. Even though I can't hear her from here, I know the version she is belting out is so much better than the one on the speaker.

Without too many people here yet, she looks to be feeling a bit freer than she usually would at a party. She lifts her hands and begins to move to the music. She's come so far from the timid little girl I met freshman year. She has found her voice.

It shows in the way she is able to gracefully navigate our friends and strangers out here today. Just like everything else in her life, she has mastered the social events that would have frustrated her back then and caused her to hide.

She catches me watching and the brightest smile spreads across her lips, the one that always appears when she sees me. She holds my gaze as she continues dancing, almost teasing me. But she knows better. She knows that is not us. She may be the woman in my life, in my house even, but she's not the woman in my bed.

Out of the corner of my eye, I catch some dork taking in the same gorgeous picture I have been enjoying. I check to see if Em has noticed, nodding over to him. She turns her gaze his way for only a second before letting her arms fall and walking off to the cooler.

Ignoring the obvious rejection, he follows her there, reaching into the cooler just as she rises from it. I'm too far away to hear what he says to her, but she throws back her head and laughs. I wonder what cheesy, unoriginal line he used on her.

Once we hit the kitchen, Cassidy breaks up the frivolity and gives Em a big hug. They may have started off a bit rough, but as soon as Cassidy realized Em wasn't a threat to her, she lightened up and became a pretty integral part of our group.

As I close in on them, Em looks to be introducing her new admirer to Cassidy. I approach the group and wrap my arm around Em's shoulder, offering my other hand to the dork, "I'm Finn. This is my place," gripping his hand until he withers in my vice-like grip.

"Finn, show me your new place," Cassidy says, winking at Em as she tugs me away from her. I really don't want to leave Em alone with this loser, but Cassidy is not easy to argue with once she decides on something.

Cassidy takes a water bottle from the fridge and leans her hip against the counter. "I was hoping to talk to you before Rhett got here."

She and Rhett have been inseparable since Freshman year and he would be crushed if she's having second thoughts. "What's going on, Cassidy?"

"I have big news that I think he's gonna hate. I don't really have to tell him, do I?"

"That depends on what kind of news." Senior year has been putting weird pressures on all of us with our scary future after college staring us down.

She takes a long draw from the water bottle before slowly twisting the lid back on and setting it down on the counter behind her. I prepare to spend the next few months consoling Rhett after she breaks up with him.

"I think I'm pregnant," she whispers as three more people bound through the door. "Do I really have to tell Rhett?"

"Yes. Immediately. You have to tell him."

"Even if I don't know for sure?" She lifts her water again, spinning the lid on and off again. "Shouldn't I wait until I take a test?"

"You tell him now. And if he won't step up, you let me know. I'll make sure he takes good care of you."

"Yeah. You're right. Thanks, Finn," she says.

"Now, let's go join the party." I wrap my arm around her and drag her outside toward the fun. "And start prenatal vitamins right now just in case. And no drinking at all. And make sure you get plenty of rest, okay?"

By the time we make it back outside, Em is still talking with the dweeb at the far end of the yard.

I join Cash and the girl he brought. "Who brought this guy?" throwing my thumb over toward the dweeb as he's juggling lemons trying to impress Em. She snatches one out of the air, throwing his rhythm off and he drops the other two. She shrugs playfully. Coyly. She's flirting back with this guy.

"Who, Tim? He came with Nick. They've been friends for years. He seems pretty cool," Cash says. Cool is not the word I would use.

As if summoned by my question, Tim and Em join our little circle. "So, I hear you all are in a rock band. Are we going to get to hear you play tonight?" Tim asks.

I'll let Cash field that one. I'm in no mood to play nice and the continued friendly conversation combined with watching Tim fit right into our friends does nothing to kick me out of that foul mood.

In the middle of some story that Tim's telling, Em leans over to me and whispers, "If you don't buck up there camper, that kiddie pool crammed with ice and drinks would work really well, don't you think?"

And she'd do it. Push me in, right there in the middle of the perfect little party she orchestrated if it meant I would stop being so grumpy. Knowing that, I head inside where I don't have to watch firsthand as this bum tries to win Em's affections.

Wandering around aimlessly, I wait for my head to cool. After dipping into the garage, pretending to look for something,

I gain enough space to chill out. I return to the house and end up waiting in line for the bathroom in my own house. Typically, I'd just go outside and take care of business, but Em would kill me if she caught me doing that at her party. Next house I rent will have to have at least two bathrooms.

The door finally opens and, just my luck, it's Tim. I don't move, taking up nearly the whole narrow hallway. He'd have to wriggle between me and the wall to get by. "Just a heads up, Em is definitely in the Red Zone, dude."

"Red Zone?" he says like he's never heard the term.

"Off limits. No Fly Zone. Stay away."

"Sorry, man. I didn't know you two were together," he says sincerely. "I wouldn't have gone there if I knew."

I don't bother correcting him. He doesn't need to know the ins and outs of my relationship with Em. As long as he stays away, it makes no difference to me.

Em deserves better than that guy. He was talking to three other girls at this sad excuse for a party before he zeroed in on Em.

When I return to the yard, Em is trying to strike up another conversation with Tim, but the sissy won't even make eye contact. Her boldness on full display, she approaches him at the food table, laying her hand on his arm. He sets his drink down and backs up a step before saying something to Em. Her faint smile holds a touch of sadness. He looks back at me to make sure I saw him and she follows his gaze.

And like everything else in this world, she has figured me out in seconds and, rightfully, chooses to avoid me for the rest of the night.

As the house empties, I find Em in the backyard, clearing the trash, packaging up the leftovers.

"This was a great party, Em."

"It had its moments," she concedes but doesn't stop wrapping up the remaining cooked burgers.

I lay my hand on hers to still her. "Like Tim?"

She stalls, still staring at the saran wrap she is unsuccessfully trying to smooth void of all wrinkles. She looks up at me. "Why'd you have to be such a jerk to him, Finn?"

"Sorry," is all I can muster. I can't come up with a real reason for the primal urge to rip that guy's head off that washed over me.

"I wasn't even really interested in the guy. It just felt really good to have a guy pay attention to me. It made me feel..." she picks up the plate of burgers, and starts toward the house. I follow close behind. "I don't know. Sexy maybe? At the very least, I felt a little bit desirable."

She stops and turns back to me, her eyes brimming with sadness. "You don't know how rare that is for me, Finn, and you had to go and ruin it."

I know there is no way I can provide the love Em deserves, but is my simple presence in her life depriving her of finding that love from someone else? I can't keep running off any guy interested in her simply to keep her in my life. I know I screw up every single relationship I have, bound to continually hurt everyone I love, but how long can I selfishly hold onto Em?

Chapter 9

EMERSON
PRESENT DAY

I never would have guessed that he had that card framed—not from the underwhelming reunion or the way he has hardly spoken to me since. I never even knew if the card got to him. I sent it to his old address nearly a year after the last time we spoke, but I'm sure he vacated it right after graduation. I suppose it did get to him—not that I ever heard a word from him about it.

But that was a lifetime ago. I was a completely different girl.

I lay Finn's clothes on the counter and peel off my gray football jersey with a huge pink 42 on the front, tucking inside the pink undies with the phrase 'I Believe in Naps' on the butt. Pulling a navy towel from the wall behind me, the smell overwhelms me. I can't quite place it, but it reminds me of caramel. Wrapping it around my shoulders, I take another big whiff. It's the smell of Finn.

I peek into his shower to see if I can find what makes it smell so good. The only thing in there is one bar of soap. No shampoo bottle to glean the name of the scent. No conditioner or body wash. Just one unlabeled bar of dark brown soap. Just like New Finn, silent and mysterious.

I slip on the boxers and fold over the band a few times. Looking in the mirror, I try to tame my unruly hair. Curls have sprung to life that won't be tamed without a hair dryer and a lot of work, so instead I decide to go along with them. I try to squeeze out the last bit of dampness, scrunching the curls with Finn's molasses-scented towel. I tug a few strands of my bangs forward.

Rustling comes from the room behind me. From Finn. Who smells of caramelized sugar and molasses and warmth.

I catch my reflection in the mirror and laugh to myself. I could go out there right now, topless, in just his boxers. Not that I would. We're not in that place. But I could.

And I could do it with utter confidence. Without hesitation. I could walk out there, push him down on the bed, and hold his hands down, teasing and taunting. I wouldn't have to research and rehearse for months on end. I wouldn't have to debate with myself if I could. If I should. If I would.

And I love that fact. I love the fact that I have come so far.

It makes sense how it all turned out the first time I tried to seduce Finn. I was so nervous I must have been a bumbling idiot. *Look how big all your muscles are.* Such a stupid thing to say.

But now? Now is a completely different story. I don't have to figure out how to seduce him, I only have to figure out if I even want to.

Either way, now is probably not the right time.

So, I dry off my top and smell that amazing scent on the towel again. The shirt he gave me is inside out. Gosh, I hope that's because he wore it already and it still smells of him.

I don't bother flipping it right side out, but rather stick my head in the hole and flip it down onto my body. I take one more look in the mirror and am smacked in the face by the block-lettered S on the front of the burgundy shirt—the unmistakable Stanford logo—and all thoughts of seducing Finn go right out the window. The only thing I want to do to Finn is murder him.

Chapter 10

EMERSON
OCTOBER SENIOR YEAR

The line in The Perky Coffee Shop is long, winding around the display of shirts and handwritten chalkboard signs with the lamest coffee quotes. "Today's good mood is sponsored by coffee," and "I put coffee in my coffee."

I'm glad to have this moment in line away from Finn who is sitting at a table in the far corner away from the bustle of the uncaffeinated patrons. I glance back briefly at him, not ready to make eye contact, but I'm dying to know how he's responding. He's holding the burgundy shirt I just gave him in both hands and staring right at it. His head is tilted down toward the shirt so I can't read his expression. And I desperately need that info.

The gift was simply a lead-in to the conversation I'm avoiding. If I'm going to ask him to pack up and move across the state with me after we graduate in June, I have to have some indication that he feels something for me.

Maybe those aren't the right words. I know he feels something for me. He has been my closest friend for the last three years.

Even though I hold people at arm's length, he has managed to inch closer than anyone ever has. He has known me in a way that no one else has been able to. I'm not a talkative person, ask anyone. But without having to use words, he has found a way to get to know me even when I can't articulate what I'm feeling, or when I'm too terrified to articulate it. He observes silently and somehow knows what's going on in my head.

And I think he has figured out the secret that has been going on in my head the last few months. It's probably been rattling around in my head for much longer than that, but it was only in the last few months that I figured it out myself. And if I'm going to lay it all on the line and ask him to come with me, I need some sort of reassurance that he's had those same thoughts, those same feelings for me.

I take our coffee from the barista and dump one pack of raw sugar and just a splash of coconut milk into his until it is barely a shade darker than the walls of this coffee shop. I watch the tops of the cups as I make my way back to our table, too afraid to see his reaction to the gift that I hope will do the heavy lifting of this conversation, or at least get the ball rolling.

I place his cup in front of him and finally force my gaze up to his eyes. He stares back with no discernible reaction.

Shoot. Am I really going to do this?

I sit down across the table and he holds up the shirt. "I'm confused."

"You know we graduate this year."

"Yeah. From UCSD, not Stanford."

"Right. UCSD." I stir my coffee with a wooden stick even though I take my coffee black.

Don't ask him. You can't ask him. He is giving you no sign that he thinks you're anything more than a friend.

He holds the shirt in the air and magically folds it perfectly in mid-air. He lays it on top of the plastic bag and smooths the top.

I had thought about wrapping it in some beautiful navy paper with white drawings of clipper ships all over it. But I knew it would be too much if I decided to wuss out and not ask. It would be too much for just a coffee day and telling him I'm leaving. The plastic bag would give me a way out.

"Em?"

I look up into his green eyes rimmed with a circle of blue

and swallow hard. "I got invited to research with Dr. Tansor at Stanford in his neurobiology department."

I study his face for anything. Joy that I'm finally getting out of his hair. Sadness that I'm leaving. Hope that I might ask him to go.

Anything.

He gives me nothing.

But I have to do this. I have to. "I start in July."

He lays his hand on the shirt smoothing out the one tiny wrinkle he hasn't already vanquished. "For how long?"

I look at the two toe-headed toddlers in red trunks playing tag around their mom's leg in line as she posts what is probably her tenth Instagram photo this morning while her kids run wild in the "too cute little coffee heaven #coffeegoals #coffeeaddict."

"Em." I look back to Finn's nudging.

"Two years."

"Two. Years."

I scratch my finger along the groove of the table.

He tugs at the hem of the shirt. "So you're leaving. Like moving there?"

Time for the speech, Em. You've practiced. You can do this. "Finn. You're important. Uh. To me."

Great, you've already messed this up.

I watch as I drive my fingernail along the crease of my other hand. I stare at it like my speech is written there. "It would be better if you were there, too." I wait for him to answer. I scratch my palm three more times to complete silence.

I look up to make sure he's still sitting there.

He is.

Sitting there looking pissed.

Damn.

Chapter 11

FINN
PRESENT DAY

The bathroom door flings wide open and Em rushes through it toward the bedroom door. "I'm going to sleep on the couch."

I spring to my feet and slip between her and the door. "Wait. What? You're not sleeping on the couch."

Her hands are folded across her chest, her face hardened and unreadable. Whatever she left open to me moments before has vanished.

"Move, Finn."

There is no way in hell I'm moving until I figure out what just happened. "What the hell, Em. You're not sleeping on the couch."

"I'm not sleeping in here with you." She lays her hand on my shoulder, trying to move the barricade preventing her egress—me.

Is she mad because I was too close, wanted too much? Is she mad at herself for wanting it, too? Looks like, in addition to all the other knowledge of Em that has slipped through my fingers in the last five years, I've lost the ability to read her, too. "You take my bed. I'll sleep on the couch."

At this, she softens. I brush past her, grab my pillow and a blanket from the foot of the bed, and then leave. I throw the pillow on the couch and my body down after it. She better not be in there crying. Pissed I can take, but hurt will kill me.

I lay awake most of the night, running events through my head over and over again, looking for what went wrong. I come up with about a hundred different things it could be, but I won't know for sure until Em tells me. Although with the stonewalling I saw last night, I'm not sure she ever will.

When I hear rustling from Grey's room the next morning, I lumber into the kitchen to start some coffee. The last thing I need is him asking about why I'm on the couch when he had such a perfect plan laid out for last night.

Grey and Charlie appear from their room first, followed by JJ and Indigo who sport guilty grins as they touch and tickle their way to the kitchen island.

"Em still asleep?" Charlie asks me.

I nod as I take down six mugs from the cupboard.

"So, I finally see what you mean about the thin walls, JJ," Grey admits.

"What can I say? It's payback for the years I've had to listen to you two."

Em pries open the bedroom door and scurries to the laundry room at the far end of the house.

JJ, Charlie, and Greyson freeze, mouths agape. Indigo runs her hand along JJ's back until it drops to his butt, giving it a big squeeze. I fill six cups with sludge and bring them to the island.

Em scurries back into the room carrying a basket of her dry clothes.

I situate the sugar and milk next to the cups.

"Holy. Crap. Finn. You let her wear your Stanford shirt?" Grey exclaims.

"No man, it's just an old tee." I dump four spoonfuls of sugar in my cup. I'm going to need all the help I can get after that awful night of sleep.

Indigo takes a cup from the island. "What's so special about his Stanford tee?"

Charlie pulls her mug to where she's standing. "That thing is precious cargo. No one touches it without fear of Finn calling down the wrath of God."

"He won't even let the washing machine touch it. He hand washes it and lays it out on a towel to dry," Greyson adds.

"It wasn't my Stanford tee," I repeat.

"What other maroon tee do you own?" JJ laughs.

No.

It wasn't.

I didn't.

If I handed her that, it's no wonder she freaked out. I'm surprised she didn't hit me with a left hook to the temple. I've seen Em's left hook. It can knock the nonsense right out of a man.

I traverse the length of the room in seconds and knock on the door. "Em."

Nothing.

"Em, can I come in?" I slowly push open the door.

The room is empty. She just went in there.

I spin back to everyone. "Where'd she go?"

Indigo bites her lower lip. "She's gone."

"Give me her number." I lurch toward her.

"It won't help. She's gone dark."

"Gone dark? What does that mean?"

"She needed some time." Indigo takes a sip of her coffee. "Turned off her phone."

"What exactly did she say? Exactly," I demand.

"She had plans for today. She needed to get her head right. She'll text when she's back, um, light?" She looks for confirmation from Charlie about that phrase. "You know, when she's reachable again. She said she won't be off the grid past six."

"Six as in six p.m.?"

That won't do. I can't let her think all day that I'm that big of an ass to throw that shirt in her face. Not after a night like that. "She said 'get her head straight'? Those were her exact words?"

"Yeah. I have her text right here." She pushes her phone toward me.

"That's okay. I don't need it. I know where she went."

Em only goes one place to get her head straight. Whenever things went wrong for Em and she needed to get her head on straight, she would "empty her salty tears to mingle with the ocean" as she would say, and fill up her reserves of strength with fish tacos. She thought that salt water and fish tacos could fix anything.

Hearing Em say how great it would be to swim at Ho'olana Bay on our way to surf on Saturday lets me know exactly where she plans on doing that.

I fly across the island like a lunatic, hoping I can catch her before she slips into the water. Apologize before she starts to cry, thinking that I'm the most thoughtless scumbag in the world for throwing that shirt in her face. Although I didn't do it on purpose, she isn't really all that far off from the truth about me.

When I pull up to the dirt lot in front of the bay, I spy Indigo and Em's rental car. One hundred yards west, a small head is barely visible above the water. I remove my goggles from the rear-view mirror and toss my shirt in the seat next to me before sprinting along the sand to get ahead of the swimmer I hope is Em.

I swim out in the sea and begin to trail alongside her for a few yards before she notices. When she does, she loses all ability to swim, jerking her head above the waterline.

"I didn't know, Em. I would never have done that," I spit out.

"What are you talking about?" She looks confused.

I raise my goggles up to make sure she recognizes me out here. "The shirt. I didn't mean anything."

"Oh, yeah. The shirt," she says dreamily. "Was that last night? It feels like ages ago."

Em isn't one to lie about being mad. If she was mad at me, she'd tell me. In a million different ways, she'd tell me. But there isn't an ounce of anger in her.

Just sad. Wistful. Heartsick. She needed to swim. So, I'm gonna let her. "How far we going this morning?"

"Till I feel like I don't have to go any farther?" she says, her anguish almost overcoming her control.

"Lead the way."

Her small smile conveys her gratitude.

We swim along the coastline at a much slower speed than we used to, Em choosing our line, me close on her heels. She pounds out a half-mile without stopping once. I pop my head up every few hundred meters to check for any signs that she is struggling but find none.

Then, suddenly, she stops. I nearly crash into her because she stops so abruptly. We're treading water just inches away from each other, our arms tangling up as we paddle.

"Okay. Let's go back," she mutters before putting her head down and starting back.

She begins to slow as we approach the lot, not from exhaustion, I suppose. She's just done running from whatever was crushing her spirit. She steers us until we are in knee-deep water where she finally pushes down her goggles until they are hanging around her neck.

I take mine off and chuck them onto the dry sand. "So, fish tacos now? Or we can stay here longer if you need to cry more?"

"Nah. I think I'm done with those tears. I've shed all the tears I have for this."

She tugs the rubber band from her hair, untwisting her locks before dipping her head under the water and standing up, letting the water run down her back. She squares her shoulders and trudges through the knee-deep water, up the steep sand berm at the water's edge. She is a vision of strength.

I'm sure she has plans for where to get those fish tacos, only, I don't think Google's gonna know where to find the best fish tacos on the island. I jog to catch up with her "So, let me guess. Siri told you to go to Paia Fish Market?"

"Yeah. Sawyer said it was the best."

"Oh, man. You've named Siri now?" It was bad enough that she set her Siri to be a guy with an Australian accent who would tell you to park in the "caaah paaak" instead of a parking lot.

Now, she's gone and named him. Either way, he has no idea where the best fish tacos are in Nalu Kai.

"Yeah. Not gonna happen. We're gonna hit up Five Ono. It's only a mile up the road. I can show you," I offer, not wanting our time to end.

"Should I drive?"

"You got your running shoes in there?"

It's only a short run to Five Ono, but by the time we're there, I'm beyond starving. Kaimana, the owner, is clearing dishes from the rows of picnic tables spread over the grass field just outside the shack that serves as the kitchen and counter. I think he does it simply to chat with everyone there. He has a knack for faces and seems to know the name of every local and tourist alike.

"Finn! What are you doing out here on a school day?" Kaimana asks.

"Showing my friend here the best fish tacos on the island." I turn to Em. "Emerson, this is Kaimana, the best chef around."

She offers her hand, but Kaimana wraps her up in a titanic hug before she has a chance to react. "So, are you the one responsible for the smile on this one's face, Emerson?" He releases her.

"I doubt it. He's always smiling like that." She looks up at me to confirm it.

"It's the first time I've ever seen it," he says. "And you got him to play hooky from work. You must be a magician."

"Ignore him," I tell her. "Go grab a table and I'll order."

———————

We take our time walking back to the cars. The dirt path along the water weaves in and out of homes that sit right on the water. From smaller two-bedroom homes on tiny lots to huge mansions with enough rooms and outbuildings for the whole extended family surrounded by lush gardens all with windswept views of the coast, Nalu Kai's waterfront is a community all its own. There aren't many places on this island where money doesn't separate people. Those who have chosen to live here understand what community is supposed to mean. Knowing your neighbors. Helping out whoever needs help. Celebrating each other's victories.

If I had known about this place when I first moved out here, I would have bought a place right in the center of it. I'm so glad Billie and Ryder have settled down here so I have an excuse to become a part of that amazing community. Even if I don't make it out here too often on a 'school day.'

As we follow the path to the inland side of another block of homes, Em shrieks, then stares at me as if asking something. I glance around but have no clue.

She points to an Open House sign. She doesn't bother to wait for my answer before skipping up the front walkway. She pauses in the doorway, turning her head slowly from one end of the front room to the other before she turns back to me. "Come on, Finny. You have to see this place."

When I meet her at the front door, she loops her arm through mine as we saunter through the estate like she's looking at a museum full of art, not a simple house for sale. We peek into a small office just off the main entry. "This would be such a cool library, filled with old books and big comfy chairs."

"The twelve-foot ceilings would give you enough room for a sliding ladder in front of floor-to-ceiling bookshelves." She used to drool over bookshelves just like that at the Living Room coffee house we haunted back in La Jolla.

"That would be perfect," she says as she pulls me to the door leading out to the garage. "This is huge. A workshop. Definitely, a workshop."

I would never leave a workshop that nice, finally having enough room to keep all my tools out, ready to use, instead of trapped in plastic storage bins.

We head upstairs to view all of the bedrooms as she points out the perfect baseboards, the perfect views out the windows, and the perfect bathroom fixtures. I've never heard her use the word 'perfect' so many times.

Downstairs, the living room and kitchen are completely open

to the backyard through folding doors that disappear when open. A long pool stretches out the back, ending in an infinity edge that looks like it leads directly out to sea.

"I could for sure see myself cooking in here." She turns to the living room filled with a deep L-shaped couch. "And watching movies in there." She spins to take in the view out the back. "And napping out by the pool. It's perfect."

If I remember correctly, the undies I found her in the night the pipes exploded declared her belief in the power of naps.

"It will need a new deck, and the stove will have to go. I'll have an aqua oven by then," she says as if it's a fact.

"And when exactly is that going to happen?"

"I'm going to retire here," she declares.

"You are. You can just will that into existence?" Knowing her, she could.

She always had the ability to dream big and make it happen. She dreamed so big, sometimes I think it rubbed off on me. Listening to her dream out loud back in college, I could almost see a future that wasn't bleak and dark and riddled with pain.

"Jimmy Buffett says I can." She turns back to me with a grin as big as the sea behind her. "'Someday I Will' and all that?"

"What if it's not on the market when you retire?"

"It will be." And with that, her tour of the future is over. She drags me out the front door and we stroll back toward the cars.

The pathway leads behind the backyards of the next block of homes, bringing into view the backyard palapas and kids' swing sets. A long slip-n-slide sprays a tunnel of water over its long yellow launchpad. In the opposite direction, out in the distance, Lanai sits with her base in the mighty ocean and top in the clouds spinning lazily by.

Em tugs on my arm, drawing me close enough for her to whisper as if there was anyone around to hear what she's going to say. "Are those public?" She points to one of the hammocks set up near the pathway. "Like, anyone can just use them?"

"As long as they're empty. Not really good form to shove someone out of one to climb in."

"Really?" Joy bubbles in her laughter and shines in her eyes. She bounces over to the hammock and climbs in. She tucks one arm behind her head, blond hair splayed around her, before taking in a huge breath and letting it out as one contented sigh. Her eyes close and peace washes over her features.

I give the hammock a small push to give her just the right amount of swing.

She opens one eye, shielding it from the sun with her free hand, and stares at me, baffled. "How are you not in here with me already?"

I thought she'd simply lie there for a second and then we'd keep walking. But, the way she's getting settled in right now makes me think she's burrowing down for one of those naps she loves so much. "That's not gonna hold us both."

"Oh, my gosh. Stop stalling and get in here, Finny." Dammit.

I do my best to leave some space between us, but it's a hammock. That's not really an option.

"So, I have two weeks left here. What are we going to do with all that time?"

"You have to see sunrise from Haleakala. And maybe hike to a few waterfalls." She rolls toward me and nuzzles into my side as I continue. "We could go find some sea turtles to swim with and.."

Em's breathing grows deep and steady. "Em?" I whisper softly. She doesn't move.

I gently tuck the strand of hair that fell in front of her eyes behind her ear. As I listen to her, my breathing slows to match hers. My shoulders unwind. I let my eyes close as the sun warms my skin. The scent of her coconut shampoo mixes with the salty air, swirling around us, wrapping us in a tropical cocoon. One that I never want to leave.

That peace quickly evaporates, though, when I remember that I'm not here relaxing with my best friend in the world, wiling away the hours. I'm sharing a hammock with another man's wife.

A place I should not be. But if I move, I will wake her, and I just can't bring myself to disrupt her respite. After all, that is the only thing I was trying to do for her today. To take away whatever it was that was crushing her this morning.

We *are* just lying here. She *did* invite me. We *are* in public. How bad could this really be?

Yeah, I know. I should wake her up.

A gray francolin decides to do it for me with his loud call. Em startles awake.

"Em," I try to rouse her so she won't fall back asleep. "We should probably go."

———

Alone, in my truck on my way home I call Justin, my business partner. "Hey, can you hold down things for the next two weeks?"

"What happened? What can I do?" he says like I just told him my dog died.

"Nothing happened. Just gonna take a vacation for a couple of weeks," I say like it's a thing that I do from time to time. In reality, I haven't taken off more than three days in a row ever. And even then it was only because the hospital wouldn't release me in under three days after my appendectomy.

Justin is understandably confused. "Okay. I can take care of everything, but you sure you're okay?"

"I'm all good. Listen, I need you to do one more thing." I turn onto The Kuihelani Highway to cross the island back home.

"You need me to hunt down the alien who took over your body?" he laughs.

"Funny. Can you put in an offer on 526 Oia'i'o Road? Forty thousand above asking. All cash offer."

"You find another house to flip?"

"Not a flip. Put it in my name, not MacGregor Homesteads."

"Really? It's that good?"

"Yeah. It hardly needs any fixing up, just a new deck and a... turquoise oven."

I've been living out her dreams for the last few years anyway, why stop now?

Chapter 12

FINN
OCTOBER, SENIOR YEAR

The Santa Ana's have been blowing a hot, dry wind for days now, the Red Flag warning predicting fires all around the county. For us, it meant perfect surf conditions. The water was still warm from the Indian Summer, the wind blowing offshore, shaping the waves into perfect faces for us to enjoy. When our arms can't paddle another stroke, we grab a couple of burritos and hike out to our hill.

Em found the little patch of grass covering a wide hill tucked into the campus of Scripps Institute of Oceanography during our freshman year. It quickly became our go-to place to warm up after a long surf, or simply a place to wile away the hours. On a clear day, we can see the Oceanside Pier up north, Catalina, San Nicolas, and San Clemente Islands out to sea, and not another soul on earth.

We toss a blanket over the tall grass and scarf down our lunch.

"I saw this video yesterday of these two guys surfing some completely empty break down in Mexico. Can you imagine that? The entire break to themselves," she sighs out.

"It's probably just some trick photography. Careful editing."

"Oh my gosh, Finn. Can't you ever just enjoy something?"

I lay back and shield my eyes with my arm. "Sorry, Em. It must have been great."

"We should go do that. You know, find some empty break down in Mexico and surf for days." She lays back beside me. "Or weeks, we could stay for weeks."

"Sure. Who needs to actually go to class."

"Don't make me throw you in the water, Frowny Finn." She bumps my shoulder. "We could go after we graduate. I have a month before I have to move to Stanford."

Damn, that sounds kind of nice. I'd love to get away from people for a while. But being alone with Em for that long is bound to go bad. I'm bound to go bad.

"And we could do it for super cheap. We could catch fish straight from the ocean and roast them over a campfire. Your van could make it down there, right? We could sleep in your van. And be crispy with salt for days."

I don't think she realizes that means sharing a bed. For weeks.

Or maybe she did. I may be able to muster the self-control for a night or two when we go on local surf trips, but weeks? There's no way in hell I could be with her alone in my van for weeks and not screw it up.

"It would be so awesome. Warm waves every day. And you could bring your guitar and I'll bring my mandolin and you could write. You could write your whole first album out there. You could call it Baja Sessions. Okay, I know Chris Isaak already did that, but you could find a new name. It would be amazing. Just music and waves. And us."

"That sounds perfect, Em."

A fluffy cloud billows overhead, changing from an ugly old man's face to an elephant sounding off. I reach for my soda and take a long sip. Weeks alone with Em on empty beaches sounds like heaven.

"And when we get back, maybe we could go to Maui. I've always wanted to live there."

There's no stopping this girl. "Yeah right. The most expensive place on the planet to live. With no jobs or stuff or money?"

"We wouldn't need stuff or money. Not much at least."

"Hmm," is all I can muster.

"We could buy a little piece of land, grow all our food, and build a little shack. Hell, I'd even live in a tent on Maui. It's not like it gets cold."

"Wow, Em. You must be serious if you're cussing about it," I tease.

"I'm a fully-grown adult, now. I can say 'hell' if I want to."

Ha. She may be twenty, but she still dreams like a child. So pure and unspoiled, she almost makes me believe these things are possible. "Could we grow bananas out there?"

"Sure."

"Okay. I'm in."

"All it takes is bananas?"

"It's been a lifelong dream of mine to grow my own bananas."

"Good to know you dream big, Finn."

I don't tell her that growing bananas is the sum total of all my dreams. When other people talk about all the dreams they have and all the things they're going to accomplish, it's like they're talking a foreign language. I can't get my thoughts that far ahead to actually want anything for my future. I have a hard enough time existing in the present.

She rolls to her side and props her head on her hand. "So, you'll really go, Finny?"

"After graduation, Mexico. Sounds like a plan."

She rests her hand on my chest. And I know where this leads. It can't.

I sit up. Create some distance. "We should go."

I slowly turn back to size up her reaction. Confusion radiates from her beautiful face. "I thought we were just gonna kill some time before we go to Mark's."

"I need to take a nap before we go."

"And there's a better place than this hill, in the sun, overlooking the sea?"

"Yeah. My bed."

Her eyebrows rise.

Great. She thinks I invited her into my bed. "Alone."

There's only a flash of disappointment before she smothers

it with her smile. "I suppose I could use a shower. Wash the salt off my skin."

Great. Now there's no chance of getting to sleep with that image in my head.

A few hours later, I'm late to pick her up to head to Mark's. It's only forty-five minutes, but I know it will piss her off. And, maybe, I do it on purpose. To really drive it home. To shout, *Keep Your Distance.*

When she answers the door, she is in a little pair of sweat shorts and a tank top that is way too tight for her to wear in public. She looks at her watch and smiles a groggy smile. "Thanks for letting me sleep. I really needed that."

Seriously? I silently yell and howl and shout, but she simply won't hear me. I can't make her understand, can't warn her. I can see the wreck happening up ahead in slow motion, but I am incapable of stopping it.

Chapter 13

EMERSON
PRESENT DAY

*U*p before everyone else, I relish the silence as I make breakfast. I toss an English muffin in the toaster then crack a few eggs into a pan. I push them around thoughtlessly as I stare out the window.

The only event I had planned for this trip was my one Dark Day. It marked the two-year anniversary of Timmy's death. In the beginning, nearly every day I was lost in the Pit of Despair. And fittingly so. You don't really get over the death of your husband only five days into your marriage very easily.

It took two years of work. Of crying and anger and of sitting with my grief.

Lately, I have gotten to a place where I have more good days than bad days. Where I can go for weeks without the waves crashing on me and taking me under. I came out here to mark the anniversary, but, also, to mark the beginning of the next chapter. One where I will be looking ahead instead of only looking back.

I had plans to take a pivotal deep dive into grief on that Dark Day. I gave myself permission for one final big cry. Not that I could actually control that. I knew I'd cry again. It would come in waves just like it had for the last two years, but I wasn't going to let those waves push me under for days at a time. I would ride those waves, miss Timmy, and then step back out into my life again.

I wanted to close that door and open the door to the next phases of my life. To build my friendships, to get in shape, to find my direction in life. Looks like God had other plans for that day. Or maybe we'll file that day under building my friendships. No one said that I can only be friends with girls.

And it was the exact day I needed. I didn't need one final cry, but one day where I was entirely in the present. It reminded me of those long afternoons Finn and I would lay on our hill and just pass the time. Nowhere to go, nothing to do, except enjoy the sun and good food and good company.

The toaster pops as I look down to nearly burnt eggs. I slide the eggs out onto a plate and bring the smoking pan to the sink. Running water over the pan creates a cloud of steam. By the time it clears, I'm greeted with a view of Finn out the window. He's talking over the fence to a really cute neighbor who is doing her best to get his attention. I don't blame her though. Finn is in a low-slung pair of red trunks. Shirtless.

Weights are scattered around in front of the garage along with a few medicine balls. I'm pretty sure she was just given a breathtaking show of Finn's early-morning strength workout, and like any warm-blooded female, has been drawn to Finn like a moth to a flame, a spectacle I have witnessed time and time again.

He's acting polite, accepting a dozen eggs from her over the fence, until he catches me gazing at him from through this window. He tilts his brow, looking at me uncertainly, before turning back to his neighbor.

And his whole countenance changes.

I didn't realize how little of flirting is actually in the words because I can't hear a word they are saying to each other, but the conversation just changed from polite to downright frisky. Their body language is screaming seduction. She tips her head down and the smile that spreads across her face is burning with a sensuous flame. His hand rests on her arm that is perched on the fence standing between them, the fence that just may ignite any second if they keep it up.

Typical Finn. We have one moment of connection, one moment where the whole world seems to slow down and I think that maybe the thoughts that have been swimming around in my head are swimming around in his too, and he bolts. Or maybe flinches is a better word.

He did it back in college all the time. We'd get a bit too close, over the imaginary line he had drawn, and he'd withdraw. Withdraw and make sure he was mean enough that I knew his true feelings for me. Usually, that involved paying attention to some other woman and making sure I had a unadulterated view of the game.

Back then, I would flinch right back in response. I'd get quiet and sad and avoid him for days. But I am not that scared little girl anymore. Two can play at this game.

I finish up my coffee and eggs before making my way outside to search out my dogfight.

JJ's joined Finn in the driveway. They're playing a game of hoops both shirtless and working out a little more frustration than is called for in a simple pick-up game.

Perfect. Finn's already a little worked up. Time to get him boiling over.

"Who's up for a little Horse?" I ask coyly.

Both boys turn and freeze.

So, I may have begun enacting my plan a little early. I'm in a pair of tight yoga shorts and sports bra, having tossed my shirt on the grass on my way out. It's nothing I wouldn't wear on a run, much more than I wear at the beach, but I figured if they're both shirtless and sweaty, I have to even the playing field somehow.

They look at each other and shrug. JJ finds his voice. "Sure thing. Ladies first?"

"Oh, she's no lady when she's playing basketball," Finn chimes in.

"Evens and odds for who shoots first, then?" I suggest.

"Odd man out loses. Rock paper scissors to break the tie," Finn finishes.

Finn looks my way and gives me two small nods. We worked out a secret code way back when so we'd always come out ahead in this game. When he nods twice, we both shoot twos. One nod, we shoot ones. That way we'd never be odd man out.

JJ counts us off, and surprise, surprise, he shoots a one and is eliminated.

I could always beat Finn in rock paper scissors. He's like most men. He'll keep showing whatever he won with last time. If he loses, he'll use whatever beat him. He's never been able to figure out how I can read his mind to always come out ahead.

But, the last time we played this was years ago. And remembering what I beat him with has been clouded by the excitement of winning that day.

"Been too long to remember my last move, huh?" Finn asks. So, maybe he had more of an idea of what I was doing than I suspected.

Without the knowledge of his last move, I fall back on typical male behavior. When all else fails, most men will start with rock. It's a move of strength.

So I display paper.

And win.

"Why don't we make this interesting?" JJ spins the ball on his finger, the teasing in his voice echoed in his smile. "Loser buys winner dinner?"

Oh, good. This will be much easier if JJ is up for a little harmless flirtation. I head his way, standing a bit too close. "Better bring your wallet, I expect a full four-course meal in a five-star restaurant." I slowly draw the basketball from his hands without moving my gaze from his eyes.

Finn growls. "Just shoot, Em."

Oh, this is gonna be good.

I walk back to where a three-point line would be on a real court and toss an easy shot, nothing but net. The ball bounces back my way. I slip it beneath my arm.

"Nice shot, girly." JJ offers me a high five. I happily oblige.

Finn snatches the ball from my arm and moves to where I shot from.

"It was back a few inches," I call out.

His jaw clenches as he moves back. And misses.

I snap the ball up and, as I walk it over to JJ, call out to

Finn, "That's an H." I hand the ball to JJ and soften my voice. "You're shot, JJ."

He holds my gaze for a moment before taking a four-foot jump shot from the left side of the key. Such an easy shot.

He's still standing where he made it from to mark the spot where I have to shoot. I slide right up next to him until our shoulders are touching and turn my head toward him to share a smile. I shoot without even looking at the hoop.

I don't bother checking to see if it went in. I can tell from the sound. And holding JJ's gaze for a moment longer is getting right to Finn.

Finn gets the rebound and nearly shoves JJ out of the way to shoot from the same spot.

"It was back a few inches," I tell him again.

He stomps back two paces before missing another shot.

I don't bother looking at him when I say, "That's an O," which earns me another grunt.

By the time Finn is at H-O-R-S, JJ is at H-O-R, and I have had more than my fair share of fun incessantly flirting with JJ and telling Finn to back up two inches on nearly every shot, I haven't earned a single letter. Which means my plan must be throwing Finn off his game because there was hardly a time that we would lose when playing two-on-two against nearly anyone. But today, he can't make a basket to save his life.

Maybe it's all that muscle he's put on his frame over the last few years. Must have thrown off his shot.

Or, I finally have an effect on him.

After I make an easy shot from the free throw line, he catches the ball, smacking it with his hand, marches right up to me, and snarls, "Do you really think I'm that bad that you don't need to even bother trying to distract me once?"

This draws a laugh from me. I've *really* gotten to him.

"Fine," he snarls and steps to the side. He waves his hand for me to move, before taking my spot on the free throw line.

Fine, it is.

But he asked for this.

I slide right up behind him and wrap my hand around his

waist, resting it low on his belly. I soften my voice, "It was back a few inches."

I ease him back, throwing him off balance. His abs tense under my palm as I draw it back along the top edge of his trunks, letting my pinkie slip under the belt line of his low-slung trunks just a touch.

I take my other hand and run it through his hair, tugging a bit as I get to the back. I lean my body against his back as I lift my lips until they touch his ear, "Don't miss, Finny."

I step back and he slowly turns to take stock of the new me, a girl he has never met before, and looks at me with a longing I have never seen before from him. I try unsuccessfully to suppress the smile that comes from the knowledge of this new power over Finn.

He tries to refocus on the hoop, but his shot misses by a full three feet, falling limply to the ground.

He scrubs his hand through his hair, growling, "I'm out of here," before stomping off into the house.

I look to JJ. "I guess it's just you and me, babe," I say loud enough for Finn to hear.

Is it wrong that I love the way Finn physically shudders at that?

I finish off JJ quickly after that without earning a single letter. But as I do, I wonder if I took things too far. My plan didn't exactly have the results I was hoping for. Finn's pissed and I feel awful. If this is the result, why did Finn keep doing it all those years ago?

JJ's voice draws me from my shame spiral. "Don't worry, Sonny. I won't say a word." JJ gathers the ball and smiles knowingly. "And I won't get any ideas."

"Huh?"

"Not that I mind being used like that. I'll sign up willingly for that kind of use. But, in the end, I know who that whole show was for." He throws his arm around my shoulder. "Come on, we have a hike to get ready for."

It's a forty-minute drive to the other side of the island. By the time we stop for sandwiches, I'm nearly asleep, having lost track of the conversation long before. I muster up the energy to walk inside the shop and order a veggie sandwich, but I'm completely spent by the time I climb back up into the truck.

I have no idea how I'm going to haul my heavy body four miles up some trail to see a waterfall. I had a hard enough time hauling it up into the truck. The only thing I want to do right now is climb up into Finn's soft bed and sleep the rest of the day away. I let my eyelids drop as the whir of conversation hums me to sleep.

"Em. We're here." Finn's hand is on my knee, gently shaking it.

I drag my head off the window and try to nudge my brain to start working. "Okay. Give me a second and I'll be ready."

He pats my knee again, startling me awake again. "You sure you're feeling okay, Em?"

"I'm fine."

"I know you are, Em. But I got you anyway."

I slide my hand to the door handle and tug, leaving me spilling my way out of the truck. "Let's do this," I say with forced enthusiasm.

Finn rounds the back of the truck where JJ, Charlie, Indigo, and Grey have gathered and look to be waiting on me. He untethers Baja and lets him hop out of the back before digging in the back of the truck, throwing around a few things. "Crap. I forgot my hiking boots."

I look down to the pair of flip-flops barely hanging onto his feet. He could probably do the hike in those, or barefoot, for how tough he is.

"You guys are gonna have to go on without me." He looks my way. "I know I promised you waterfalls, but any chance you'd keep me company, Em?"

Baja approaches me and sits right in front of me. I swear he smiles up at me with his big puppy dog eyes, asking me to stay. If it means I don't have to move for the rest of the day, I'd be willing to do anything. "I could do that."

"But, Sonny, this is the one I was telling you about," Charlie begs. "The waterfall's like a hundred feet tall. And you can swim under it."

Charlie picked out the Pipiwai Trail to Makahiku Falls just for me. When we were planning this trip, I told her I wanted to meander through bamboo forests and scramble up steep jungle climbs to a waterfall that felt like it was in the middle of nowhere. Pipiwai Trail hit the mark, but now that we're here, I can't imagine having to do it.

Indigo tugs Charlie's arm and gives her a wink. "I think Sonny will be just fine here."

"Ohhhh. I see." She fastens the chest strap on her day pack. "Text if you need anything."

Finn glares at Charlie. "There's nothing to see, Charlie."

Grey throws his arm around Charlie, looking back at us. "Better get out of here before he goes all caveman."

"We'll be down at the beach when you get back. Just text me," Finn says and the others take off up a trail that seems insurmountable at the moment.

Finn wrestles two towels from the truck bed and grabs our sandwiches and drinks from the cab. "It's about four hundred feet to the shore. You think you can make it?"

Four hundred feet feels insurmountable. "I'm fine, Finn."

"I know you are, babe, but I got you anyway." It's like he hears a completely different set of words when I say I'm fine.

Baja leads as we follow a dirt path through a forest of banyan trees toward the light pouring through a small opening at the end. Halfway through, I know Finn must have lied. It feels like I have already walked ten miles.

As we move through that final opening, the whole Pacific comes into view. We trudge through tall grass to the edge of this volcanic island. Finn spreads out two towels in the shade of the lone tree on the hill that rolls off into lava rock being beaten by waves.

There couldn't be a more perfect spot right now with the cool breeze floating off the ocean, the dappled sun dancing through the trees warming my skin just enough, and the sound of the waves scrambling up the rocks and shimmying back down again.

I flop down on my belly on one of the towels and kick off my shoes. Too tired to roll over, I use my toes to squiggle out of each sock and enjoy the feel of the wind over my feet.

Finn sits on the towel beside me as Baja snuggles up between us. I prop my head on my hands as I watch the waves roll in and out.

"Do you remember that time we tried to surf Santa Cruz in February? And I kept telling you that your regular fullsuit wouldn't be warm enough." Finn starts recounting the story that has me laughing at my innocent naiveté every time I think about it. "But you were totally convinced that you'd be just fine. You'd just visualize being in Hawaii and it would be enough to keep you warm. I don't think you had any idea what real cold water would be like."

I lay my head down on the towel and let the sound of Finn's soothing voice recounting one of my favorite memories and the smell of the salt air almost lull me to sleep.

Until I bolt up onto my forearms.

Baja whips his head my way on alert for any threat.

"Dammit. I forgot my meds." I'm normally forgetful, but have found ways to make it easier to remember my daily meds at home. I have my routines and my meds are right by my bedside so I see them each morning. But on vacation, everything is different, and I don't have any visual cues to remind me.

"I'll drive you back." Finn sits up and starts gathering his towel.

"Nah. That's alright." My pump will compensate for the lack of a morning insulin shot. And I won't die from not having my thyroid meds. I'll just be exhausted. At least it explains why I'm so tired today.

"Seriously, Em. They won't be done for another three hours."

"I just want to lay here and rest."

"Okay, babe. Whatever you want." Finn lays back on his towel as I rest my head on Baja and stare at the clouds passing by overhead.

The sound of Finn's phone wakes me after what feels like days of sleep. When we get back to the truck and hook Baja back in, I spy Finn's hiking boots. He quickly tosses the towels over them, his brows arched mischievously.

I don't know how he figured out that I was sick before I did, but it's not the first time.

Chapter 14

EMERSON
NOVEMBER, SENIOR YEAR

By the time midterms roll around, the stress finally gets to me. And it isn't pretty. I'm cranky, short-tempered, and irritable. I can't focus. I fall asleep in class, but never in bed at night.

I have my last exam tomorrow morning in Developmental Neuroscience, but I cannot for the life of me put any more information inside my head without it exploding. Though, maybe if it exploded, at least then, I'd get some sleep without it taunting me all night by not slowing down one bit.

I've taken to mainlining coffee to deal with the fogginess of not sleeping, but I think it may be hitting me on the back end by keeping me up the next night. Unfortunately, without it, I'm completely worthless.

Since I hate the taste, I have to cover it with chocolate syrup and whipped cream. And I don't think the barista quite understands what "a quarter of the cup of chocolate syrup" means. She laughed it off when I asked for it that way. In a place where the typical coffee order consists of fourteen adjectives, you'd think they'd be more accommodating. Or at least be able to follow simple directions.

"Fill up a quarter of the cup with chocolate syrup." I lift the cup that she already screwed up and point at it. "Right here. Fill it to here with syrup. Then top it off with espresso. It's not that hard."

As I bring my now possibly correct drink back to the table, Finn flips the cover of my Physics book closed. "Pack it up. You need a break."

"I'm fine, Finn. She just totally messed up my order. I mean how hard could it be to get it right? It's not like it's O-chem. Seriously." I flip my book back open and flop into my chair.

"Em?" he says softly. "Want to hit a few baseballs? Give you something to hit?"

Hitting something really hard right now sounds perfect. "Fine." I slam my book and notebook into my backpack before tossing my caffeine in the trash. She probably screwed it up again anyway.

By the time we hit the field at the local park, my previous caffeine fix must have worn off. The walk to the backstop looks way too far. And the five-gallon bucket of balls is much too heavy to lug all that way.

"Let me have that," Finn says as he lifts the bucket from my hands. "You can carry this." He tosses me his old mitt.

I think he knows how badly I need to hit something so he lets me bat first. He trades me his mitt for the bat and drags the bucket of balls to the mound.

"Let's go, MacGregor. Pitch me something I can hit," I tease. I swing and miss the first one.

"Maybe try to actually hit it this time," he laughs.

Ten misses in and I can barely drop the bat from my shoulder, let alone make contact. The fierce anger I was burning with just moments ago has been replaced by an overwhelming heaviness and apathy.

I drag the bat behind me as I walk to the mound. "Your turn." Maybe throwing pitches will be easier.

I slide the worn-in glove on my left hand and it takes a few shoves to get it on. As Finn throws the balls I missed from the backstop, I try, mostly successfully, to catch them and dump them in the bucket. I stagger around to the ones I missed and gather them in my glove before returning to the bucket. I dump all but one, grasping it, ready to pitch.

Finn takes a few practice swings before squaring up in the batter's box. "Let's see if I can hit more than you did. Couldn't do much worse," he laughs.

"Oh shut up, Finn." I toss the first pitch his way. He connects and sends it flying over my head.

Whatever. Like I even care. I bend down to grab the next one and send it in his direction. He hits it right back toward me.

I can see the ball coming straight at me, but I cannot get my body to react. It's like it doesn't care. Or maybe, it's on strike. Either way, I simply stand there as a ball heads my direction at what has to be close to eighty miles an hour.

It whizzes past my ear so close that I can feel the air move.

"Oh, crap. Em. I'm so sorry." Finn sprints my way. "Are you okay? You didn't even move."

"I'm fine, Finn." It seems to be the only thing I can come up with to say to him lately. And I say it on repeat. Fifty times a day after he asks if I'm okay, if there's something wrong, if I'm mad at him, why I'm mad at him. And fifty times a day, I have to tell him that I'm fine.

It's good enough to convince him to return to the batter's box. But that heaviness and apathy have now increased exponentially. When I bend to pick up another ball, I hover there for a few minutes while I try to convince myself to put out the effort to stand back up.

I toss the next pitch and it doesn't even make it to the plate.

"Come on, Em. Seriously? I gave you some real pitches."

I close my eyes, trying to muster the strength for one more pitch. I lower my glove and let it hang loose at the end of my arm. I stare down at the bucket of balls so far away.

"Em! Let's go. Come on," he shouts to me.

The last thing I want to do is move. All I want to do is lay down right here on the mound and sleep for a week.

"Quit being such a wuss and pitch something," he taunts.

I know he's joking, but thinking of having to move at all only ignites a fire within me. I lift a ball from the bucket and launch it at him with all my might.

Not over the plate.

At him.

He flinches at the pain, tucking his shoulder. I take another ball and hurl it at his back. Then another and another. Until I'm completely spent.

I collapse onto the red dirt of the mound, as tears stream down my cheeks. All the energy used to keep them at bay used up in my fit.

And then Finn is there, next to me. His legs wrapped around me as he tries to get close enough to hug the freak of a person in front of him. "It's okay, Em. Everything's gonna be okay."

He doesn't ask me to explain the freakish outburst, which is good because words right now are coming out all mushed up and backward. That is if I can even find the right one back in my brain files.

I sag into his chest, letting his arms hold me up. "I'm so tired, Finn."

He holds my head to his chest and runs his hand over my hair. "I've got you, Em."

After what feels like an eternity, he draws back to survey my face. "Better now?"

I nod.

"You ready to head to the van?"

Another nod.

He unwraps himself from me and my body craves the missing protection immediately. I'm left to support my own body weight and every muscle I own is screaming at me about that.

Finn hauls me to my feet and we begin to slowly move toward the van. Halfway there, I realize his arms are empty. "The balls, Finn. And bat."

"I'll worry about them later. Let's just get you to the van."

When we pull up to my place, I peer through the window at the neverending expanse of grassy yard between the van and my front door. Then, I picture the miles from the front door to my bed.

I lift my hand to the car door handle and pause. "I'm so sorry, Finn." I crack the door and slide out.

I'm hit with the pulsing sound of music pouring out from my small house. There is no way I'll be able to sleep with my roommates' music. And they won't turn it down for me. I know. I've asked.

Dragging my lagging body up the incline toward my front door, my ability to propel myself any further fails. And, once again, I crumple to the ground.

Finn is there in an instant. "Em, are you okay?

"The music."

"The music?"

"Tired. And the music. And sleep." I begin to cry again. I've done more crying this semester than in my whole life.

"You could crash on my couch?" It sounds more like a question he's asking himself.

I look up at him, too tired to even form the words. But he knows my answer.

He stands. "Come on."

Sadly, I'm too tired to stand. Every last ounce of energy I have is currently being used to sit upright.

So, he scoops me up and carries me to the car. He settles me in the front seat and buckles me in.

And takes me home.

Chapter 15

FINN
PRESENT DAY

Seeing Em flirt with JJ pissed me off, but her hands on me like that just about killed me. Maybe she's punishing me for the way I left—I know I deserve it. I more than deserve it. But feeling her arms around me, her body pressed up against mine, that was damn near torture. To get a taste of everything I've ever wanted, everything I would never deserve, and to know she didn't mean any of it was a harsh truth.

And, of course, she didn't mean any of it. How could she? She's married to a man who is perfect. Em would never settle for less. I'm sure he's everything I'm not. Reliable, trustworthy, safe. Someone who would never let anything bad happen to her.

Last night, when we finally got back home and Em got her meds, she moved her medical bag to the nightstand where she'd see it and remember to take them tomorrow. I should have told her to do that from day one. See, unreliable. I can't even keep her from missing a day of her meds.

At least I did one thing right. And that was to never cross that line with her. It would have only been an unmitigated disaster.

I look up from my stool at the kitchen island to see Charlie, Em, and Indigo chilling in the living room, killing time until we do another Game Night. They're laughing so hard about something Charlie said that they're crying.

Em looks happy.

Content.

Peaceful.

And if me walking away made that happen, then I'm content, too.

Content and alone.

The way it should be.

Charlie rises from the couch heading toward me before bracing herself on the back of the couch. "Whoa."

"You okay?" Indigo asks.

"Yeah. Just got up too fast."

Em glances my way and raises her brows as if to ask, *What was that?* We've always had a way of having silent conversations. I make a face as if to say, *That was weird.*

Charlie makes her way to the kitchen and begins digging through the pantry. She brings a bag of my Cheetos to the island and raises them up asking if she can have some.

"Queen of all-natural? You want Cheetos?"

"It just sounds really good. You okay with that?."

I shrug. "Go for it."

She adds a bowl and the sour cream onto the island before mixing them with the Cheetos and then brings the crazy concoction back to the living room. "Anyone want some?"

"No, thanks. I think I need a refill of tea, though." Em brings her half-filled cup my way. She pulls the pitcher of tea from the fridge and sets it next to her glass on the island right next to me. She whispers, "I think I know something that I shouldn't say," and the sound of her whispering brings back the sensation of her lips against my ear the last time she whispered to me. "But if you know, too..." she continues.

"About Charlie?" I whisper back.

She nods.

Charlie has been off the past few weeks. Ever since she got what she thought was the stomach flu for a week straight. The weakness, weird cravings. The other night she convinced Greyson to run to the store at midnight to get her mint chocolate chip ice cream and pickles.

"I might know something, too," I admit.

Her smile grows exponentially. Man, it feels good to have a secret with her again.

She rubs her belly and lifts her brows.

I nod. "I think they've been trying." I try to plaster on a smile to cover the worry that erupts whenever I hear someone's pregnant.

Em looks back at Charlie and her smile falls for just a second.

"What's all the whispering about, Sonny?" Charlie calls to us.

"Oh, nothing." Em turns toward me trying to hide her guilty smile from the girls. I love that she doesn't try to hide it from me.

"I've been meaning to ask, what's with the new moniker?" I really want to ask, what's with the new Em? She is a completely different girl than the stifled one I met years ago who hid behind her intellect and kept people at arm's length.

She shrugs as if it's nothing. "Timmy started calling me that when we met and it just kind of stuck." She fills another tall glass with tea, tosses a spoon of sugar in it, and slides it my way—just how I take my tea. "Why? You don't like it?"

"It's not really you," I say over the brim of my cup.

"Timmy thought it matched my sunny disposition. *He* thought my wide-eyed positivity was something to be celebrated instead of shunned."

I knew her indefatigable hope and optimism should be celebrated. It was one of the things I loved most about her. I just knew I couldn't be the one to destroy it. I wouldn't let myself do that.

Em grabs the pitcher and returns it to the fridge without even filling her glass. She walks to the living room and dissolves back into the girls' laughter.

And our tenuous moment of connection is gone. Like it never even happened.

I turn back to my sketch of a yard I've been working on in one of the flips we are almost finished with. Though, I'm merely using it as a cover to sit here and soak in every moment I can of

Em's sunny disposition. I can use as much of it as I can get. There hasn't been a whole lot of sunshine in my life in the last four years.

"Soooo," Charlie practically sings at Indigo. "You and JJ seem friendly. You two a thing?"

"Oh, my gosh. No. JJ's just a big ol' flirt," Indigo protests.

"You know we can hear you two giggling in that room every single night. You sure there's nothing going on there?"

"Can we not talk about this?" Indigo throws a pillow at her completely missing and slamming into the guitar suspended on the wall like decor instead of a usable instrument. "I'm so sorry, Charlie." She hops up and straightens the guitar, picking up the pillow on her way back.

Em checks out the guitar and then glances at me, a sad smile tugging at her lips.

"Is that yours or Greyson's?" Indigo asks Charlie.

"I think it's Finn's. It was here when we moved in," she says.

I pretend not to notice the girls looking my way for confirmation. "*You* play guitar?" Indigo sounds stunned. "There's no way. Play something for us."

"I haven't touched that thing in years." I try my best to avoid Em when I say it, but I cannot convince my eyes to stay off her.

She looks at me with such disappointment in her eyes. I know she's thinking I'm a shell of the man I once was. And she'd be right.

She unfurls herself from the couch and walks to the ukulele on the wall next to my Ovation. She removes it from the wall and, as she walks back to the couch, gives me a look like, *Come on, I'll do it with you.*

The thought of getting to hear her voice again convinces me. There was nothing that could wash away a bad day like hearing her sing.

I set my pencil down and retrieve my guitar. As I tune it up, she strums out the beginning of the Jimmy Buffett song, "Souvenirs." I watch trying to pick up the chords, but my ukulele fingering is a little rusty.

She fills in the gaps. "It's E, B, C#m, E. Then A, E, F#m, B. The chorus is only a little different. There's a G#m in there. You'll figure it out."

We play it through once. Then she looks down and asks, "Could you play it with open power chords? It just sounds so amazing for this song."

I make the adjustment and play along with her once through, and then she starts to sing.

I can feel every muscle in my body go slack. It's like the tension that I had been carrying around with me for years vanishes into thin air. I join in with her, harmonizing on the second line.

When she gets to the line about her memories being like ghosts, I can hear my voice getting tight, my throat throbbing at the strain of trying to hold back something I have been clinging to for years.

Just in time, Billie pushes through the front door with Ryder following closely behind. "You all ready for Game Night? I got a special one you're all gonna love."

Em stops singing, but finishes off playing the song before returning the ukulele to the wall. I keep playing while everyone files out the door to go play another game. From the smirk in Billie's voice, I can tell she's come up with a game that I'm going to hate even more than usual, and I'm in no hurry to play.

When we're all seated around the fire, Billie lets us in on our punishment for the night. She calls it Truth or Darehole. She says it's a grown-up version of the stupidest game ever invented, truth or dare, but with a cornhole twist.

I stand, nearly ready to bail before this one even begins.

"Wait, Finn. I promise it's not bad," Billie begs, before setting off into an explanation about how she made truth or dare more fun.

Someone will roll two eight-sided dice to decide whose turn it is. Then, those two people toss a beanbag onto the cornhole board fifteen feet away. You make it, you don't have to do the truth or dare.

Which is perfect. For years, I've been using that cornhole game as a way to distract myself from thoughts I'd rather avoid. In other words, I have spent way too much time perfecting my game. Looks like I won't have to be peer-pressured into doing something totally idiotic for Truth or Darehole tonight.

Because that was the whole purpose of playing this game as a kid. You didn't have the guts to do something on your own so your friends would get you to do it by suggesting truth or dare. I don't think, in the history of this game, things didn't dissolve into chaos and hurt feelings when all was said and done.

Billie collects a box of her premade Truth or Darehole cards from a table filled with props, trying to convince us that this will be an innocent game of doing silly things, but I know Billie. She always has a trick up her sleeve.

"Okay. Fine. I'll play, but nothing sexual okay? We're not in sixth grade anymore and peer pressure is stupid."

Billie hands the dice to Ryder who rolls them on the small table next to her. She looks down to read the dice. "Finn and Indigo." She actually made dice with our names on them.

Indigo hops up and drags me to my feet. We step up to the pink chalk line Billie sprayed on the grass and she hands me a bean bag. I toss it perfectly and swagger back to my chair. Indigo hits the board, the bag sliding up until it's nearly in the hole, but it hangs on.

"Truth or dare, Indigo?" Billie asks.

"Dare," Indigo replies.

Billie draws the first card from the deck and reads it off. "Read out the last five things on your search history."

"Can I switch to truth?"

"Sure. Your truth is, What are the last five things you searched for on your phone?" Charlie counters.

"Fine. Hold on." She pulls out her phone to look and scrolls down a bit before reading, "Water temp in Maui..."

"That is so not the last thing you searched for," Charlie shouts. "Hand it over."

Indigo reluctantly complies.

"Oh, this is good. I can see why you wanted to cheat," Charlie teases.

"Whatever. I am who I am. No shame in my game," Indigo says, with a bit too much bluster in her voice.

Charlie raises her brows before reading, "JJ Gerdis Instagram, JJ Gerdis Police Detective, JJ Gerdis shirtless. Need I go on?"

"No need to Google that Indie." JJ whips off his shirt, flexing over the fire. "All you had to do was ask."

"Sit down, JJ," Ryder says with a laugh.

"And put your shirt on," I add.

"You afraid your lady's gonna get some ideas?" he throws back at me.

She's not my lady. And we all saw what happened last time he was shirtless in front of her.

I growl my reply.

After we find out that Billie would choose Bear Grylls in his younger years to be stranded on a deserted island with, Em tells us, with a bit too much enthusiasm, that she would rather skinny dip with someone she knows than a stranger, and we watch Ryder down a raw egg mixed with five different condiments, Billie rolls the dice again.

"Finn and Emerson. You're up," Billie says with suspicious glee.

I walk to the board and retrieve two beanbags, handing one to Em, letting our hands touch for a moment too long. The smile in her eyes contains a sensuous flame.

I step back to let her take her turn, but mostly to keep myself from doing things I shouldn't. I can't.

Em tosses the bean bag and misses pretty badly. She turns to me and lifts her brows at me, daring me to do the same.

No way I'm gonna do that.

And what the hell is she doing flirting with me like this when she has a poor husband at home waiting for her, thinking she's faithfully hanging with Indigo and the girls?

Unfortunately, the pounding in my heart and the adrenaline from having her this close to me and flirting makes me overshoot the entire board.

Well great, now we both have to truth or dare.

"Truth or dare?" Billie asks.

Truth is safer, right? "Truth." I look to Em to see if she agrees. She nods. Thank God, no dares.

Billie sneaks a card from the bottom of the stack and hands

it to JJ to read. Like I said, always a trick up her sleeve. I know I'm in for it, now.

"What is your biggest regret in life?"

My face flushes hot with the recollection. There's no way I'm going to tell this whole group that my biggest regret is not having the balls to tell Em how I really felt all those years ago and I'm a terrible liar.

"Dare," I blurt.

Em stares right at me like she can read my thoughts. "Fine, dare."

JJ reads, "Kiss each other."

"That's not what it says," I protest.

"Fine. It says kiss someone. But you both have to do it, and good luck getting anyone else to agree to that."

"We all agreed. Nothing sexual," I add.

"You keep saying you're just friends. So, there shouldn't be anything sexual about it. If you want, I'd be happy to step in and kiss her for you," JJ taunts.

I'm not letting you kiss my Em.

"Oh, my gosh, Finn," Emerson says, looking a little too into this. "You are such a baby. It's not a big deal."

That's it. I'm not standing for this nonsense for one more second.

I take a step toward her and she gravitates toward me. I grasp her hand and growl, "We need to talk." I drag her over to the side of the house where I hope we can get some privacy away from the prying eyes of the happy couples we are constantly surrounded by.

"This has to stop," I growl.

"Simmer down. It's just truth or dare," she says lightly like this isn't the hardest thing in the world to do.

Because, for me, it is. "What do you think your husband would say about that?"

She dips her head and speaks softly, "I haven't had a husband in two years. Actually, two years and a day." She deflates against the side of the house.

No husband. She isn't married? Wait, two years and a day. That was her Dark Day. She was out there mourning her divorce. I step closer so no one can overhear us. "You left him?"

She scrunches up her face with bewilderment . "Why would you assume I left?"

"Any guy would have to be a complete idiot to leave you."

"Present company excluded," she adds with a slight smile of defiance.

No. I am the biggest idiot on earth, but, I did that for you, babe. Not me.

"Intracerebral hemorrhage," she mutters like she's repeated the phrase in her head a thousand times.

I wait until she lifts her eyes to me before I speak. "He must have been a good man if that's what it took to pull him away from you."

She nods her head and smiles. "He was."

"Kiss, kiss, kiss," the mature couples behind us begin chanting.

I look at Emerson not wanting to add to her pain. I lean my forearm against the side of the house behind her. "If I put my arm here, and we move close enough," I take another step toward her, "they'll never know we didn't kiss."

A devious smile washes across her face as she leans in and covers my lips with hers. It's a surprisingly gentle kiss. She pulls away and flashes me a satisfied smile.

She kissed me all sweet and innocent, and it unlocks something in me that is not sweet, nor is it innocent. It's hungry and carnal. And, in that moment, I decide that, though she kissed me like the kids we had been, I would kiss her like the man I'd become.

I push her up against the house and kiss her greedily, leaning my whole body against hers.

I drop my lips to her neck, kissing my way over her jaw to her cheek and back to her lips where I take long tastes of her mouth and that coconut chapstick she has been putting on all day.

She slides her hands under my shirt and up my back, begging me to take it off.

I'm seconds away from ripping it off, needing her skin to press against mine when I hear Greyson's voice. "Damn. Get a room already."

I step back and look at Em, to see if I've taken things too far.

She gives me that devilish grin and slips out of my grasp returning to the circle of chairs around the fire.

Come with me.

That's all I had to say.

Come with me.

I could have grabbed her hand and led her into my bed where we could have finished what we started.

Instead, I head inside to gain some time to gather myself before having to face a crowd that I'm sure has something to say about what I just did. I open a beer, taking a long draw, before setting it on the counter. I brace myself with my hands on the island, questioning what I just did.

It was only truth or dare. Maybe she won't think anything of it. She is so carefree and flirty now. But the way I kissed her was not a dare kind of a kiss. That was a decades-of-yearning kind of a kiss. And I did it mere moments after she told me about her dead husband.

Her. Dead. Husband.

I must be the crappiest person on earth to do that to her after she reveals her deepest pain.

I leave my beer, and march back outside ready to face the music. Billie eyes me as I make my way around the fire to my empty chair. She almost looks reticent. I know she planned this all out, but it's not her fault I can't control myself.

That's all on me.

The motions of the game continue in front of me but they aren't loud enough to capture my attention over the screaming in my head.

Two years ago, Em went through more pain than any human should have to endure. And she did it alone. I should have been there for her. To console her. To take care of her. Like the friend I always said I was.

But, like the reckless scumbag I really am, I burned that bridge years before into a pile of ashes, covering all my days since in a smoky haze.

Emerson smiles at me over the fire. Her cheeks are red and spotted around her lips.

Somehow, Em, my bright and joyful Em, has found a way to look past my failures, and can still stand to be around me.

She lays her head back laughing at something JJ said. I see her neck and remember being able to kiss that neck. I think about her telling me how her skin gets super sensitive from her thyroid stuff. And I realize I did that to her. Pushing my scruff across her lips, on the delicate skin of her neck.

My leg starts shaking on its own.

I couldn't control myself and that is what happened. I caused her more pain than she's already had to endure.

I grind away at my fingernails. I can't sit here and pretend to play a junior high game. I stand, calling out, "I'm gonna grab another. Who wants?"

Ryder holds up his empty bottle. Billie shows me her wine glass, "Some red?"

I don't bother remembering because I have no intention of coming back out here tonight. I'm going to bed.

Chapter 16

FINN
DECEMBER, SENIOR YEAR

E'm finished finals that year a totally different person. Deep purple bags under her eyes, a grumpiness I had never seen. She was constantly tired and wanted to stay in every weekend. She would skip classes to sleep. Never wanted to surf. When I could convince her to go, she'd paddle out, sit for twenty minutes not even trying to catch a wave, and then paddle in and lay on the sand until I was done.

The last Friday before Christmas Break was the first of my shows that she missed since before school started. Before each show, we began this little pre-game ritual. After I had warmed up with the band and finished with sound check, she'd bring me a beer and before handing it over, she'd take a huge sip. She hated beer, so she'd scrunch up her face, shake off the bad taste, and say, "Poison-free, Finny. Not a big enough star yet to be poisoned, so go out and play hard."

That adorable face of hers, all sour and scrunched up, was the fuel for my show. Without her there last night, without her face in the crowd giving me someone to sing to, something was off. I stumbled through my performance so distracted with worry that something had happened to her. It had to be one of the worst shows of my life.

I didn't hear from her until the next afternoon. I called and texted about a hundred times last night, even stopped by her place to make sure nothing had happened. But, no Em.

I spent the whole next day horribly imagining the worst. Not that she had been kidnapped or was laying in a ditch somewhere after being thrown from her car in a crash, but something much more agonizing.

The image I could not get out of my head, the one that kept me up most of the night, was that she had met someone. Maybe he saw her studying in a coffee shop somewhere, started up a conversation, and hit it off right from the start.

Justifiably, he was so taken with Em that he took her to dinner, joking and laughing the whole time. Em was so into this guy that she forgot all about my show. About me.

As I was pounding on her door well after midnight last night, I was struck with a much more excruciating thought. She might still be out with the guy. Or, even worse, she could still be at his place at this hour of the night.

Too wired to sit peacefully on the beach to watch the sun rise, I sprinted up Mount Soledad to catch it. After a stop at Gino's Bakery on my way home, I spent most of the day in the backyard breaking up old pallets for beach bonfire fuel. Nothing like taking an ax to a pile of wood to get out my frustrations.

I toss the last piece of firewood on the ever-growing pile before the desire to hit stuff completely subsides, so I send the ax flying into the old metal shed at the edge of the yard just as Em slides through the side gate nearly getting pummeled.

Crap.

Just like the last time I nearly took her out with a baseball, she barely registers the ax heading her way. I watch in slow motion as my anger nearly ends her. But for the mercy of God, it misses her by a foot.

I sprint over to her. "Em, are you okay?"

"I'm fine," she mutters like my anger didn't nearly kill her.

Something's off.

Something bad.

All the anger I was trying to get rid of with attacking inanimate objects vanishes instantly. I don't care why Em missed my show, as long as she is okay. And right now, she's not.

"Babe, what's wrong?" Whatever it is, I will fix it, whatever it takes.

She wipes at the tears now flowing over her cheeks. "I'm horrible. You just need to walk away, Finn."

"Em, you are the farthest thing from horrible." I take her hand and lead her to the chairs overlooking the little snippet of ocean visible from the yard. "Talk to me, babe." The 'babe' slips out before I have a chance to catch it. It does that when she's down.

"I missed your gig. I fell asleep in the back yard. When I woke up, I was in such a daze, I totally forgot. Like, completely forgot." She looks up to me like she just killed my dog.

"Hey." I run my hand over her hair. "It's okay, Em. You didn't mean to."

Horror suddenly washes over her face. "No one was there to taste test your beer, Finny. I'm so sorry." More tears pour out. "I can't believe I did that."

"I'm still alive. Not that big of a star yet," I joke, trying to cheer her up.

"It's not just that. I'm awful lately. I'm mean to you. I screamed at my professor. I tried to take a nap in a booth at Chipotle, right there in the back of the restaurant."

"You've just hit a rough patch. You'll pull out of it soon."

"But you don't get it, Finn. I'm horrible. And I hate myself for being this way, but I can't fix it."

"Look at me, Em. You are not horrible. You could never be horrible. You are the farthest thing from horrible, even when you miss the most important show in the whole wide world," I say teasing.

She hits me in the shoulder. "Finn. You're awful."

About that, she's right.

I slide the pizza box onto the coffee table and throw on another episode of *Lie to Me* on the TV. "So, how long do you think you've been feeling like this?"

"I haven't slept in weeks," she answers from the kitchen.

"Except for Chipotle," I tease.

"Yeah. That's the weird thing." She brings our drinks and slides under the coffee table. "I lay in bed for hours and cannot get my brain to turn off enough to sleep. I just lay there thinking. For hours. Do you know how long eight hours is if you're not actually asleep? It's For-ev-er," she draws out like the kid in Sandlot. She takes a big bite of her pizza. "And then, in the worst times—in class, at a red light, or," she pauses and drops her head, "just before your gig—I fall asleep. But even that's not a real sleep. I don't wake up refreshed. Just more tired."

"That alone is enough to explain the... uh... personality changes?" I suggest.

"I guess. But, it's not just sleep, Finn. I'm so angry all the time. The other day I was driving and all of a sudden I started getting really mad at all the red things I saw. There were like five red cars and they were all a slightly different shade of red and moving at different speeds and I got totally pissed at that. Like screaming mad. And then I passed a McDonald's sign and it was a whole different shade of red and not moving at all. And I was ready to run someone down with my car."

"That's not like you, babe."

"But it is, now. This is me." She nabs a few more slices of pizza from the box.

"We can fix this, Em." I cannot let her continue to suffer like this. I have to help.

While she finishes off nearly the whole pizza, I take out my phone to do some research. There has to be something to help her sleep.

Scrolling past too many ads for sleeping drugs, I find an article entitled, "10 Secrets to a Better Night's Sleep". And I'm gonna try every single last one of them.

She slides up on the couch and tugs a blanket over her. "One more episode?"

"Sure." I draw a pillow against my leg and motion for her to lie down. She draws her legs onto the plush couch and curls up against me.

When four more episodes end—I thought I'd try that first—I pull up the list again. "There's some things we can try to help you sleep. You want to try?"

"I'd try anything at this point. What's first?"

I glance at the list. "Number One. Take a hot bath."

"Here?" She sounds as hesitant as I feel, but if we're gonna get through the whole list, she can't very well go home to do it.

"Sure. I can go set it up."

I begin filling the tub. I don't exactly have the usual bath stuff, so I pour some body wash in to get it bubbly before heading to the garage for my emergency kit and find some candles and a lighter. I light the candles on the sink and flip on my bluetooth speaker, starting Em's Playlist. I have secretly been compiling the list of songs I know she'd love or songs that remind me of her. I had no idea it would come in so handy.

First song on the list is 'Souvenirs' by Jimmy Buffett. Why not start with her favorite? But I can't get myself to hit play. It's a little creepy that I keep a playlist just for her. And some of the songs are a bit too revealing.

I turn off the water and call to the other room, "It's ready."

"Do you think I could borrow some sweats for after? I hate trying to put leggings back on after a bath."

I've seen her struggle to slip into leggings after a surf and it's hilarious. She has nearly lost her towel a time or two in pursuit of that goal. I steal into my room, fish out a baggy sweatshirt and pair of basketball shorts, and set them on the sink. "You got everything you need?"

She inches toward me and reaches behind me before the lights flick off. "There. Now, it's perfect."

With the candlelight making her face glow, I'm paralyzed. I

glance down at her lips before dragging my gaze back up to her eyes. "I'll leave you to it," I say weakly before extricating myself from that oncoming disaster.

With the safety of a closed door between us, and knowing her state of mind is way more important than guarding my secret playlist, I get up the guts to hit play.

I hear the opening beats play, and within the first measure, I hear Em practically sigh, "Finny, that's perfect."

Although this plan may be working to get Em more sleepy, it has done just the opposite for me. Knowing Em is in the next room, in the bath, has me more alert than I should be.

It's still quiet after about thirty minutes. Too quiet. She could have fallen asleep in there and drowned. I should have made her leave the door open just in case, but that was not something I was going to ask her to do.

I lean my head against the door and tap quietly not wanting to jar her awake. "Em, you haven't drowned in there have you?"

The door pops open and I'm greeted by a relaxed Em who is once again standing much too close for comfort. I step back. "You tired?"

Her face falls. "Not yet. But like I said. I've already tried everything."

We make our way back to the couch and I make sure I'm sitting on the far end.

"What's next on the list?" she asks.

I skip over a few steps hoping she dozes off before we get to those. "Have you tried meditation?"

"Yep. Doesn't work. Remember the anger from the color red? Meditation is even worse."

"Chamomile tea?"

"Gallons."

I read the next bullet point on the list. "How about alcohol?" Great. Now I'm offering alcohol to an under-aged girl. But, I'll do anything to get her some rest. "It says that for some people it makes sleep worse, but if you're so wound up, maybe it will help you unwind."

"I haven't tried."

I escape to the kitchen and dig through the alcohol cupboard. "You don't strike me as a bourbon drinker. Maybe a margarita?"

"Whatever you think best."

What I think is best is not offering alcohol to her. Not being in a tiny candlelit bathroom with her. Not laying on a couch with her in my clothes. But she needs my help. And I can control myself enough to do that.

I fire up the blender, going easy on the tequila. I don't think any real amount of alcohol has ever touched those virgin lips, and I'm not about to overdo it.

Em wanders in and leans against the counter next to me. "All of this is really sweet, but it's not going to work."

"Sure it will. We'll find something. I promise, Em." I hand her a salt-rimmed glass, half full.

She studies the drink and then looks up at me, brows raised inquisitively. "And you think a half of a margarita's gonna do the trick?"

I reluctantly fill up her glass with more from the pitcher. She takes a big sip, bringing a smile to her face that I haven't seen in far too long. "Ooh. This is good, Finny."

Back in the living room, she sits a little too close to me on the sofa, drawing her legs up under her, before setting her drink on the table and running out of the room. No way it could have hit her that fast.

She returns with my speaker from the bathroom, mutes the TV, and hits play, before grabbing her drink and sitting even closer. "So, what's next on this master list of yours?"

"You just knocked off number six, music. So... how about number eight, meds." Usually, a good shot or two of bourbon is enough to throw me over the edge when I can't sleep, but I've been sleepless enough to have tried every sleep med around.

"No way. If I got low and had a sleep med on board, I might not ever wake up. Way too scary."

"Okay. No meds. Let's see what else there is." We're running out of easy solutions that I'm willing to entertain. "Hmm," I stall.

"None of this is going to work. I've tried everything, meditation, white noise, sleep apps, audiobooks, math in my head. I got so good at doubling numbers, I would be into twelve digits before I got bored and moved onto something else."

I scroll up and down, passing over the tips I don't want to try.

"You out of ideas so soon?" she tugs at my phone to study the list. "Massage. I haven't tried that yet." She shrugs. "Can't really give myself a good back massage." She looks up at me with those huge brown puppy dog eyes.

I head to the kitchen to pour myself some of the leftover margarita to deal with this new development, bringing it back to the living room before I sit on the rug with my back against the couch. I polish off half of my drink before begrudgingly asking, "So, we gonna do this or what?"

After a few beats of silence, I tip my head back to look at her.

She points to the rug. "Down there?" I'm reassured that she's as hesitant as I am.

She rises from the couch and polishes off her drink before rounding the coffee table the long way and sitting in front of me.

I lift my hands and hover above her shoulders. This won't be so bad, I try to convince myself. At least she's got my thick sweatshirt on.

I hold her shoulders and squeeze.

"I'm a tough girl, Finn. You can be a little rougher."

Not if she's gonna talk to me like that, I can't.

I increase the pressure a bit.

"Hold on," she says before leaning forward and yanking off my sweatshirt, leaving her in a thin white tank. She scoots back toward me. Far too close.

I scratch my hand back and forth over my scruff.

You're just trying to help her sleep. This doesn't mean anything.

But her skin is so soft under my hands, I can barely focus. My sweaty hands stick to her skin and snag it as I try to work out a knot in her traps.

She flinches. "Ow."

"Sorry. That's not really working, is it?"

"Not so much."

I put my hands on her shoulders and push her forward a bit, giving me enough room to escape from behind her. I stand and make my way to the kitchen. I swing open the cupboard and stare down the coconut oil.

This doesn't mean anything.

But even I am not convinced.

I return to the living room and slide in behind Em, showing her the jar. "You good with this?"

"Anything is better than whatever that was that you were doing before," teasing overflowing in her voice.

I take a dab, letting it turn to oil in my hands before sliding them over her shoulders, then up her neck.

She leans into it. "Much better."

I run my hands down her traps to her shoulders, starting to work the taught muscles under my palms.

She relaxes into my hands, letting her head drop forward.

I slowly work my way back to her traps finding a knot on her left side. I move both hands there and rub my thumbs over the tender spot.

She lets out a nearly silent moan and purrs, "Oh, damn, Finny."

I reflexively yank my hands back, letting them hang in the air above her like I just touched a burning flame. The sound of her saying my name in that tone is too much.

It is doing way too much to my body.

And to my heart.

She turns back to look at me. "Why'd you stop?"

There's no way I can tell her that the sound of her moan has me thinking things I should never be thinking about Em. I can't tell her that I'm the darkest of dark and doing what I swore to myself I would never do. I have gotten her drunk and now I'm rubbing her down and getting turned on by the sounds she's making.

With no other way to answer her question, I lie. "Sorry. Hand cramp. I'm fine now."

I turn up the music, hoping to avoid the sound of her enjoying my touch. And I go back to the massage, running my fingers from the base of her skull down her back until I hit the top of her tank top, over and over.

Thirty minutes later, I'm running out of self-control. "Tired yet?" I ask, hoping to end this torture.

"Relaxed, but not tired. Let's see that list again." She spins around in front of me, leaving my legs wrapped around her and her face way too close. With a mind of their own, one hand continues to lightly rub her back, the other rests on her knee.

Taking my phone from the table, she holds it up to my face to open it and continues reading the list. "Number nine. Cold, dark room. My roommate threw a fit the last time I tried to sleep with the window open. There's no way I can do that."

At least I know we won't have to do everything on that list. Number ten, sex, is a no-go for me.

She scrolls down before blushing, then quickly scrolls back up. "Number four. Avoid blue lights."

She hits the TV remote on the table and the room goes dark, the only light coming from my phone, lighting up the most beautiful face I have ever laid eyes on.

I snatch my phone away before she gets any ideas from the other tips on that list. This only draws her closer, leaning over to see the screen, laying her head on my chest, lazily scrolling down the list.

She fits so perfectly, it makes me stupidly imagine that there might be a chance that I could do this without breaking her. That we could be more.

But I know how that ends. And I'm not that guy. I'm the guy who isn't fit to be anyone's husband.

I push up onto the sofa and lean over to flip the light on, jostling her as I do.

She lays her hand on my sweatshirt lying on the table and stands, making her way toward the door. I may not want to fall into bed with Em, but I also never want her to leave. "What are you doing?" I ask.

She slides her keys off the hook next to the door. "Going home to sleep."

"By the time you get home, all the work we've done will be wasted. Just sleep here. I'll even let you keep the window open."

She looks at my room and looks at me, weighing her options. "In your bed?"

Unable to get words out, I shrug.

"I don't know. I'll have to check it out, see if it's up to my standards." She hooks my gaze as she saunters into my room. I follow behind her like a fish caught on the line.

I slide the window fully open, letting the cool salt air fill the room.

She pushes down on the mattress, testing its firmness. "I suppose this could work." She lowers the blanket while staring at me, sliding in on her side and innocently throwing down the other side of the blanket.

I pick up my pillow and start toward the door. I see a flash of disappointment on her face before she covers it up with an easy smile.

"I'll see you in the morning, Em. Sleep well."

I know I won't. Not with her sleeping in my bed and guilt fully awake in my head.

Had I taken it too far? She was onboard and we were simply trying to get her to sleep, but it was still way too much. I knew the consequences. And she'd be the one paying for it.

I always knew the consequences when it came to getting close to people. I would eventually screw it up and they'd get hurt. Or worse.

Em would be no different. How could she? My curse was too strong for even her sweet innocence to combat.

Chapter 17

EMERSON
PRESENT DAY

I cannot believe the amazing community Indigo has allowed me to be a part of here. In addition to a weekly game night, the girls also have their monthly Crunch-n-Brunch where they do some sort of crazy adventurous activity and then celebrate surviving it over brunch. It is everything I have been missing the past few years—built-in friends who care so much for one another and really know how to have fun. And it's calling out for me to stay here forever.

Today, Harley has joined us at a local pool and is in charge of what she is calling Tactical Water Training. We're all standing in a circle on the deck of a huge pool in our bikinis. Billie says Harley's got some experience with the Navy SEALs and I can only imagine what she has in store for us. I just hope it's complicated enough to require my full attention. I need something to stop the wash-cycle of thoughts and emotions over that kiss last night.

Which was, hands down, the best kiss of my life.

And, what makes it even better, was that I was the one to instigate it. I didn't have to plot or plan or research. I just reached out and did it. I have grown so much that I feel like I'm almost a normal girl.

And, damn, if Finny didn't respond like he had been hiding

those feelings for me for decades. Like pent-up desire has been raging just below the surface for far too long. I've never seen that side of Finn, all passionate and intense. He's usually so reserved and in control.

But everything from him after that kiss is the same old Finn, a thoroughly-expected Mega-Flinch. He didn't say a word to me, avoiding me for the rest of the game. Or at least for the five minutes he spent out there before disappearing inside for a refill and never coming back.

After the game, I headed into Finn's room to change. He's been nice enough to let me have the bed all week while he crashes out on the old couch. I had my shirt halfway off when I heard him snoring quietly. I finished putting on an actual set of pajamas and slipped in beside him.

I wasn't about to sleep on the couch. And if he could kiss me like that, he could certainly share his bed.

Harley's instructions bring me back to the present. With all the equipment she has unloaded and either dumped in or strapped down to the pool, my fear has me paying attention to every word. "We'll get to all the sets and equipment in a bit. For now, I want us to do a little breathwork. Let's try a little diaphragmatic breathing. So, put one hand on your chest and one on your belly."

She lays one hand on her navy blue Speedo two-piece, so sturdy it could never be called a bikini, and one hand on her abs, so ripped she puts all the guys on deck to shame. We all follow her lead.

"Good. Now we're going to breathe in for five seconds through our nose, trying only to let your stomach move. Chest stays still."

We breathe in unison for a few minutes before hearing about how today's workout is all about finding our limits and then relaxing through them. Standing here doing breathing exercises, just imagining what we're going to do with all of Harley's gear already has me at my limit. So, I try to relax my muscles and just go with it.

We spend the next hour retrieving masks from the bottom of the pool with our mouths, swimming across the pool underwater only to have to tie and untie knots on the bottom of the pool, and then bobbing up and down like we have our feet and legs bound and are trying to still survive. That one actually is a bit relaxing once I get my rhythm down, releasing all my air to get to the bottom and springing off the bottom to get another breath of air at the surface before repeating it all over again. Like scuba diving without all the air tanks and gear.

We tread water while holding bricks over our heads, and do burpees and squats on the deck before jumping in again and trying to swim the whole length of the pool without taking a breath. By the end of this workout, I can barely manage to haul myself out of the pool.

I'm so grateful that food is part of this whole Crunch-n-Brunch thing because after a workout like that, I'm starving. We pile into a large booth at The Painted Lantern and pass out menus. The cloudless sky pours in its bright happy light into the restaurant. The open wall of windows lets in the salt air, making for a perfect brunch spot. I only hope the food can rival the view over short palms straight to the tranquil, blue water.

"Harley, that was the hardest workout of my life," I start. "Where'd you learn to do all that?"

"My dad had me training like that as a kid, but I've been experimenting with using it with sailors with PTS as a way to retrain their nervous system."

It still sounds weird to me when Harley, and Billie for that matter, call PTSD PTS. But after hearing her explain how the change is intended to put the emphasis on the stress instead of the person suffering, and to make it easier for people to seek help, it started to make a little more sense.

"I'm starting to think about looking for funding for a new medical study," Harley continues.

Wow. That sounds so interesting. I haven't thought about

neurobiology since my Stanford days, but what a great way to apply it.

"So, is that what you do? Medical studies?" I ask.

Harley sets her menu on the table. "Medical research. Mostly focused on PTS in Special Operators."

It's the first itch I've had to go back to my studies. It would be so fascinating to write up my own study. To design it and get funding and actually discover something totally new. Something that could help people. Had I just stayed with Dr. Tansor, that's what I'd be doing by now. But my life has taken too many wild turns since then.

"Billie, here, was my first guinea pig," Harley adds.

"I didn't know you were in the Navy, Billie," I say, confused.

Billie laughs. "Nope. Just ended up in the wrong place at the wrong time. It took me a bit to fight my way back to my old self. Harley was invaluable in that fight. And the pool training we did helped so much."

"Yeah, that and all the sexy training with Ryder," Charlie laughs. "If I had that man pushing me up against walls I'd be feeling better in no time, too."

A fierce blush rises on Billie's cheeks. She shrugs. "It sure didn't hurt."

Our waiter swings by taking our drink orders.

"I don't know what was wrong with me today, but I just couldn't keep up," Charlie complains.

I wonder if Charlie really doesn't suspect she's pregnant. I mean, I could be totally wrong, but who eats Cheetos and sour cream unless it's a pregnancy craving?

"Weren't you high all day yesterday?" Indigo asks. "That could definitely make today harder." High blood sugars will, for sure, make you feel hungover the next day.

"It's been like that all week. I changed everything out; my insulin, pump site, I even changed my Dexcom in case it was just reading off."

Pregnancy will do that, too.

I don't want to jump the gun here and diagnose her. I've learned you jump in too early with medical advice and diagnoses and people don't react too kindly. Sometimes they have to come to a conclusion on their own.

"Are you sick?" Billie offers. "Bacteria will make you high for days."

The waiter drops off our drinks and takes our orders.

"I did throw up the other morning. Maybe I still haven't recovered from the stomach flu I had last week." She drinks half of her water.

"Yeah, but that's a virus. Viruses make me go low," Indigo says.

"So, tired, throwing up, high blood sugars," I say, trying to lead them. "And do you always eat Cheetos and sour cream?"

"No. That was so not me. I never touch that stuff," she says, almost embarrassed.

Then they all look at each other, eyes going big.

"Do you think?" Billie asks.

"We have been trying!" Charlie squeals.

The table erupts into overlapping conversation and more squeals. I'm happy for Charlie and Greyson—I really am—but right alongside that happiness is that familiar haze of grief. I excuse myself to go to the bathroom so I don't rain on their parade.

On my way, I bring out my phone and start typing.

EM:

> **So that thing we suspected? We were right. But don't tell Grey. I'm sure Charlie wants to do that.**

I erase it before hitting send. That's not the first thing I want to say after kissing Finn like that last night and then watching him disappear. What I need to say to pull him out of this flinch, I have no idea, but it certainly isn't that.

When I return to the table, it's like walking into a funeral.

"We're so sorry, Em. Is this hard for you when I'm going on and on about getting pregnant and how awesome Grey has been?" Charlie asks with such concern in her voice.

"No, it's not bad." It's not *really* a lie.

I learned long ago that I wasn't going to get the same milestones as everyone else. From skipping grades to not having a graduation party because I was done at fifteen and had no friends at school to celebrate with, anyway. No prom. No grad night parties. No parties of any kind for that matter. No college boyfriend—couldn't get Finn to bite on that one.

I thought things would be different when I got married, but that was just a blink of an eye, the fluttering of a butterfly's wings, for how long it lasted. I never really get to enjoy having the same things everyone else does.

"How's it been being back here?" Indigo asks.

"Wait. It happened here?" Billie gasps.

"Oahu. So not *here,* here." I can do better than that. I used to shut down when things like this came up. I'd eke out a tiny answer when someone would ask me something deep and then they'd move on.

Unless it was Finn. But, even then, I could barely expound on my thoughts.

When I met Timmy, he was so interested in me that he'd sit with me for however long it took to get me talking. And when I did, he loved every part of me. He was so accepting and never judged me. I realized that maybe other people might like me, too, if I shared with them all my weirdness.

"It's been easier than I expected. This year didn't seem like I was grasping for the past. In the beginning, I was doing anything I could to feel close to him, being in the water, playing his favorite song or wearing his favorite shirt. But lately, it's been less about wanting to bring him back, and I've started being able to celebrate the time we had and what he gave me. How much he taught me about this world and my own place in it."

"That's a hard shift to make," Billie says. "That part took me years to get to."

"Can I ask?" I say softly.

"I lost Brent, my twin brother, about eight years ago and kind of got stuck in the denial phase." She takes a long drink of her iced tea. "So, it's great that you've taken the time to really process your grief. I didn't do that until much later. And it sounds like you're doing really well."

"But that has been hard in its own way. Like, I feel bad that I don't feel as bad anymore. Does that make any sense?"

"That makes so much sense. But even that fades away. And then it's just the good stuff left," she reassures me.

It feels like I'm getting very close to that part. "Okay. Enough of the sad stuff. This is Crunch-n-Brunch. My guess is it's supposed to be about fun."

"I have something fun to ask." Indigo wags her brows suggestively and stares at me. I know that look. It's one that usually ends with my embarrassment.

"What," I say flatly.

"Oh, you know, that little makeout session last night?"

All eyes snap to me.

"We noticed that he wasn't out on the couch last night, either. You want to explain that?" Billie teases.

I'm not sure I can. I haven't really made sense of it myself. "He was already asleep when I got in his room. So, I crawled in right next to him, all loud and stuff. I tried to move around a bunch to wake him up, but he didn't move a muscle. Clearly, my kissing skills are so bad that I put him to sleep."

"That's not what it looked like from where we were sitting," Charlie says, a little too excited.

On my end, it was an incredible kiss. One I have set on replay all night and into the morning.

But, it's Finn.

So, there are repercussions.

I just hope I can figure out some way to sneak around his defenses so he doesn't run.

"It's not that easy with Finn," I try to explain. "After that kiss, he wouldn't even look at me. Like everything shut down again. That's what he does. When things get blurry, he shuts down or picks on me to gain some distance or he completely leaves." That was a fun one.

"You guys have kissed before?" Billie practically freaks at the thought.

Not ready to tell the hungry eyes before me the story of my failed seduction, I give them the next best thing. One that's humiliating in a whole different way.

"Not kissed. But I did flash him my boobs."

That leaves them all staring and speechless.

Chapter 18

EMERSON
JANUARY, SENIOR YEAR

ou get some rest over break?" Finn asks like everything's normal between us like he didn't totally bail on me.

Finn never goes home for Christmas, doesn't really ever talk to or about his parents. When my mom heard about that Freshman year, she demanded that he spend Christmas with us up in Seal Beach. And he's been spending it with us ever since.

This year, though, he called with some lame excuse that he got the flu and couldn't come up. The only flu he had was the flinching flu. One massage and he freaked.

But his flinches only last so long. If I give him enough time to mellow out, he's back to good ol' Finn.

When I get back to school, I find myself back at his place Saturday morning for our cinnamon toast ritual, trying to get things back on track.

He grabs two plates of toast and leads me to the backyard. I pick up my iced tea and his coffee and follow. "Not much rest, really. I mean, it was nice having my mom cook for me and take care of my laundry and all that, but I'm still so tired."

He sits, handing me my breakfast. "Em, does all this sound normal to you?"

"No. I'm a total freak. That's what I keep saying." I look

out to the sliver of ocean glistening in the morning sun. "I'd understand if you need to just walk away."

"Don't be stupid. I'm not walking away. And what I mean is, this isn't normal for you. I think you need to see a doctor, Em, because something's off. You didn't turn into a horrible person, as you put it, overnight. You might be sick."

"I don't even have a doctor down here and, even if I did, I'm afraid to drive. I fell asleep at a red light last week."

"You're still on your parents' insurance, right?"

"Yeah."

"Give me the card."

A week later, Finn insists on coming with me to the appointment he set up. He said he had to make sure the doctor was competent. I didn't mind so much, though, since he was willing to drive.

"So, what seems to be the problem?" Dr. Babcock asks without looking up from his computer screen.

"I can't sleep and I'm always tired."

"Hmm." He clicks away on his keyboard. "And you have Type 1 diabetes?"

"Yeah. For eleven years now."

"Hmm." More typing. "Are you in school or working?"

"I'm a senior at UCSD."

More typing.

Then silence.

I look at Finn trying to figure out if this is going well.

"Well, Emerson. It looks like it's probably just stress. You're working and going to school and probably partying too much. And the diabetes can keep you up at night." He shuts his laptop and stands. "Maybe take some time off, stop partying. Or take a vacation."

"Doc, this is not just burnout," Finn interjects. "Em doesn't party. And school is a breeze for her. She wouldn't know how to stress if her life depended on it. It's more than that."

The doc sits back down and finally looks up.

"She isn't sleeping at all. And then she gets all this energy at night. She's got these bruises all over her body and has no idea how she got them. She's got bags under her eyes and she is way more pale than she should be. And she has these…" he looks down at me like he doesn't want to have to say it, "fits of rage? And, Doc, if you know anything about Em, it's that she's the mellowest, sweetest girl. Wouldn't hurt a fly. But, recently, she's changed. We were playing baseball the other week and I was giving her crap about not being able to strike me out, stuff I've done a thousand times, and she threw an entire bucket of balls at me. And this girl has an arm." He pushes up his sleeve to show off the patches of purple and dark yellow as the bruises from that night fade.

"So, look doc, you run all the tests. You do whatever you have to do to find out what's wrong because this isn't my Em. This isn't normal."

"Anything else?" the doc asks, like all of this isn't enough to convince him that I'm sick.

I whisper, "I've put on like twenty pounds in the last two months."

He thinks for a minute. "I suppose it could be low thyroid. I can do a blood test if you want."

I have to face my next appointment alone. Finn had band practice and I wouldn't let him miss yet another thing just to humor me. I know what the doc is gonna say anyway. "Sorry. Nothing's wrong with you. You're just overworked and a total freak. Time to get used to it."

But, by the time I stumble back to Finn's after the appointment, my head is spinning.

Hyperthyroid. That's what the doctor said. My thyroid has decided to stop listening to directions and just pump out a boatload of hormones into my body at all times. And, unfortunately, that one hormone regulates a ton of stuff in your body. Metabolism, blood clotting, sleep, and energy, even oil production for your skin and hair. No wonder I had to start washing my hair every single day.

And, especially in me, it has a huge effect on my irritability and aggression.

It wasn't what I was expecting. After hours of medical research of all my symptoms, the weight gain made me think hypothyroidism was a shoo-in. That's when you have too little thyroid hormone and all the opposite things happen. But, I guess I'm just one of those lucky ten percent of people who gain weight with hyperthyroidism instead of losing it all.

Once again, I'm a total freak.

After explaining the results to Finn, he goes into fix-it mode. "What are they going to do?"

"They can't do much. Some pills to slow it down, but that won't take it away and they only work for a few months."

"Seriously? There's nothing else they can do?"

"They can make me radioactive to kill my thyroid, but I have to stay twelve feet away from all other humans for ten days."

The doctor explained this like it was normal. They give me a radioactive iodine pill that the nurse has to bring to me in a lead-lined vial so they don't get irradiated, and I have to *swallow* it. It accumulates in my thyroid and, for the next two weeks, kills my thyroid so it won't overwork again. In fact, it won't work at all for the rest of my life.

I, then, have to take thyroid replacement for the rest of my life. But, unlike the insulin hormone that I've had to replace since my pancreas broke over a decade ago, thyroid is a much simpler hormone to dose.

The procedure still makes me radioactive for two weeks, kind of like a superhero, or maybe a supervillain, who can secretly kill bad guys with radiation just by being near them. But, I won't be able to control who I shoot out my radioactive rays at. And, my roommates may be completely inconsiderate and selfish, but I'm not about to secretly kill them.

"I live in an apartment with five other girls. I can't exactly kick them all out. So, if I want to live in a tent on the beach for ten days, I can do that."

"You're doing it."

"Did you not hear the whole twelve-feet thing?"

"It will fix this right?"

"Yeah, but..."

"Then you're gonna do that. You can stay with me."

"Your place is twelve feet from front to back. You can't stay that far away from me and there's no way in hell I'm gonna give you cancer from this."

"I have a yard. I'll sleep there. The rest of the day I can hang outside if we're both home."

I spend the next half hour trying to convince Finn why that won't work. I have to treat myself like a toxic chemical. Everything I touch has to be thrown away in a separate trash can at the edge of his property or washed separately several times. The bathroom is especially going to be toxic.

He spends that time destroying every one of my perfectly logical reasons not to do this. He can buy paper plates and cups. He has his own washer and dryer. He has no problem peeing under a tree. And it will be spring break in a week, so he has all the time in the world to take care of me.

From a distance.

The perfect solution for Finn.

By the time I drive home from the radioactive lab, Finn has his whole place set up for me. Stacks of paper plates, cups, and paper towels in the kitchen next to a whole box of trash bags. Stacks of new towels in the bathroom next to a hamper that had never been there before. And, out back, he has a tent set up next to his camping hammock.

"You need two places to sleep out here?" I call out from the back door as Finn stands after finishing driving in the last of the tent spikes.

"The hammock is for sleeping. Tent is for my clothes and to change."

"Not for all your overnight guests?" I know Finn dates a lot. He is a musician after all, so he always has girls throwing themselves at him. I'm just not sure how far he takes it.

"You're my only overnight guest here, Em." He moves toward me to hug me.

"Stop! Twelve feet!"

He freezes. "Sorry, Em. I forgot."

"Air hug?"

He lifts his arms and squeezes the air in front of him. "So, do you feel it yet? Do you have some new spidey senses?"

"I can read minds," I tease. "But I've always been able to do that."

"Don't I know it," he mutters.

I settle in on the couch to watch one of the dozens of movies I've put on my Netflix playlist in the last week preparing for ten days of recovery. I don't know how I'm going to fill the entire week when I barely have the energy to watch a full movie.

Since I don't have to worry about Finn complaining about my movie choice, I flip on a sappy chick flick, hoping it distracts me from my despair. Not five minutes in, my phone beeps.

FINN:

> **Come out here quick!**

I toss my phone and sprint out to the yard to find the sky lit up in oranges and pinks. Finn is hanging on the back fence. When he sees me, he slides down to the opposite side of the yard. "There," he points to the spot he just vacated. "It has the best view."

I walk up to the fence and take in the view. Finn's house is on a hill with his backyard pointing toward the ocean. His backyard neighbors are down a sloped common area, so from here, you don't even notice them. His view points out over a small valley leading to the ocean. And right now, the sun is setting directly in the middle of that valley, like it was framed there just for us.

The deep blue chases the colors away as we sit in the oncoming dark, talking. It's nearly midnight by the time a strange and beautiful sensation washes over me. It's faint, but I feel it.

Tired.

But, tired in a new way. Maybe it's better described as sleepy. I'm sleepy and I cannot express how amazing it feels.

"I'm going to try to sleep. Wish me luck," I say hopefully.

"You got this. I believe in you, Em." I was kind of hoping he'd try to help me sleep again. Because that night was amazing.

———————

Finny! I slept. I ACTUALLY SLEPT!!!!!

And it was the most delicious sleep I have ever had. When I laid down my head, I felt this magnetic pull, like I was sinking into the bed. Like gravity had been turned up and it was planting me deep inside a magical land where all my exhaustion was being sucked from my body, only to be replaced with energy and vigor and brightness.

I woke this morning with my head more clear than I've been in months. I hadn't noticed how groggy I had become because it all happened so slowly. But waking up from it was like... well, waking up.

Each day after that, I feel more and more like myself. I'm thinking clearly and have my energy back. The low-level depression that had been sitting on me for months even lifts. I head out for morning walks and by the fourth day, I'm lifting weights.

Our nightly talks begin just before sunset, and, I don't know what it is about that setting, but it's letting Finn open up in ways that he never has before. He's answering questions that I've wanted to ask for years but never had the guts to ask.

He said he'd answer questions on one topic a night. And when we get to ex-girlfriends, I'm starting to doubt my tactics to get Finn to talk. It's weird to think of him living with his last girlfriend. I guess because he never talked about his past, I began to think he didn't have one. But hearing about Sophia has me feeling more naive and young than ever before. Unfortunately, the long nights have loosened my tongue and I keep asking questions I don't really want the answers to.

"So, you lived with Sophia? Like shared-a-bed lived with her?" I ask, not wanting to know the truth, but not being able to resist asking.

He tugs at the back of his neck, before sitting up. "Hey, I just forgot. I've got a date tonight." At this, he stands and heads into his tent, zipping it fully behind him.

I'm not even that upset when he flinches this time.

But, even the small glimpse into his Nashville year has me overwhelmed and fidgety and needing to process. So, I take off on a run to clear my head.

I spend the first two miles trying to put together the little bits of information that Finn shared to make some sort of cohesive story. He moved to Nashville right after graduation to pursue his music. He found Sophia that first week. They moved in a few months later.

I may be naive, but I'm not a complete idiot. I know what that means. But, it's so hard to reconcile that version of Finn with the guy I know. The guy who hasn't dated anyone seriously in the four years we've hung out. The one who hasn't let on in the slightest that he's sleeping with any of the women he dates casually. And I've never seen any evidence of that.

It's weird to think he could have gone from that, to this.

I head back at mile three, not wanting to do too much with this new healthy energy that I've been experiencing this week.

Heading toward a shower, I stroll into Finn's room and start peeling off my sports bra. It gets stuck halfway off, so I have to give it a bounce or two to get all the way off. I toss it to the floor and hook my thumbs in the hemline of my running shorts and skivvies to whip them off.

As I push through the bathroom door, I look up to find Finn standing in front of me shirtless, hair dripping, jeans on but unbuttoned over a pair of black boxer briefs, looking like he just stepped out of a Calvin Klein ad.

And I don't know if it's my newly acquired healthy energy or what, but the sight of his massive shoulders and bare chest quicken my pulse. When I finally drag my gaze up his body from his undone jeans, over his rippling abs and chest, so packed with muscle it takes hour-long seconds to move my eyes over it, I see his face and it's brimming with so much longing that I can't look away. He takes one step toward me, not moving his eyes from my face.

Until I realize I'm topless. A foot away from a sexy-as-hell Finn and I'm half-naked.

I cover my chest and look for my sweaty bra. "You're not here! You're gone. On a date," I say as if that could make it true. I scour the room for my bra.

"I..." Finn struggles for words as I have accosted him in the bathroom.

My gaze catches on my bra hanging from Finn's desk.

He takes another step toward me.

"Twelve feet!" It's all I can think. "I'm killing you."

I spin and reach for my top, but hear him sigh, "You are Em. You so are."

Chapter 19

FINN
PRESENT DAY

*A*t one point last night, I remember the smell of Em, citrus and mango and peace, like she was lying right next to me. But, by the time I wake, I realize I must have been dreaming, right before realizing that meant I was once again a selfish swine who made her sleep on the couch.

Flashes of that kiss waft through my mind. I never imagined that kissing her would be that breathtaking. I had imagined it a million different ways over the years, but none of them held a candle to the real thing. It was like she breathed all her Emerson brand of joy and peace directly into me.

For the first time in years, I felt like I was alive again. Alive and happy. There has to be some way that I can hold onto that.

It was always easier thinking about things with a guitar in my hand and there's no sign anyone is awake out front, so I crack open the door and steal my guitar from the wall and hop back in bed. As I strum, my thoughts start to organize themselves.

For years, I have been so tired of hurting that I think I turned my emotions off. Every one of them was no longer functioning. I was just all cold and dead inside. I felt like I was losing my passion for anything that has to do with life.

But the moment Em arrived, everything started waking up.

I know I can't be with her, I know how that ends. She's already lost her husband. The last thing I need to do is bring more pain into her life. She deserves someone real who can take care of her.

But, maybe there's a way I can keep her close to me, just while she's here. I'd be happy to be her rebound. Her vacation from all her grief. If that's what she wants.

And while she's here, I'll try to breathe in all the life she brings. Try to wake myself up. And then, when she leaves, this time, I'll try to keep that life going.

And this time, we'll both walk away unscathed.

I allow myself to revel in the memory of last night, something I have, over the years, trained myself to never do. The little moan she let out when I pressed her against the wall and really kissed her. Her hands on my back, grasping for more of me. The delighted smile on her face after we were ungraciously interrupted.

And the red on her skin afterward.

I'm not about to do anything ever again that will bring her pain. So, step one is to get rid of this beard.

I pad into the bathroom, swiping the scissors from the top drawer, and stare at my face in the mirror. I grasp the end of a clump of hair and raise the scissors. "Looks like your time is up."

I snip the rough hair, grabbing one clump after another until my beard looks like two day's growth, and wonder if I've aged under this thing. It has been four years.

I wipe up the sink that looks like it's halfway to turning into a werewolf and hop in the shower. In there, I finish the job with my four-blade titanium razor that so far has only had the task of tidying up the edges of this beast of a beard.

I hear the mina birds singing a cheery tune this morning out my window. For the first time, I don't consider bringing out my pellet gun to scare them off. Instead, I'm humming along with them, stealing their melody to put to the phrase that was running around in my head all night. Now, it almost feels like the start of a song.

I wrap a towel around my waist and open the bathroom door to find Emerson facing the window topless, in just a pair of shorts. She must not have known I was in here.

She looks over her shoulder at me, mischievously, letting her eyes roam over my bare chest, and then, spins a little more toward me, not enough to get a full glimpse at what the myna birds outside that window must have been singing about, but with that small shift her confidence spills over, and she is captivating.

So much for her not thinking anything of that kiss last night.

I step back into the bathroom and close the door. I'm not ready to have her that close. If I let myself fall into her that much, I won't walk away unscathed when she leaves. I have to do this in a way that keeps her near, but not too near.

I wait a good ten minutes until I hear her voice out in the kitchen gabbing with Indigo and Charlie.

A few moments later, I join them at the kitchen island fully clothed.

"What the hell?" Greyson says.

"What did you do?" JJ asks at the same time.

"So, that's what you look like," Indigo adds.

"What prompted that?" Charlie inquires.

"I don't know. It was time." I reply, trying to avoid any eye contact with Em, but I can feel her gaping.

When they have all finished making me totally uncomfortable, Charlie lays her hands on the table and says, "Grab a towel, and let's do this."

"Do what?" I ask.

"After that workout, we've earned a recovery day, so we're going to lay out and float in the ocean all day."

I look to Em and wait for an invite to come, but it never does, and soon, the girls file out the door for the day. And I feel the loss.

Greyson nods to the door Em just exited. "So, that for her?"

"Nah. Just sick of the beard. It was too scratchy," I deflect.

He's not deterred. "So, where do you think it's going with Em?"

"It's not going anywhere, just a momentary vacation illusion. It's not real. Nothing you do on vacation is real. In one week, she'll leave and move on to the guy she should be with. The one who will keep her safe. The one who isn't me."

"And why exactly can't you be that one?" he presses.

Because I'm not fit to be anyone's husband.

I shrug my reply. "Whatever. I'm gonna go run." I head off to my room to change.

Greyson laughs, well acquainted with my silent ways. "We're heading out at five. Don't be late. The girls will freak out."

I wave over my shoulder, not bothering to turn around or even ask what they have planned. If Em is gonna be there, so will I.

On my way out, I check in on the crew I have working on the flood in the Ohana. Stepping over a line of fans and dehumidifiers on the porch, I tuck inside the door. Luckily, the building was already ripped to the studs so the cleanup is not as bad as it could have been.

"Looks like you guys are making good progress," I say to Justin who is heading up the crew.

"I don't think it'll set you back in the renovation much at all."

"Awesome. Thanks for helping out."

"Hey. Are you gonna be able to stop by the office today to sign the papers for Oia'i'o Road?"

I check my watch. I should be able to work that in. "Around three?"

"Sounds good. I'm heading out now, just wanted to check up on everything this morning."

I walk him to his truck parked next to mine in the driveway.

He opens his door and calls me over to his truck. "I see now why you took a vacation. I'd be at home, too, if my house was overrun by girls that pretty," he calls as I make my way across the yard.

I can't really deny it. But, it's just one pretty lady I'm interested in.

With Baja in the back of the truck, I pull up at the bottom of Kahakapao Loop Trail. It's one of my favorite ways to clear my head. But, this morning, for the first time in a long time, my head is already clear. I've found a way to have Em and not hurt her.

I let the tailgate down and Baja jumps out, waiting patiently by my feet. I secure his retractable leash that lets him go off-leash while still having something to tug on in case I meet someone on the trail who doesn't understand Baja.

Because Baja is not like any other dog. Since the day I met him, he hasn't wandered far. But, knowing where he came from, it makes sense.

The second week I was in Mexico, I had finally caught a fish and was roasting it over a bonfire. He sat on the sand at the waterline for over an hour before slowly inching his way toward me.

When my dinner was ready, I took a small piece of fish and offered it to him. It took him over ten minutes to trust me enough to come get it. He was so scrawny and dirty, I ended up giving him nearly the whole thing.

He ended up staying with me the rest of the trip and, I have to say, I didn't mind the company. Forcing myself to take the trip that Em had dreamed up for us was more lonely than I expected. Having Baja there with me eased that a bit. Nothing like having Em there by my side, but his presence kept me from walking out into the water, never to come back.

Once I got him to Maui, he was so attached to me, I never had to put a real leash on him. He never left the yard and would walk next to me like I was the most disciplined trainer ever to walk the earth. The reality of the situation was, he was too scared to venture far.

He still has some of those traits he picked up begging for food on the streets of Mexico. When he wants me to feed him, he'll sit just outside the kitchen door until I fill his bowl. And if ever I even show him a broom, he takes cover. I think he was chased out of far too many restaurants with a broom. No matter how long he's been with me and how safe and cared for he is, he just can't let go of old habits.

We make our way through the Makawao Forest Reserve, past tall eucalyptus and pines surrounded by plush ferns, red dirt sticking to my shoes and Baja's paws. The sound of a trade-wind breeze in the trees and the rhythm of my shoes on the soft earth lull me into a happy rhythm.

At the halfway point, I stop, taking a moment to enjoy the array of beautiful flowers along the trail. Baja keeps running until he notices me stopped. He turns in circles, totally confused by my behavior. I never stop on runs. When I stop, the thoughts I'm trying to escape have a chance to catch up. But today, I don't mind the feelings that flow through me.

I have finally found a way to be close to Em without any risk. And sure it's only for a few more days, but I'll take anything I can get.

Chapter 20

FINN
JANUARY, SENIOR YEAR

EM:

You up?

The text comes on the fourth night Emerson has been living with me while she recovers from radiation treatment.

FINN:

What's wrong?

FINN:

Are you sick?

FINN:

You need something?

I'm in full-on alert mode. But all I see are three little dots. I sit up in my hammock, judging if it's worth the radiation dose to go check on her in person when her text hits my screen.

EM:

So, what sort of skeletons am I going to find in your room?
You got anything in here worth snooping for?

"Ha," I laugh to myself before laying back down, trying to slow my heart rate.

FINN:

> **You better not be snooping. I'll have to come in there and tickle you.**

EM:

> **NO! That'll kill you! I won't snoop.**

She's the only person I actually trust enough to allow unsupervised in my room.

EM:

> **I promiZZ**

Or, maybe not.

FINN:

> **Emerson Mahershalalhashbaz Malone. Don't you dare.**

EM:

> **You can't stop me <winking face with tongue>**

FINN:

> **I can handle a little radiation. I'm getting up right now.**

I slide out of my hammock just in case she's at the window watching me.

EM:

> **No! Don't!**

I take two steps toward the house and see her face peek out from behind the curtains.

EM:

> **I'm naked**

I freeze.
Em is naked? In my room?
Or is she just saying that to keep me from coming in there?

EM:

> **HA! You should have seen your face.**

EM:

Don't worry. Fully clothed

She stands in full view of the window now, waving. I wave before settling back in my hammock.

EM:

So, what exactly do you not want me to find?

FINN:

I don't hide anything from you, Em.

Though that's not exactly true, I do tell her a whole lot more than anyone else in my life. But some things you just don't share.

EM:

Yeah, right. I could fill a whole songbook with the stuff you don't talk about.

FINN:

Like what?

EM:

Your childhood. Where you grew up. Your parents. I don't even know if you have siblings.

EM:

Ex-girlfriends. Current girlfriends. Current groupies.

EM:

And don't even get me started on the whole Nashville chapter. Oh wait, I couldn't get started cause I don't know anything about it.

Her texts come in like gunfire, one right after the next. Like she's been loaded up with those questions for a while now. Maybe I've been hiding more than I thought from her. But sharing that stuff is the quickest way to send her fleeing from my life forever. And that's something I won't survive.

EM:

It's fine Finn. I'm just giving you a hard time. I know you don't like to talk about it.

No, I don't. But, she clearly does.

Maybe I could give her the sanitized version of things. The one where I don't end up looking like the reckless dirtbag that I really am.

FINN:

Tomorrow. We can talk tomorrow.

EM:

What?!?!? Really???

FINN:

Tomorrow. You need your sleep.

FINN:

Goodnight, babe.

EM:

Night, Finny.

The next night, a little earlier than usual, Em appears with her iced tea and takes her chair toward the far end of the yard. Looks like she's anxious to hear stories of what a bum I am. I hesitantly drag my chair closer to her. I really don't want to have to yell the things she wants to hear tonight. Or maybe she forgot all about it, and I won't have to share my biggest failures with her.

"You're too close. Back up," she demands.

"Em, it's been like a week. You're not that radioactive anymore."

"Okay, fine. But only because I want to hear every word you say tonight."

Great. She did remember. And she looks excited.

"How about just one question tonight? Childhood or siblings?" I offer the two easiest topics.

She sits quietly for a moment. "Were you always so distant from your parents?"

"Okay. Jumping right in."

"I did save you from having to talk about ex-girlfriends." She angles her chair toward mine.

"Thank you for that."

"That's what tomorrow is for," she says with a mischievous smile.

"Uhh. So, growing up wasn't so bad. My parents were parents."

"Don't spill all your secrets at once," she says, thick with sarcasm.

"I don't know what you want from me, Em," I snap.

"I'm sorry, Finn." She tucks her legs up under her. "We don't have to do this. I know you don't like sharing. Let's just watch the sunset."

Her disappointment tugs at me.

She leans back in her chair, turning away from me to the view. "It's a pretty one tonight. The clouds help," she says half-heartedly.

"My parents were patient with me."

At this, she doesn't move, probably afraid she might scare me off.

"I got into a lot of trouble as a kid. I hated school. But, they were always there trying to make things better for me."

She turns her head my way.

"They weren't really happy when I put off college and went to Nashville. They were worried I would get mixed up with the wrong crowd. And they weren't entirely wrong."

"Is that why you stopped talking to them?"

I can see the look of disappointment on my mom's face the last time I talked to her. Or maybe it was more disgust. Either way, she and my father made it clear they wanted nothing to do with me.

"They didn't like what happened in Nashville. And they let me know about it." I don't tell her why they hate me. Why I'm not worthy to be called their son.

Em leans toward me, face abounding with compassion. "Oh, Finny. That must have been so hard."

I nod.

"Have you tried reaching out to them?"

There's no reason. They were right to be done with me.

I interlace my fingers behind my head as my frustration rises.

"Finny?" she begs.

"I think we're done here." I push up from the chair and duck into my tent, zipping it behind me.

A few moments later, I hear a faint sarcastic, "That went well."

The next night, I distract Em from the harder topics of ex-girlfriends and my Nashville year by telling her stories of my easy summers in Seal Beach. I entertain her with stories of hustling money for ice cream at Mother's, jumping off the pier, and running from the local cops when they caught us. She's so excited by the idea that we could have been at the same beach at the same time so many years ago, she forgets the heavier topics we're supposed to be discussing.

I'm reminded that, when I was there at fourteen, she was barely ten. And the creep factor gets bigger. Her age doesn't bother me so much anymore, now that she's twenty, but thinking about how young she was during those summers, just reminds me of how sweet and innocent she is.

And how much of a careless scumbag I can be.

A few nights later, because of her patience with me, I tell her a little about my ex. About my parents. Not everything, but way more than I have ever shared with anyone else.

And each night after we talk, after I get all riled up having to think about my past, I pull out my guitar to calm my nerves and suddenly I'm overflowing with all sorts of song ideas. Em digs up things in me I had long since buried. And those painful things seem to be filling page after page in my songwriting notebook.

Maybe she's right about Mexico. If she's there with me, maybe I could write my whole first album. And, if she's right about Mexico, maybe she's right about Stanford.

She hasn't broached the topic since she brought it up last Fall, but after my reaction to it, I get why. I've been thinking about it lately, though. I've even checked out a few apartments. The prices up there mean I'd have to rent a shoe box, but a shoe box near Em is better than a mansion anywhere else.

And if this is how I'm feeling after having her by my side for a week, I can't imagine ever letting her go after spending a whole month with her in Mexico.

Chapter 21

EMERSON
PRESENT DAY

I wake up Tuesday morning looking forward to my Day Of Me. Greyson and Charlie are at work, while Indigo and JJ took off for some romantic hike. Finn left early this morning, doing his best not to wake me as he slipped out of bed.

I have the house to myself and I'm going to make the most of it. Gonna lay in bed until I'm good and ready to get out, make some pancakes, do some yoga. Enjoy the day. Read in the sun. Try to capture the Expansive Now.

I slip into my bikini, throw on a pair of jean shorts, and finger-comb my hair back into a ponytail. I pluck my book from the nightstand right next to *that* framed card. Man, I loved that boy all those years ago.

I slip out of the room to find Finn sitting at the kitchen island scribbling in his notebook.

He throws me a smile and then reaches back to push down the toaster. "Morning, Em."

"Morning, Finny."

He finishes capturing his thoughts in his notebook, closes the cover, and slips his pen into the spiral. He slides the notebook to the far end of the island.

My eyes follow his movements.

"You hungry?" he asks, trying to distract me.

I cannot tear my eyes from the turquoise cover sitting there just out of reach. I want so badly to dive for it, to get to it before Finn could stop me. To see if it's true. If he's writing again.

See, that's not just any notebook. That's his songwriting notebook. I know it well. It's the only type he would ever use to work out the lyrics and music to his songs.

We were at my place one day when he had filled up all the pages in one of those notebooks, and he nearly went crazy when I offered to give him an extra one I had on hand. You'd have thought I handed him a live snake.

I guess 6x9 narrow ruled, poly-covered, top-spiral notebooks in teal are hard to find the first week of a new quarter around UCSD because we spent the next four hours driving to every Target, Staples, and Office Depot within twenty miles of campus to find one.

But I thought he gave that up. He said he hadn't touched a guitar in years. And I haven't seen his name in the credits of any songs in the last few years, either.

Early on, he let it slip that the song we were listening to was originally written differently.

"You read that in Luke Monroe's biography?" I teased.

"No. I wrote it that way, but Luke didn't like it. We argued for days about it. So, when he debuted the song at one of his concerts, he changed it. He knew when people heard it that way, he'd never be able to record it differently. Sneaky bastard."

"There's no way you wrote that." Finn always was trying to get me to believe his wild stories.

He pulled out his phone and showed me the album liner for *Still Water Trails*. And there it was—Finnegan MacGregor. He was listed as the writer of four songs on that album. Four songs.

"What are you doing taking music classes at UCSD if you are a professional songwriter?"

"Needed a change. You can't write a good country song unless you have a life you left behind," he deflected. He always did that when I asked about life before he showed up on the shores of La Jolla.

Over time he shared the other songs he had sold. We'd be listening to Spotify while lying on the hill overlooking Scripps Pier or in a car with friends and he'd look over to me with this smile, this proud, knowing smile, and nod his head so slightly that only I would see, and I'd know. It was another one of his songs.

Soon, I started secretly searching for his songs, loading them onto one big playlist of *Finny songs*. I never got the guts to tell him I did it. After all, it was such a girly thing to do. And whenever I did something so girly, he'd flinch. Sometimes it was small. Sometimes the flinch turned into a full-on retreat.

I never gave up the habit, though. Which is why I know he hasn't written in years. Or maybe he just hasn't sold anything in years.

But with the Finn I've come to know again, a Finn who barely speaks, a Finn who hasn't touched a guitar in years, it wouldn't surprise me if he hasn't picked up a pen in years, either.

"You still start your day with a sugar bomb?" He spins around to the counter and plucks two slices from the toaster, tossing them on a plate.

The scent of cinnamon wraps me in wistful nostalgia that nearly overwhelms me. "On a Tuesday?"

"You didn't seem hungry last time. So, I thought I'd try again this morning."

He rounds the island to place them in front of me. He holds up a bag of icing and a pair of scissors moving them up and down across the corner of the bag. "Thick or thin brush today?"

I move his hand a few millimeters from the corner of the bag so I can get a thin icing line to make my icing art. I haven't painted cinnamon toast in ages. What would be the perfect subject today?

Finn leans a hip against the island. "Out of ideas?"

I take a few paces toward his notebook. "I'm sure I could find a few in there."

He lurches toward me, wrapping his arms around my waist. "You promised."

I spin in his arms. "Did I? I could have sworn I said, 'I Promizz to never read your songbook.'"

He pulls his arms from my back and begins tickling me until

I'm a squirming mess in his arms. "Okay. Okay. I give. I promise. Promise with an S."

He raises his eyebrows at me to confirm.

"I promise I said Promise with an S."

He shines a devastatingly irresistible grin. "That's more like it."

My heart does a flip when I see him like this. Happy. Truly happy. A relaxed and unshielded happy.

I lift my hand to his cheek, sliding my fingers to his neck. "I can't believe you did this. I can actually see your face again."

He skims his fingers along my still-red neck. "After what I did? I had to."

I capture his gaze. "That was not your fault."

My words land on him, touching something much deeper than guilt about roughing up my skin.

I lay my hand on his chest. "Finn, it was not your fault."

A flare of gratefulness is gone before it is fully formed. Replaced by something else entirely.

"Well, then, I guess shaving was a stupid thing to do." And with that, he was out the door.

Four years later and I'm still falling into the same trap. And I just can't do it anymore.

I thought things were different now. He's become so flirty and physical, touching me, and laying his hand on my knee, cuddling up on the couch. He never did that before. But it looks like the deep emotional stuff is still off the table.

If only I could find the magic combination of things, words to say, topics to avoid, ways to touch him, to stop him from withdrawing.

I lift the icing bag and sketch a portrait of his grin. That's the Finn I want to remember. That's the one I will hold onto.

Not the moody, retreating Finn. Him, I could do without forever.

When I finish my breakfast art, I move to the sink to tidy up. Through the window above the sink, the north end of the compound Finn has built stretches out.

It is an incredible refuge. A sunken, sandy fire pit sits to the right of the wrap-around porch on the Ohana that we were supposed to be staying in before lightning struck and flooded the whole thing. A raised veggie and herb garden spilling over in greens and reds and yellows is ringed by a fruit orchard. Bananas, oranges, mangoes, lemons, limes. Any sort of tropical fruit you would need, hanging there for the picking.

Just beyond it, wrapping all the way around the property is a wall of bamboo making this place feel completely separate from the world. A sanctuary apart. And with all this food growing, you would hardly need to ever leave.

Perfect for Finn.

I lift a dish towel to dry off my plate when Finn lumbers across the yard lugging an ax along with him. He stops in the middle of the yard looking to the left and then the right, like he somehow got lost on his way to the lumberyard.

He must spot his target because he moves to the far end of the yard before setting the ax on his shoulder and then slamming it down against the bamboo. He lifts the twenty-foot pole he severed and tosses it behind him like a toothpick.

He lifts the ax again and attacks the next pole, blow after blow until he has amputated an entire row. He tosses the ax to the ground and rips off his t-shirt, wiping his face with it. Then he collects the fallen shafts and tosses them in the pile.

He picks up a four-foot crowbar and pummels it into the ground beneath the row of bamboo he just cut down, then rocks it up and down until a huge chunk of earth pops out. He picks it up by a dangling root and flings it into a new pile.

I could have sworn that Finn developed his massive shoulders and tight abs from years in his outdoor weight room in front of the garage. Never would I have guessed it was from leveling fields of bamboo. But watching the way his biceps and back muscles flex with each blow, it is no wonder he looks like he is built of steel.

Lifting his shirt from the grass to wipe his face again, he catches me ogling him, which seems to ignite his frustration even further. He hoists his ax and goes back to work assaulting plants.

I finish wiping the dish that has practically air-dried in the time I spent leering at Finn before setting it back in the cupboard. Looks like I'm back to trying to capture my Day of Me, which doesn't sound as exciting as it did before the prospect of spending a day with Finn took root.

I take my book, swipe a beach towel from the shelves above the laundry, and make my way out the door just as Finn lumbers through with his shirt wrapped around his hand.

"Are you alright?" I ask.

He doesn't even slow down on his way to the sink. "I'm fine."

I follow close behind. "What happened?"

He unwraps the makeshift bandage and lets it drop into the sink. "I'm fine."

I peer into the sink and his shirt is now painted crimson. "You're not fine. Here let me look at it."

He turns to me and offers his hand. There's a three-inch gash on the outside of his palm.

"First aid kit?" I demand.

He kicks at the cupboard door under the sink.

I open it and dig around until I find a red box and a bottle of hydrogen peroxide. Laying the kit open on the counter, I open the lid to the peroxide and hold Finn's hand over the sink. "This might hurt."

He nods, and winces when the cool liquid hits his hand.

"How'd you do this?"

He shrugs.

I tear some clean paper towels from the holder and blot his cut gently. The scowl that appeared on his face when I touched him earlier still hasn't budged.

I try again. "You auditioning for a new hot lumberjack Instagram profile out there?

That elicits a growl. A growl?

I smear some antibiotic cream on the cut, a little less gingerly this time, and cover it with a bandage that I'm sure to apply enough pressure to.

"Ow." At least it's a word.

"Oh, did the little lumberjack get an owie?" I tease.

His eyes grow openly amused. He plucks his hand from mine and runs his hand over the bandage. "Thanks."

"It was nothing."

He heads back outside without another word.

I sigh. "Nothing at all."

I take my book and towel to the grass out front. Two can play at this game. I shimmy out of my shorts, lay down, and hike my bikini bottoms up a little.

To avoid a tan line.

That's all.

I try to lose myself in the story, but the images of Finn shirtless and sweaty dance in my head. I end up reading the same line fourteen times before I give up just as Finn appears from the garage carrying a skateboard, heading over the gravel driveway to the street.

Without a helmet.

Oh, crap. He's skating without a helmet.

I'm on my feet and sprinting toward him before I fully process what is going on. Just as quickly, tears begin to stream down my face.

"Stop! Finn, stop!" I scream at top volume.

He glares at me, "What, Em!"

"Helmet," is all I can get out between sobs. I try to catch my breath as I keep blurting out, "Helmet, Finn."

His annoyance with me fades as he takes in the raving lunatic I have become. I can see it, I know I have come unhinged, but I can't stop it from coming.

He drops the board and wraps his arms around me. "Em, babe. What's wrong?"

I suck in a halted breath and manage to mutter into his shirt, "You have to wear a helmet, Finn. Promise me you will. Promise me."

"I promise, babe. I promise," he says, drawing out the 's'. He wraps his arms tighter around me. "Em, what's this all about?"

All the energy that had flooded my body to try to stop him from going has fled, and, in its place, only weakness remains. I droop into his arms. He holds me up as he guides me to the log that serves as the edge of his driveway. We sit as I struggle to regain some bit of composure, but it won't come.

And so my story comes out as chopped-up bits and pieces. "Timmy." I sniff, wiping my nose with the back of my hand.

"I'm so sorry, Em." Finn gathers me into his arms and rocks me while I let down a flood of tears. I guess I wasn't done crying about him. I know I owe Finn an explanation, but the words are slow to form.

"We were on our honeymoon on the North Shore." I wipe my eyes. "We ran into one of his old friends who owned a legendary house right on Pipe with a mini-ramp in the backyard."

I tug on the back of my neck, trying to finally tell the story I usually avoid even thinking about. "We spent the afternoon surfing very small Pipe, then had a barbecue with our new friends. We all were hanging out in the backyard, eating, skating, watching the sun go down over the water when someone offered Timmy a board."

A breeze sends a chill over my skin. I wrap my arms around my bare arms.

"Here." Finn pulls his shirt over his head and hands it to me.

I slip it on and can still feel his warmth. He lays his arm on my shoulders again.

"I don't know if it was the new board or warped plywood from the ocean air, but he didn't make the drop. His board shot out in front of him and he fell on his back. Everyone yells, 'Oooh' and 'Damn,'" but he jumps right up and pumps his arms in the air. They loved that."

Everyone loved Timmy. No matter what he did, he could always capture people's hearts. He could be the biggest fool and find some way to make it cool.

"He sat down next to me and says, 'I can't believe I did that. I'm such a kook.' So, I tell him, 'But you're my kook. Forever and always.' And he kisses me. We were so absolutely happy. It was perfect."

I wrap my hands up in the bottom of my shirt. Stalling. Wanting to stay forever in that perfect moment. But we can't. We can't just pick one moment to stay in forever. Not even when simply telling a story. The rest of the story will come crashing in to ruin every perfect moment. I unfurl my hands from the shirt and rub my sweaty palms off on my knees.

"A few minutes later, he turns to me and says, 'Why don't, why, wha,' he shakes his head, 'baby, wha, why' and his face gets funny. Scared, maybe? And that was it."

God, the look on his face. He was so scared and he had no way of telling me. I could tell he wanted to say it. But his words were all messed up.

Finn nods his head. He knows how this story ends. He somehow knows without me having to say the words. Or maybe he knows so that I don't have to say the words.

"I'm so sorry, Em. I am so sorry," he whispers.

"I am too."

He kicks his skateboard aside, pushing it out of my view like he is protecting me from even the sight of a skateboard. That elicits a smile from me.

I bump his shoulder. "Thanks for listening. And for not running from the crazy lady assaulting you."

"You're not crazy, Em. Loud, but not crazy," he teases. He bumps me back. "So, Timmy always wore a helmet, huh?"

"I told him he didn't need one." The words are out of my mouth before I can catch them. Big sobs overtake me again.

I never told anyone that part. The part that I was too ashamed to admit to myself. When he was standing on the coping with a borrowed board, he tapped his head asking for a helmet. I shrugged him off.

Because nothing bad could ever happen to break us from that happy bubble. Plus, there was no need for a helmet, it was only a quarter pipe. Five feet tall. I'd dropped in on those when I was eight. And he'd have to borrow someone's nasty, sweaty helmet.

Stupidest decision I've ever made.

And I won't let it happen again.

"Finn, you have to promise me you'll never get on anything without a helmet. I don't care how safe you are or how good you are or how invincible you think you are. You're on a skateboard? You wear a helmet. Bike? Helmet. Wakebording? Zip-lining? Hell, even jumping on a trampoline, you wear a helmet. Promise me."

"I promise, babe. I will always wear a helmet. Promise, with an s. I promise."

He rises and pulls me to my feet, and lays his hands on my hips. "Em?"

I wipe my eyes and look up at him. "Yeah?"

"It wasn't your fault. You know that right?" He pushes a strand of hair behind my ear. "It wasn't your fault."

I have heard people tell me that for years now, but they never knew the whole story. They didn't know the part I played in it.

I have been telling myself that it isn't my fault for the past two years, trying to get my brain to agree, but it's not until I hear Finn say it out loud after he heard the whole truth, that I finally start to believe it.

Chapter 22

EMERSON STANFORD

Two weeks after graduating from UCSD and making my move to Stanford without Finn, it all became too much. I dropped out, moved home with my parents, and wallowed. I had never quit anything like that before. Never failed. And I had no idea how to deal with it.

Somehow, Indigo found out about it and demanded I come down to San Diego to visit. I wasn't really in the right mindset to hang with Indigo, but she isn't someone easy to say no to.

She planned the whole day to cheer me up. Coffee at Goldfish Point, an unhurried morning surf at Wind-an-Sea, and one-pound burritos at Roberto's in the sun for lunch. And, although I enjoyed the day, being back in La Jolla just served to remind me of Finn. I couldn't shake the feeling that I would run into him at any moment and I was nowhere ready for that.

We headed out that night to The Twirling Stone for trivia night and games with a group of Indie's friends. And that's where I met Timmy. Or I guess I should say met Timmy again. He was quick to tell me about the first time we met at one of Finn's parties.

"You were wearing this amazing yellow sundress. I was trying to do anything I could to get your attention. I think I may have even juggled?" he said with a laugh.

"No way. I think I actually remember that," I admitted, though I had no idea how I didn't immediately recognize him. He was gorgeous and I think might have even been flirting with me at that party. How could I possibly forget that?

"I never got to apologize for that night."

"Apologize for what?"

"I had no idea that guy was your boyfriend. Really, I never would have been flirting like that if I had known."

"Who, Finn? Wasn't my boyfriend. So, no apologies needed."

He took a sip of his soda. "So, just to be on the safe side now, no boyfriends currently?"

I tried to suppress my grin, but it was no use. "No boyfriends."

His smile matched my own. "Good."

We spent the rest of the night beating the pants off the other Trivia teams. Timmy was outgoing and funny and just the right kind of intriguing to draw me out of my funk. We went out on that mortifying first date the next weekend and were inseparable after that. Two years later, we were married.

And five days after our wedding, he was gone.

Everything had evaporated. Like it had only been a dream and now I was awake. But, really, I was forever trapped in a new nightmare.

It took me days to speak to anyone afterward. We still had four days left on our honeymoon and I had no idea how to tell people. Or who to tell. Or what to tell them. My whole world had collapsed.

When I left the hospital, I crawled back into our hotel room and laid comatose in complete darkness for days.

When I could finally muster up some logical thought, I still couldn't figure out how to tell my parents. Or how to even *call* his. I didn't have their number. I had only met them once before the wedding and the day of our wedding was such a blur I don't remember even talking to them.

I'm sure I did, but the only thing I remember from that day was the smile on Timmy's face. And the thoughts of how amazing our honeymoon was going to be.

Boy, was I wrong.

So I sat.

For days.

Alone.

A completely new type of alone.

Now that I had fallen so deeply into another person, I felt the gaping hole of loneliness even more than before.

And there were so many things that I had to do that I was utterly unprepared for. How do you get a body moved back home? Plan a funeral? Or even just move after losing your other half. I was just a kid. I was way out of my depth.

I didn't find the strength to tell anyone anything until the last day of my honeymoon. I couldn't put it off any longer, so, using Timmy's phone, I called his parents and, although they were devastated by his unexpected death, they stepped in and did all the stuff.

And I got on a plane and left alone. What was supposed to be the start of my new life, became the start of my new life, just not the life I had envisioned, not the life we had planned together. Not a life I wanted at all.

When I got home, I tried to handle the pain. I didn't feel like a widow, so I didn't feel comfortable seeking out other widows who had years or decades with their husbands and kids. I hadn't even moved in yet with Timmy.

But he wasn't just a boyfriend who died, either. We had plans. We were married. I didn't have time to change my name on all the paperwork, but I still wanted to be Sonny Starkey. I lost that chance before it was even mine.

So, I faced the agony alone.

Slowly the seasons of grief washed over me. That first phase is total shock, where you are just enduring each moment waiting for things to happen. A dead spot like the moment at a stop sign where you finally stop and roll back on your wheels before you have to take off again.

Then it switches from an impatient grief to an oh-crap-it's-really-here-grief. When people around you start back into their everyday lives, and you are still left with nothing, doing everything you can to stave off starting that new life. You cling to your old life so tightly you almost strangle yourself.

Then there are the months of pretending to live, but not being able to do anything effectively and having no emotional energy for anything. Not to connect with other people. Not to deal with the slight disturbances of everyday life. Where everything angers you and brings you back to a pile of soul-crushing tears.

And in the midst of that, you begin to have these little fleeting moments of peace. The first time I could listen to music again, I could only listen to it for a few measures. But those transient seconds were the first time I had felt anything even happy-adjacent.

Eventually, I found the moment when the first real wave ended. When I thought I might actually move through the grief one day. That I could imagine a time in the distant future when I wasn't at the very bottom of this deep dark hole.

On the first anniversary of Timmy's death, I made the decision to spend the next year getting to a place where I could ride the waves of grief without it taking me down. I would never stop missing him, but I needed to get to a place where grief would not overrun my life.

Somewhere in the middle of that year, I ran into an old friend at Roberto's and as we caught up, I realized I was a completely different person than I was the last time we spoke before I even met Tim. I now spoke my mind without hesitation and had no problem expressing my feelings. I was open and affectionate. That was the gift Timmy gave me.

So, on that day, I decided I was going to be happy that I had those two years with him. And I was going to be everything that he always thought I could be. The open person he worked so hard to find behind my wall. And once he found me, and was so loving of who that was, I was able to let others see me too. And to show them how much I cared.

I had changed by loving Timmy, and by letting him love me, but I was still stuck in all the pain. My entire life was smothered by a fine layer of grief like June Gloom on a misty morning in La Jolla. And although I was grateful for all the amazing things Timmy gave me, I had to find a way to become unshackled from this pain. Not to erase it, but to set it beside me so that it was a part of me, but not something that was keeping me from being fully me again.

Being here, being around Finn, somehow reminds me of the girl I once was. Before I knew more than my fair share of heartache. Being around him reminds me of the girl I used to be before all the pain took over. When I was happy. Free. Filled with unbounded joy. And that's a girl I so want to be again. A girl who laughs and smiles and loves music.

Becoming her again is now number one on my goals list.

Chapter 23

FINN
PRESENT DAY

The grungy chords of the iconic electric guitar riff of Nirvana's timeless anthem, "Smells Like Teen Spirit," ring out from The Painted Lantern's karaoke stage as JJ tries to embody a disillusioned teen in the 90s. But when it comes time for him to sing, JJ belts out the first line to Weird Al's *Smells Like Nirvana* in a horrible falsetto, and I can't tell if the crowd loves it or is about to rip JJ to shreds for crapping on their precious Kurt Cobain. I'm fine either way because I'm sitting next to Em, who is thoroughly enjoying his performance. And that's all I need. For Em to be happy.

After sharing her story with me this morning, she hasn't left my side. I knew I could cheer her up with lunch at Five Ono's and a long surf at Westies. When we got back home, we curled up on the couch to watch North Shore because she swore she could point out every single mistake in the whole movie. And there were a ton.

I was bummed when everyone came back home and dragged us out to karaoke, but seeing the smile on Em's face now, I'd endure years of JJ's horrendous singing if it made her this happy. And it sure doesn't hurt that she's still snuggled up next to me as we take in the show. My arm is slung over her shoulders and I let my thumb rub slow circles on the bare skin there.

JJ finishes off his song and collapses into the chair next to mine as an old man with white braids down to his belt gets up and belts out a rendition of Tennessee Whiskey so smooth that I have to double-check that it's not Chris Stapleton in disguise.

When he finishes up, the mic stands empty for far too long as the heads around our table begin to turn toward Em.

Charlie is the first to break the silence. "You said you'd switch out your no's for yes's. From the looks of it, you really want to say no."

Charlie's barking up the wrong tree here. Back in college, Em never sang in public. Every now and then she'd sing when it was just the two of us and I'd play, but involve a stage and a mic and she would cower.

She takes in a huge sigh and her whole body wilts as she lets it out. She replies in a low, resigned voice. "Fine."

Approaching the host, she makes her song request, then drags herself on stage. Fear, stark and vivid, glints in her eyes. When they find mine, I lift her drink and take a sip, holding it up to her afterward as I mouth the words. "Poison free."

She nods, the beginning of a smile tipping the corners of her mouth as the backing track begins.

I don't know who signs off on the horrific versions of karaoke songs, but they could take the greatest song and make it a miserable experience. It's like one guy with an electronic keyboard and three weeks of piano lessons has made every single track.

But when Em belts out the first line of "A Piece of You", everyone goes completely still. The backing track fades in my head, replaced by the guitar, mandolin and violin of the original track. I know that one all too well.

After all, I wrote it.

Her voice washes over me, relaxing every single cell in my body. And I'm instantly back in college, singing in my backyard, watching as the sunset fades into deep night, the only place where she found the confidence to sing her heart out without any insecurity. I would let one song bleed into the next, terrified that if I stopped playing for even a moment, the spell would be broken and she would stop singing, only to cover herself back up with caution and self-control. I lived for those nights of abandon.

After the first verse when the mandolin starts to fill in, she begins to find the strength in her voice and she's really meaning every word of the mournful chorus. She can barely make it through the chorus because she's fighting back tears and her voice gets tight. But she grins and bears it, and when the chorus comes out the second time, she is nearly screaming it, and I swear her voice lifts that song to an entirely different plane.

When I wrote the song, before I sold it to Jerry Guth, and his producers forced me to change the last verse, it was a sad song of loss and despair. The way it should have been. But they wanted a happy ending. So, I complied and begrudgingly rewrote it.

Now, hearing Em sing the final verse that I was forced to wring out of my head, I am so glad I did. They seem to bring the joy back to her.

And for the first time, I see this song in a whole new light, as an anthem for Em. She knows every word by heart. I wonder if it was what brought her through losing Timmy. Through the grief and mourning. To the other side where she found her joy again. Did she play it on repeat in those days as that one song that everybody has that can drag you through the worst of times?

I would love to think that I at least gave that to her at a time when I should have been there to help her get through the worst days of her life.

Em jumps off the front of the stage and snuggles back up to me.

"Why on earth would you not want to sing on stage, Em, is beyond me. You were incredible," Charlie gushes. The others all erupt in praise, too.

I drop my hand from her chair, suddenly feeling very uncomfortable being so close.

"It's weird. I used to be so afraid of that. But I guess after everything I've been through, it doesn't seem so scary anymore," she admits.

The sudden agitation in my body drives me to move. I snatch my glass and head to the bar looking for a refill.

When I get back to the table, it looks like they've already started singing Timmy's praises.

"I remember after that first night when you came out to trivia with us," Indigo says. "He would not shut up about you. Swearing that you were the one. That he would marry you one day."

"Oh my gosh. That is so sweet. Love at first sight," Charlie swoons.

"It was weird," Indigo adds. "It took that kid ages to make even the simplest decision, but he knew immediately with you."

Em smiles and looks down at her hands which are fiddling with a napkin under the table.

"Do you remember, at your wedding, when your pump kept alarming right in the middle of the toasts, but you had tucked it into your dress so you couldn't silence it and you couldn't leave the speeches to fish it out of your cleavage either? So, right after his best man's speech, he pulled you to your feet and spun you around. And everyone thought he was just being romantic, but, really, while no one could see, he pulled out your pump so you could silence it before the next speech."

"That was totally him. He could figure out a solution to any problem and find a way to do it so you'd never be embarrassed. The perfect gentleman," Indigo says, melancholy overcoming her happy demeanor.

"Em, you remember when we flew out to San Diego to surf with you guys and you had that last-minute job interview? So, Timmy drove like three hours up to LAX to pick us up before he had ever even met us. And he brought us burritos from his favorite little, authentic Mexican restaurant in LA because our flight got delayed another two hours and he thought we might be hungry after all that. What was that place called?"

"Aldeberto's. We would stop every time we were up there," Em says, wistfully.

"That's right and we kept going on and on about all the -erto's restaurants in So Cal the whole ride home," Charlie adds.

"Oh, yeah. Filoberto's and Fancyberto's," Billie says.

"And Superboberto's," Charlie barely gets out between laughs. "Man, Timmy was hilarious."

Em looks at me. Trying to catch my attention. I can't give it to her. She deserves so much more. Someone like Timmy, a superhero who is the perfect gentleman and hilarious and selfless. Not a screwup like me. I don't know how I forgot that today.

"I remember when he nearly ruined my birthday that first year because I couldn't figure out what to wear to my surprise party. He kept pushing me to go and he was pacing around my place, and complaining so much that we were going to be late that we ended up fighting the whole way over there. I was nearly in tears when I had to walk into the party for everyone to yell, 'Surprise.' Damn. I was so pissed at him."

No one knows what to do with that. JJ clears his throat. Greyson takes a huge sip of his beer so he doesn't have to talk. Even the girls, who are usually so sweet and comforting, don't know how to react.

"When people die," Em tries to explain, "everyone is so ready to turn that person into a saint. To only ever speak the good things. You want to make it hurt less so you convince yourself that you were once in the presence of greatness. But, then, you end up misrepresenting who they really were. Timmy had some amazing qualities, and I'm so glad I got to love him, but I want to remember all of him." Em wipes the condensation from the side of her glass. "He was impatient and he would come up with these outlandish dreams that sounded fantastic, but were so impractical. And he would insist on trying them."

"Like the, what did he call it? The beanie for your beard?" Indigo asks.

"The Beardie," Em concedes with a laugh.

"He swore he was going to get so rich off that." Indigo says.

"Right? And then he was totally convinced that we should become the caretakers of a lighthouse on Tukammaksa Island off Tasmania for six months. With no cell phones, no Wi-Fi, no communication with the outside world at all. No doctors and no med shipments, either. Oh yeah, and no electricity besides the light for the lighthouse. Like it would be super simple to leave everything behind like that."

"How would you keep your insulin cold?" Charlie asks.

173

"Or even get supplies out there for that long?" Billie adds.

"Exactly. He never knew how to think through all the details of how to make something like that happen. He just had the idea and insisted it would just happen," Em lets her voice slide into her version of Turtle from North Shore, "'No problem, eh?'"

"Oh my gosh. He loved to quote Turtle," Indigo says.

"But it's okay that he wasn't perfect. I mean, can you imagine being married to someone who *was* perfect?" she asks.

Em was always able to overlook other people's flaws.

"Anyway, I had my own faults. And some of them I actually improved on. I still have a bunch more areas I need to grow. But that's just the thing. People suck." She takes a sip of her tea while everyone is still stunned into silence. "Okay, maybe they don't suck, but they're people. They have their strengths and their... rooms for improvement," Em says.

I study her for a minute trying to decide if she really means it. Does she really think every disgusting, deplorable tendency can improve?

Chapter 24

FINN
NASHVILLE

hen I first got to Nashville, everything went right. Here I
was, a kid fresh out of high school in North Carolina, on
my own for the first time in a big city and everything I had
always dreamed about was falling into place.

The first week, I found a shabby apartment, but thought it
was the greatest thing in the world because it was mine. And since
Nashville was the place for young musicians to try to make it,
finding friends was like shooting fish in a barrel. And these friends
had the same goals in life. So, we would all play and write and
drink our days away.

I found Sophia that first week. She moved in a few months
later and everything was perfect. Within a month there, I even
had a lead on selling my first song.

I was showing my parents that everything they had worried
about happening, every horrible thing they swore would happen
to me if I went there, was completely wrong. I wouldn't even need
to go back to my deferred admission to UCSD like they made me
swear to do. They were wrong. And I was right.

The only problem was, living with a woman brought all the
complications of living with a woman without any of the security
or commitment of marriage. Every time we would fight, I became

more and more fearful that it would be our last. I'm sure it didn't help that Sophia would threaten to leave, too.

So, instead of bringing up anything that I didn't like or things she would do to piss me off, I would push those feelings down and, instead, avoid her. Which, of course, led to a really crappy relationship.

We were at the point where I could tell it wasn't working anymore, but I just didn't want to do what needed to be done.

One night, we went out with friends to Santa's Bar. It was one of the dive bars we frequented as a warm-up to our night. They had decent food for cheap and could put up with a little more rowdiness than some of the other places in town, which made it perfect for us, as long as you could overlook the Christmas-themed decor.

Tommy finished off his beer and slammed it on the slightly sticky table. "Who's ready for The Local?"

The Local was a good place to scope out our competition or look for upcoming artists to round out our sound. We had been looking for a mandolin player for the last few weeks to help with one of our latest songs.

"My tummy hurts," Sophia demanded like a petulant child. That was her code for wanting to go home. Her moods had been more mercurial for a few weeks and she was dipping out of nearly every night out. I didn't want to fight with her, so I gave in.

"Looks like we're going to head home. But make sure you guys check out the River City Wranglers tonight. I really like Danny Curt on mandolin."

Sophia didn't say another word on our way home, which I didn't mind. It made it that much easier to ignore her pouting. Once at home, she locked herself away in our room while I cracked another beer and watched some old black-and-white movie on TV.

A few hours later, she got bored and probably mad that I didn't go chasing after her to make up for whatever imagined slight I had dished out. "My tummy hurts, Finn. You need to take me to the doctor," she whined.

"It's almost midnight, Soph. There aren't any doctors open. And besides, you don't have insurance. Do you really want to

pay two hundred dollars for him to tell you to take some Tums?"
I snapped.

"Fine. Then get me some Tums." Like she wasn't capable of
crossing the puny living room to get to the cupboard.

Silently, I crossed the room and dug out the meds. Anything
to get her to crawl back into that room and go to sleep. I tossed
them to her and fell back into my chair, leaning over to look
around her as she blocked the TV.

She stood in front of the TV with her hands on her hips, her
face mimicking a chagrined elementary school teacher.

"Goodnight, Sophia," I practically sang.

Satisfied that she got her way, she practically skipped into our
room and shut the door behind her.

I woke around three, still in my chair, to the sounds of Buddy
whimpering in his sleep. Only, my childhood dog was back in
South Carolina with my parents. But the sound persisted.

I struggled to a stand and followed the sound to the bathroom.
Sophia was lying on the bathroom floor in pain, pale as a ghost.
"ER," is all she said.

I scooped her up and drove straight to the Emergency Room.
An orderly met us at the curb and wheeled her off while I parked
my car. By the time I got to the front desk and asked about her, the
nurse told me she didn't want me back there. I knew Sophia was
mad the night before, probably even more mad that I didn't take
her complaints seriously, but to be that vindictive was shocking.

I collapsed in the gloomy waiting room and... waited.

For hours, I waited.

Every hour, I would ask the nurses again to go back and see
Soph, hoping that maybe she had changed her mind. Maybe once
they got the pain under control, she'd be thinking more clearly.

Six hours later, after shift change, I tried charming the new
nurse to no avail. But I did, unfortunately, catch the attention of
a very stately-looking couple.

"What do you want with Sophia?" the man demanded. His
gleaming blue eyes reminded me of Sophia's and I put it together.
They must be her parents.

"Hi, Sir. I'm Finn. I'm Sophia's boyfriend. Do you know how she is? They won't let me back there."

"Oh, we know who you are," the woman spit out. "You're the dirtbag who got our Sophia in this position in the first place."

I know Sophia talked on the phone with her mom every now and then. Maybe she had complained a bit too much to her about our recent problems, but even that didn't seem to explain this hatred that was radiating off of Mrs. Astor.

"How is she? Do they know what's wrong?" I begged.

Her dad wrapped his arm around his wife. "She's in surgery, you little prick."

"Surgery? For what? What's wrong?" They must have known. The doctor must have talked with them.

"What's wrong? What's wrong?" her mom shouted. "You're what's wrong. You convince her to move in with you and get her pregnant and don't even have the decency to take her to a doctor." She moved closer, began poking at my chest with her bony finger, and raised her volume even more. "And now, she's laying on a cold metal table with doctors cutting into her trying to save her life. You've been playing house with our girl, but you're not fit to be anyone's husband."

A doctor stepped between us. "This is not the place for this, Mrs. Astor. Let's go over here and I'll tell you how things went." Mr. Astor led his wife to the other side of the waiting room, far away from me.

Pregnant? She never said a word. I had no idea.

And then surgery? What could have possibly gone so wrong?

When the doctor was finished and led Sophia's parents through the protected double doors, he came back my way. "I assume you're the father, so I'm legally allowed to share this with you. Sophia had an ectopic pregnancy. The fetus got lodged in her fallopian tube which is not an organ that can allow the fetus to grow to term. It, unfortunately, grew too large and burst the tube causing internal bleeding, which is what caused the pain. She came out of surgery fine, but for now, it's probably best if you aren't back there while her parents are around." And, with that, he disappeared behind the double doors, too.

Internal bleeding? Surgery? Pregnant? And I ignored her. I shoved her aside for another beer and some dumb movie that I don't even remember now. She was in the next room in massive pain and bleeding to death and I went to sleep. It's no wonder that she doesn't want to see me. That her parents hate me.

I was supposed to take care of her and I almost let her die.

With no hope of getting to see Sophia to apologize, to try to make things better, I went back to our apartment and waited to hear from her. I figured she would call when her parents weren't around.

But she never did.

And every time I went to the hospital to check on her, three or four times a day, the nurses sent me away.

The last time I went, the nurse looked at me with such pity. The pity I could handle. It was not being able to talk to Sophia that got me. Most times, the nurses had come to avoid eye contact with me. They knew they'd have to tell me once again, Sophie wouldn't talk to me. But this time, the nurse came right over to me.

"I'm so sorry."

"She still won't talk to me?"

"It's not that." A shadow of grief touched her face and I knew. I didn't need to know the details of how it happened. Sophia was gone. I left without another word.

For months, I tried to keep writing music in Nashville. To keep pursuing a career, but my heart just wasn't in it any longer. And songwriting and performing is not a job you can do half-heartedly. It demands your entire soul, and mine was in no shape to write or play music. So, I tucked my tail between my legs and went limping back home.

After a week of sulking and grieving the loss of a family I never knew even existed, my parents' patience wore thin. They demanded I tell them why I was back. I think they wanted to hear me say I was wrong, that Nashville was the wrong path for me, and that they were right, more than they actually cared why I was so broken.

When I finally told them, they were no more sympathetic. While my dad yelled at me about being a sinner and reaping what I've sown and feeding the flesh, my mom was in my room packing up my things and throwing them out my second-story bedroom window. The only thing she said to me was, "We can't have that here. You need to leave. You're not even worthy to be called our son."

I got in my van and drove down the coast until I hit Florida. I fell asleep in my van in a parking lot at the north end of A1A. When I woke up the next morning, I had to decide whether to take A1A to its other end in Key West and follow in Jimmy Buffett's footprints drinking and writing music and performing in bar after bar each night, or take the academic path like Miles Davis and make my way to UCSD on the other coast.

I had had enough of the East Coast's sweltering summer humidity and I figured the farther I could get away from Nashville, the better. So, I took off on a cross-country road trip with only the items my mom threw out my bedroom window, ready to start a whole new life.

Chapter 25

EMERSON
PRESENT DAY

*I*can't believe that my two weeks here are almost over. I feel like a whole new person. Or maybe not a new person, but definitely like I have fully entered a new season. The joy and beauty of Spring has sprung.

In twelve short days, I have made some incredible new friends who I know will be a part of my life for the rest of my life. Billie and Charlie, Harley and Indie. Amazing girls who love challenging themselves to pick up new and incredibly demanding sports. Girls who pursue creative and artistic expression. And girls who love each other deeply and are so ready to support each other and offer really good advice.

I have finally found those friends that I have been searching my whole life for. Friends who push me to follow through on my grand ideas. Friends who could convince me to take the stage and sing a song that was way too personal. The ones who make me feel like my freakish ways aren't really all that bad. Like they're just a part of what makes me an interesting person. Maybe I should have been looking for girlfriends whose names end in 'ie' my whole life. It would have saved me a lot of time.

I came here looking to build a support system for the next time life turns into an unholy mess. And that's exactly what I found.

What I didn't expect to find is a Finn.

And that's the only way I can describe him. I can't seem to fit him in any other category. I kiss him and he unleashes himself on me, but then he acts like it never happened. He cannot keep his hands off me since then but hasn't come anywhere near kissing me again.

Sometimes, it's as if we are somehow alone together in the midst of everyone, giving each other looks across the room, understanding each other without having to talk.

We flirt and cuddle on the couch. We have even been sleeping in the same bed for the past few nights. And still, I have no idea where we stand. It's like his body is saying one thing but his mouth refuses to admit it.

The line that was so freakin' easy to find before, has gone completely fuzzy. I have no idea where to find it. And no idea of how to make sure we land on the romantic side of that line when this is all over.

Indigo pops out of JJ's room, giggling as usual. "We gonna do this bio-fixing thingy?"

JJ steals a kiss from Indie on his way out the door. "Sushi, tonight?"

"Yeah, sweetie. Seven."

It all seems so easy for them. They've known each other for twelve days and have fallen into a very easy relationship. No confusion. No doubts. No drama. So lucky.

"Come on, Em. Let's go get our gardening on." Indigo hauls me from the sofa, dragging me outside to where Billie has set up what looks like a whole movie set.

Indigo is helping her with a promotion video for her Biovandal Art Subscription Boxes and her movie-making skills are going to make Billie's art look incredible.

Most of the time, her monthly subscription box of art goodies focuses on a new art style. They come with all the supplies and inspiration needed to try your hand at something new to bring a little joy to the public space. Whether that is sidewalk chalk challenges to cover a whole city with words of encouragement, huge magnetic words to leave poetry on public spaces, or even a hydrophobic paint that only becomes visible when it rains.

But since the wildfires took down Lahaina last year, Billie has been looking for a way to support the community. She teamed up with local scientists to develop a kit that has everything you need to start using native plants to clean up the toxins that were left behind and prevent those toxins from spreading further into the watershed and wreaking havoc on wildlife in the area. And to give the people affected a feeling that they have at least a little control over the devastation.

I love that after everything Maui has given me in the last two weeks, I get to give back a tiny fraction of that.

Since these are a little more complicated than most of her subscription boxes that are more freeform expression, she is making an explanatory video to accompany it.

"Okay, girls." Indigo puts on her director's voice. "Each girl behind a table. Billie here will explain a little bit about the project and then walk us through how to build them. Just pretend the cameras aren't even here. I'm gonna hit record on all of the cameras and then not touch them so it might make that a little easier. Just focus on Billie and having fun."

Indigo walks to each camera, hitting a few buttons, before standing behind her own cheerily decorated table filled with supplies. She nods to Billie.

"Hi everyone. Thanks so much for helping me with this project. It is such an important one. Usually, I.. No wait. I usually send out. Shoot." She looks at Indigo. "Do we have to start all over now?"

"It's totally fine. Whenever you want to, you can just start over. But remember, it's just us girls here. You don't have to be perfect."

Billie manages to fall into a more conversational tone and explains bioremediation, which, I learn, is using living things to clean up disaster sites. I guess a lot of the homes built in Lahaina from the 1930s to the 60s were built with a drywall type of product made out of recycled sugar cane rinds called Canec, which is an awesome use of a byproduct. The only problem is that little termites love the taste of all that sugar cane waste. So, they doused it in arsenic to stop them. When the fires burned, all of that arsenic was released into the ash and soil. Then the rains came and washed it into the beautiful ocean at the edge of town.

Add to that all the asbestos from building materials, lead from paints, melted pipes, and roofing, and a whole host of toxins from all of the vehicles that were trapped and burned, and you are left with a toxic soup that becomes very difficult to clean up.

But there are these incredible plants and fungi that can clean up those toxins.

After her introduction which has me hanging on every word, Director Indie steps in. "So, I was thinking for the actual step-by-step part we can do a voice-over and some written steps on screen. So, you can still walk us through each step, but I won't be using the audio, so feel free to have fun and just chat."

"And there's the printout card on everyone's table with the directions. I was hoping to see if you girls could put it together with just that," Billie adds.

We each dive into creating our mycosocks, which look like giant nylons filled with straw and soil, and then they get rolled in mushroom babies. Billie explained all the biology behind it, but what I got was these are little guys that grow into big mushrooms.

We move onto seed starter packs that will help grow a couple of plants that will further help remove toxins but also look great while they are doing it.

Finn and Greyson slip out the front door.

Charlie sprints to Greyson, wrapping her arms around him. "Bye, Babe. Be brave, be smart, be strong, and come back home safe. Both of us will be waiting."

He rubs her tummy and then gives her another big hug.

Finn leans over the open truck door as he takes in the two of them. He glances my way, melancholy written all over his face, while Greyson hops in the passenger side of Finn's truck.

As Charlie skips back our way, Harley leans towards me and points toward Finn. "So, you guys finally official?" Can't get anything past Harley. She's constantly noticing every single detail of everything around her.

"I wish I knew." I stuff more straw into the sock, almost ripping the fragile material. "He couldn't be harder to read if he were *War and Peace* written in Greenlandic. Half of the time I swear we've moved way past just friends. Then others, he is making it perfectly clear that's all we are."

"Yeah. Greyson did that too for a long time. So did I. Poe friends." Charlie wipes her brow with the back of her muddy hand. "Yikes. I can't believe I used to use that phrase, it was so dumb."

"Poe Friends?" I ask.

"So, so dumb. No one ever got the joke," Charlie laughs. "Friends, like Edgar Allen Poe's poem, *Nevermore*. Get it? Yeah. I know. So dumb."

"Ohhhh. Okay. That's not totally dumb," I assure her. No dumber than the Pro-Con list I made last night that was more of a He Loves Me, He Loves Me Not List. All the proof I had that he thought we were more than friends on one side. Proof that we weren't on the other.

"Maybe you need to find out once and for all one way or the other," Indigo suggests.

I would love to know one way or the other, but pressing Finn usually results in him running.

"What did you do, Charlie?" I ask.

"He did it. He just snapped one night. When we were on a double date."

Billie interrupts, "With other people."

"Yeah, and it was the last straw." Charlie packs another huge handful of mycclium into her sock. "But thinking about it, I may have pushed that line a few times before that moment. Nothing as far as making out with him in the middle of a truth or dare game, though."

"Right? That had to mean something." Harley shakes a muddy hand in my direction. "A guy doesn't do that and not have feelings for you."

"Yeah, but then he goes running off. And the last time I pushed that line, I lost him. Gone. For good. No closure. No nothing.

He fled to Baja and I never heard from him again. I'm not sure I could take that again."

"But could you *live* with not knowing? With missing an opportunity because you were too afraid? Are you willing to risk an incredible forever because you don't want to mess up a muddled "best friendship" that may not even endure you going home?"

"I hadn't even thought about our friendship not withstanding me going home. I'm not sure I could go back to another Finn-less world."

"So, don't go home," Indigo says it likes it's that simple.

"Don't go home? Like ever? How would I even do that?"

"You could crash with me as long as you need," Billie offers.

"I'm looking for a research assistant to carry on my research while I'm back in San Diego," Harley adds.

That would be so much better than being a paint waitress for half-drunk moms painting pottery. And so much better than my tiny, dark apartment overlooking a biker bar in Pacific Beach.

I could stay.

But that doesn't fix the whole Finn conundrum. I still don't know where we stand. What he wants.

As I try to scrub the dirt and fungi from beneath my nails for the fourth time tonight, scenes flash through my mind from the last time I tried to push Finn for an answer to the question that has been plaguing us since we met.

The cacti. The ice cream. That damned Stanford shirt. It took a week of research and planning, all for me to make a total fool of myself.

"Ooh, what great big muscles you have, Finn." I must have sounded just like Little Red Riding Hood to him. No wonder I made it a failure of cataclysmic proportions.

But I'm a whole new woman now. I don't need to research and plot and plan. I just need to tell Finn what I want and hope he doesn't disappear for another four years like last time.

Billie flies down the stairs. "It's done! Everyone into the viewing room."

I dry my hands on a kitchen towel. "There's a secret viewing room I don't know about?" Wouldn't surprise me if Finn built a hidden room for movies.

"The couch, Sonny," Billie says. "Come on. I can't wait to show you. Indigo is a genius."

We all settle into the sofa as Billie pushes play on the remote with a grand flourish.

Indigo certainly is a talented filmmaker. It couldn't look more professional.

"So, I also took a lot of the footage you captured from your launch last year and spun it into a bunch of shorter clips and videos that you can use on socials and on YouTube."

"No way,' Billie sequels. "Is that on here too?"

"In the main menu."

Billie plays through short fifteen-second clips of chalk art and poetry magnets, then some longer ones. There's a slow-motion video of what looks like water rushing down a gutter until it hits something that makes it barrel into a standing wave. With tiny little figurines surfing it. I pull out my phone to sign up for Billie's kits immediately. This stuff looks so fun.

The last video starts with a close-up of a dingy sidewalk. A wave of water splashes over it, darkening the sidewalk. As the camera draws back, there are lighter parts of the sidewalk that somehow escaped the deluge.

I look back to my phone to complete my subscription.

"No way," Charlie gasps.

"That's why it always looked so familiar," Billie adds.

I hit the subscribe button and peer up, trying to catch up to all the excitement.

And, there, on the paused screen, Finn stands looking down on a face that looks all too much like mine. Around it in handwriting that I have seen fill hundreds of songwriting journals is the phrase, "Be good and you will be lonesome."

I look to Indigo to back up my theory. If he was painting my face on the streets of Maui before I ever came back into his life, maybe there is more to Finn's feelings than he is letting on.

Her knowing smile confirms it. "Well if that's not a sign, I don't know what is."

Chapter 26

EMERSON
JUNE, SENIOR YEAR

I'm sitting in the Earth Science class that I put off all four years, trying to focus on the least interesting science ever created. Rocks that sit there, don't move, don't hunt, don't even have little rock babies, don't really hold my attention.

The professor is going on and on about how all these geological processes had to take millions and millions of years to form the Grand Canyon because the river is only eroding the land by 0.1524 cm per year right now. Since the Grand Canyon is 1829 meters at its deepest, it must have taken blah blah blah years.

"It's Uniformitarianism," he says, like the fancy schmancy capitalized term makes it true.

And, for the first time in my life, I think I might finally relate to rocks. Finn and I have been hanging out non-stop for nearly four years and we are still creeping toward that friendship-romance line slower than a turtle limping through cold molasses. At this rate, it would take nearly 4.5 billion years to get there.

And, perhaps, that's the answer to the question that has been plaguing me lately. Things will never change. Or at least not in my lifetime. And certainly not before some other girl catches Finn's attention and snaps him up. Some girl who could barely be concerned enough to even learn his name, more interested in the things he could give her, the fame and riches of a future country star. One who would leave him alone and destitute if her dreams for him never came true.

And I'm left stuck in a Uniformitarianistic trench.

The thought throws me into a daze. I'm not sure I can even picture my life without Finn in it, without him being the most important part of that life. He is so ingrained into every aspect of my life that I wouldn't know how to exist without him. And the thought of some other girl getting to have that life with him is enough to kill me.

That thought drives me out of my head and back into the lecture where the professor decides that everything he lectured about during the first forty minutes of teaching isn't actually true. Or, more precisely, he gives a big EXCEPT...

"Cataclysms happen," he says. He goes on to explain that the rate at which things are currently happening doesn't necessarily mean that they have always been happening at that speed. That it is totally possible that the Grand Canyon was carved out much faster than we would expect, as long as there was a whole lot of water draining really, really fast.

Maybe that's what Finn and I need. I just need to create a cataclysm.

The only problem is, I have no idea how to even do that.

And I'm running out of time to make it happen. We leave for Baja in just one week. There's no way I would try to cause a cataclysm when it's just Finn and I on some secluded beach in Mexico. Can you imagine having to drive eighteen hours back to the US in silence as Finn pouts because things got murky? That would be torture.

If I'm gonna take a chance of messing things up, I'm gonna do it here in the safety of my home, which means I have exactly four days to figure out how on earth I'm gonna make it perfectly clear that I want more. One day to implement it. And two days to convince Finn that I meant nothing by it and we can still go to Baja as the plain old friends we have always been when it all blows up in my face.

Since I have absolutely zero experience with this, I do what I always do when I get interested in learning something new. Research.

I start with all the famous movies about friends crossing that line. Harry and Sally took decades to figure it out, so I skip that one. And then, I'm ruling out a whole host of other movies that took that long. *One Day*, *Love, Rosie*, and *My Best Friend's Wedding*. I'm not waiting until Finn's married to tell him.

Then I take out the ones where the couple ends up drunk and sleeping together. Or crying and sleeping together. Or fighting like dogs and then sleeping together.

Though with Finn, the fighting part might be easier to accomplish.

By the time I watch four of the movies that made it past my standards, I don't see myself in any of those women. They all knew what they were doing or were completely okay with putting themselves out there in crazy ways. Not me at all.

I move on to my favorite TV shows that aren't classically thought of as Romances and study even further. I fly through episodes and seasons of *Bones* looking for that one moment when it all changed. After being forced to face their growing love by their therapist, Booth finally confesses everything. And, sure, it takes them a few more seasons for him and Bones to get together, but then it only happened after a crying fit and sleeping together. And a surprise pregnancy. Okay, not the best playbook.

And anyway, I'm no good at big speeches. Tried that one back in the Fall when I plotted and planned to ask Finn to come to Stanford. And we all know how poorly that went. "You're, uhh, important to me, Finn." So dumb.

Next, I play and rewind scenes from *Prison Break* where the inmate Michael crosses that line with Sarah, his prison doctor. And he just went in for the kiss. No warning. No lead-up. No speeches. He just went for it. That sounds doable.

But how sad is it that the game plan I find most feasible is an illegal relationship propelled by a male convict.

That has to be the exact opposite of what I should be doing.

I cannot believe I have spent twenty years on this earth and I still have no clue what I'm doing when it comes to boys. Once again, I feel like a total freak. I swear if I didn't look so much like my parents, I would think I was an alien.

Even if that were true, I need to figure out how to blend in with my human counterparts. Time for a little written research.

I hop on my bike and head to Verbatim Books. Wandering through the magazine section, I pluck every women's magazine I can find. Plopping down in a big comfy chair, I sort through my stack of research. I scan headings of *How to Seduce a Man Using Only Your Tongue, 9 Things Every Naked Man Wants to Hear,* and *Lingerie to Make Your Thigh Gap Pop.* I am so out of my depth here.

I should start at the beginning, learn to walk before I run. Teen Vogue Magazine it is.

The cover boasts an article entitled, *5 Signs You're Ready to Take Your Friendship to the Next Level and How To Do It.*

Okay, so maybe I'm not the only one who needs help figuring this out. Of course, this magazine is directed at twelve- to seventeen-year-olds, but I'll rack it up to just one more thing I have done at the wrong age. And if your average teenager can figure it out, so can I.

I skip the part about how to tell if I'm ready. I have already decided I'm doing this and the last thing I want to do is second guess that decision. No need to add even more insecurities to the mix. So, I dive in.

1. Set the scene. Make it romantic. Lay out a few things to enhance the theme. Think about good lighting. Candles. Twinkle lights. The golden hour right before sunset.

Added Bonus: If you take him to watch the sunset, it will get dark soon after sunset which gives you a lot of privacy to celebrate your new relationship.

2. Cook for him. Get those scents going. There's a reason they say the way to a man's heart is through his stomach.

3. Wear something revealing. No need to dress like a professional dancer, but consider stepping up your usual casual look for something a little more sexy.

4. Complement his body. Every guy wants to think he's attractive. So go ahead and lay it on thick.

5. Go in for the kiss. It's an unmistakable sign that you want this friendship to evolve into something more.

So, maybe I wasn't a total freak for thinking Michael from *Prison Break* had it right after all.

I spend the next four days implementing my master plan.

And trying to force my resolve to not back out of this.

Chapter 27

FINN
JUNE, SENIOR YEAR

We graduate in two days, then we take off for Baja in my truck for four weeks. Together on empty beaches, eating fish straight from the ocean, doing all the things Em has been dreaming of doing for years.

I'm just afraid that I won't be able to stop doing the thing that I have been dreaming about incessantly for the last few months. Being with her. Really, being with her. Being completely with her. Which can never happen.

She convinced me she needed to cook a special dinner for me tonight. She said it was so she could practice cooking Mexican food before we go down to Baja. She somehow got it in her head that if she didn't know how to cook Mexican food before we got to Mexico, we'd starve to death. I don't know why. She has some convoluted explanation that just meant she has been stressing about this for weeks and there'd be no way of appeasing her without letting her just do it. So, I agreed.

But when I came home from my Contemporary Performance final to find my whole dining room decorated like a cantina, complete with bright paper banners on the walls, serapes over the chairs, and a table covered with candles and flowers, it felt like a whole lot more than Em practicing her survival skills.

I swing open the fridge searching for a beer. I can tell I'm gonna need it. I pop the top with the magnet on the side of the fridge before taking a long draw.

"Aww, Finny, no beer tonight. Especially not a San Diego beer. It's our Baja Preview Night. I made margaritas."

It's then that I see what Em is wearing. Which isn't a whole lot. Jean shorts that are way shorter than she usually wears. Much tighter too. A belt that draws your eye to the way those short shorts are slung far too low on her hips. And a tank top so tight, I'm not sure how she's breathing. Maybe it's the long slit right down the front that lets her get any air at all. Though right about now, the way it's put her chest on full display, it's making it hard for me to draw in a full breath.

As I stand here like a fool, gaping at Em, she removes the beer from my hand and holds up a margarita in a fancy blue glass I know she didn't find in my kitchen. "Bienvenido a Baja," she says in a cute accent as she waves her arm toward the rest of my apartment.

There are tiny cacti in pots around the room, a Mexican blanket slung over the back of my couch, and matching pillows slung over the floor. She has gone all out. Which worries me.

"Here. I even got you a shirt." She holds out a white linen button-down. "You'll need it if we go to a fancy restaurant down there."

She tosses the shirt at me. "Put it on."

She spins back around and pours another margarita from the pitcher. Right to the rim.

"Slow down, Em. I'm not even done with my first one," I say as I slip the shirt on.

"Oh yeah, like you ever drink more than one." She shoots me a mischievous grin before taking an enormous gulp. "This one's for me."

"Em," I say in my most disapproving tone.

"Oh, come on. I turn twenty-one in, like, a month. And in two days we'll be in Baja where I could have drank when I was eighteen. Drank? Drunk? Drinked? Imbibed. I could have imbibed years ago. Stop being so uptight, Finny."

Setting the drink on the counter, she swings open the oven and removes a dish. "Now, come on. Let's relax and eat."

I join her at the table where she dishes up what looks like some sort of enchilada casserole. "You know we won't have an oven down in Baja, right?"

"Yeah, I know. I just thought it would be nice. You know, have one last really good Mexican meal before we are only eating over a campfire." She laughs like it makes perfect sense.

As we dig into what she calls Enchilada Pie, which is actually a lot better than it sounds, things go back to normal. We chat and joke and it feels like whatever big scheme Em had planned has been forgotten. Maybe she's gotten better at taking a hint from me and knows when to call it quits.

She drains her drink before sensuously licking the remaining salt from the rim.

Or maybe not.

"Mmmm. Salty. I need more of that."

And I need a whole lot less of that.

When she makes it to the kitchen, she looks at the pitcher like she's reconsidering, and boy, do I hope she does. Her hand rubs back and forth lightly across her bare stomach as she contemplates. The image of my hands across her stomach, arms wrapped around her as I kiss her neck, flies unbidden into my mind and it takes everything I have to not indulge in it.

"Can you do body shots with margaritas? It's salt and lime and margarita, right? Is that how they do it?"

"No." I shake my head. Em and tequila are not mixing well. "It's tequila. But you're not doing body shots, Em. Ever."

"Okay, Finny." She shrugs me off. "Guess it's more margarrrrrita," she says, rolling her r's far too long.

She sloshes her way back to the table, surprisingly able to make it without spilling a drop. "So, are you excited for our trip?" she asks while stirring circles in the few bites left of her enchilada pie.

I spent the last few weeks steeling myself for this trip. Not that I wasn't going to enjoy it, but just making sure I was ready to do the heavy lifting to guarantee our boundaries stayed firmly in place. After tonight, I'm not sure I did enough preparation.

"Oh, darn it," she exclaims. I look up to her rubbing a napkin over her cleavage.

I drag my gaze away as soon as I can muster the strength. "What happened?"

"Of course. I dropped red sauce on my new shirt. I'm gonna have to get this in water as soon as possible. Can I borrow a shirt?"

Now that's the first sensible thing she's suggested tonight. "Yeah. Take whatever you need."

As she disappears into my bedroom to take off her shirt, I try to distract myself by finding all of the little things Em set up for tonight. My record player is spinning with an album I know I don't own but somehow reminds me of every cantina I've ever been in. Beside it, is another of the small cacti that have been scattered around. Alongside the paper flowers in old corona bottles that have been painted bright pink and neon orange are a tiny pair of maracas.

This whole night must have taken her hours to set up, let alone the time it took to dream up. And it's all too much.

Em emerges from my bedroom draped in the Stanford tee she bought for me back in the fall. I thought the wardrobe change would be a good thing, but the way I can't tell if she even has shorts on under that tee has my mind in the gutter again.

She heads toward me and runs a hand along my shoulders as she moves behind me before settling in her chair. She tugs the collar of the burgundy shirt out a bit. "Is this okay?"

Back in the Fall, when she gave me that shirt and told me she'd be moving after graduation, I knew without her having to say it. She wanted me to come with her. To follow her to Palo Alto. To start making life decisions with her in mind. Like we were a couple in love.

It is one thing to spend time with her when we're both here at school, I'd be a fool to give that up. But to purposely decide that the next phase of our life would be done together is too much. There is no way I could anchor myself to her. I'd inevitably drown her.

I saved her the indignity back then of having to ask me and listen to me reject her. Instead, I avoided the whole conversation. Changed the subject. And she never brought it up again.

But this whole night certainly feels like a setup for something just like that. And it's not something I can let happen.

I push my plate away from me. "That was really good, Em. A little spicy, but good." I pull my phone from my pocket and check the time. "I'm pretty beat from finals and all that studying, though. Maybe we should call it a night."

"But, I bought ice cream. Every Mexican meal has to end with ice cream. It will take care of all that spice. I can't leave your tongue all hurty." She jumps up before I have a chance to argue. "Come on," she says, waving me over. "It's a Sundae Bar. You have to make it yourself."

I clear our plates while she sets out the ice cream and more toppings than a frozen yogurt place on steroids. She takes out the whipped cream last. I turn away from her so she cannot read the lascivious thoughts going through my head. She leans up behind me, reaching her arm around me to set it on the counter, and whispers in my ear, "Don't worry, Finny. I remembered the whipped cream."

I grasp the counter with both hands.

Do not move, MacGregor. You move, you're done.

It takes everything in me to not turn around and gather Em to me. To kiss her until we're both drunk off it. To keep her next to me for the rest of time.

Instead, I busy myself with ice cream. Because the faster we get this part over with, the sooner I can convince her to leave. Where she'll be safe from me.

I dish out a minuscule scoop of vanilla into my bowl and take a bite. With my hands full and my mouth busy, I finally dare to turn around leaning back on the counter.

Em is next to me making a sundae worthy of a four-year-old. Three kinds of ice cream. Sprinkles. Syrups of all kinds. M&m's. Chocolate chips. The works. She looks up from her sugar long enough to smile at me with a savagely angelic grin, completely contented. Entirely unaware of the places my mind's been.

And everything is right again. Em is my happy little Em. And I haven't broken the one good thing in my life.

She peers over into my bowl and gives me her cute little puppy dog eyes. "JPV? Really, Finn."

"JPV?" I ask.

"Just. Plain. Vanilla. After I bought all of this for you. That's just not gonna do." She spoons up a huge bite of her concoction and lifts it to me.

I twist my mouth into a threat. No way I'm letting her feed me.

She is undeterred, though.

Until a huge blob of mixed chocolate and caramel syrup loosens itself from her spoon, rolls off my chin, and lands squarely on the white shirt she forced on me earlier.

Before I have a chance to move, she reaches past me, pushing her chest into mine. She retreats with a towel in hand and begins dabbing at the stain. She unbuttons my top shirt button and slips her hand inside to get a better handle on it.

She pulls back to appraise the progress before pressing herself up against me again, this time to wet the towel in the sink behind me. She rubs at my shirt until she's satisfied she has every remnant of chocolate vanquished.

She leaves her palm on my chest and tosses the towel to the counter. Her eyes roam over my face. "Oops. Looks like I missed a spot."

She lifts her hand to my face and slowly swipes her thumb down my cheek letting it drag over the corner of my mouth. And that small touch nearly undoes me.

I try to throttle the intoxicating torrent flowing through me. I dip my chin and turn my head away from hers because if I look for one more second at those full lips of hers, I'll screw everything up in one amazingly beautiful, thoughtless tragedy.

"You know, you've gotten so much bigger since we first met," she lays her other hand on my chest. "Not that you were scrawny or anything, but you've put on so much muscle." She runs her hands down my arms. "I mean look at this. I can't even wrap my hand halfway around your bicep."

I lock my hands against the counter behind me so I won't reach out and touch her, take her.

She slowly runs her hands up my shoulders to my neck, taking her time to feel each inch. "And you have these things. What are these called again?"

She won't take this anywhere. She is way too young to know what she is doing to me. If I just wait her out, she'll stop. "Trapezoids?" I mumble.

She's smiling and babbling like the alcohol has taken away the filter of her thoughts. Which is exactly why I cannot do anything about this.

Nothing.

She giggles. "And your thighs. Damn. They're huge." She lays a hand on my thigh and it lights up my entire body.

Her eyes lift to the hem of my shirt. "But, your abs..."

Good, she is coming back down and ready to insult me, back to the old ways.

She sneaks her hands below my shirt and splays her hands over my stomach. "Your abs have always been perfect." She begins feeling my stomach and everything comes alive.

She traces the lines of my obliques, drifting lower each time, and the way she is eyeing my belt, I have to stop this.

I wrap my hands around her wrists and drag them off of my skin. "Stop."

She takes the restraint as an invitation, stepping closer and leaning in.

Unwillingly, I'm drawn forward, inching closer and closer until I'm hovering just a breath away from her.

But I can't do that. I can't go there with my little Em. It would be so incredibly wrong to take advantage of her like that. Especially when that second drink has hit her way harder than expected.

"Emerson Mahershalalhashbaz Malone," I say in my most disapproving tone. "You have to stop playing this little game of yours."

Her hands drop. Smile dims. Eyes well-up. Until the hurt is

smothered in a layer of rage. She shoves my chest hard, throwing me back against the sink.

"Screw you, Finnegan Ruth MacGregor. See, I can use your full name to make you feel like crap, too. I can't believe I do all of this," she waves her hand to the remnants of what I thought was going to be the perfect night, "and all of this," she drags her hand over her body, "and you'd still rather be with some groupie who can't even be bothered to learn your first name."

She stomps out the front door slamming it behind her.

By the time I shake myself free from my stupor and rush out to the yard, the only thing out there is a burgundy tee in a sad pile on the front lawn. No Em. No chance to fix things. No hope.

I didn't even go for what I wanted this time and I still destroyed us.

She left.

As I survey my empty yard, I'm struck by a singular thought. I finally broke us.

Chapter 28

FINN
PRESENT DAY

When I finally came home late last night from effectively avoiding Em all day, she marched right up to me and demanded I pay off our basketball bet before she leaves. I could tell she wouldn't settle for me trying to worm my way out of it. And honestly, I'm not sure I wanted to. One last dinner with Em all to myself sounded nearly perfect.

But, now that I'm shaving and putting on an actual button-down shirt and messing with my hair for way longer than any self-respecting guy should, I realize that a night out with Em is much more nerve-wracking than it should be.

It's just a meal. One friend paying off a debt. This isn't a date. It's not the start of something. In fact, it's just the opposite. It's the end of a pretty great two weeks, but it's time for Em to go home and start her real life. And time for me to live off of the joy that I've absorbed for the rest of my life.

We will both walk away this time unscathed.

I knock on the doorframe of the finished ohana. Justin finished it yesterday and Em decided to give it a spin by getting ready out there.

"Just a second," Em calls from inside.

I turn to inspect the fine woodworking on the railing, running my hand along the varnished Koa wood.

"Ready?" Em's voice comes from behind me.

"Yep, let's go," I say as I turn.

Em's dark-tanned skin glows from under her delicate white tank top and nearly-white denim skirt. A bright red strap peeks out next to the white tank strap and I have to drag my eyes from the faint red blazing through that tank top before I foolishly let myself wrap my arms around her and never let her leave.

There is no way I'm coming out of this anywhere near unscathed.

Ryder convinced me to take Em to Barometer Soup. He said it with a weird grin so I'm not quite sure what's in store. But as we are seated at a low table with a sunset view of Lanai and see the delight on Em's face, I realize she might be thinking this restaurant with the stunning views and romantic live music playing in the background means this night is more than me paying off a bet, too.

It would be so easy to let her keep thinking that. To slip into a whirlwind of falling in love and overwhelming happiness and dreams of the future.

But then what? What happens to her when I inevitably screw it up? When my selfishness takes over, and she is left having to deal with the fallout. She's already endured the unimaginable agony of losing her perfect husband. I cannot allow my own needs to add even one more ounce of pain to that. I won't.

Needing a minute to think, I stand and make my way to the stairs.

"Where are you going, Finn?" Em asks before I get too far.

"Bathroom." At the bottom of the stairs, I bolt for the boardwalk in front of the restaurant. Needing to burn off some of the anger filling my soul, I take off in a sprint. After a good three hundred meters, I slow to a walk.

The sun brushes up against the ocean. I look back to the restaurant to realize I've left Em sitting alone to watch the sunset. My feet eat up the boardwalk, not wanting to allow Em to see one moment more of it on her own.

I catch her eyeing me as I approach on the walkway below.

By the time I make it upstairs, the sun is only halfway gone. I sit down to a beer and a plate of steak, a pile of mashed potatoes and green beans next to it.

Em looks up at me with a smile, her voice soothing. "Did I get it right?"

Not an ounce of judgment from her. And I'm pretty sure she knows I bolted from the restaurant. Nothing but joy from my Em.

"Perfect, Em. Exactly what I wanted."

I turn my chair to take in the rising swaths of color as the sun continues its voyage. When it finally leaves, I spin my chair back so I can take in a full view of Em. She is even more beautiful in the waning light of the evening, highlighted by the yellow glow of the string lights on the patio above us.

I reach for my beer, but she nabs it before I can, taking a sip. "Poison-free, Finny," she laughs.

"Go out and play hard?" I reply.

"Always. Go big or go home."

I carve up a chunk of my steak. It's the perfect blend of salty and smoky with a caramelized crust. Ryder was right about this place. Some of the best food on the island.

"So, do I still get one question each sunset?" Em asks, her voice a little shaky.

I finish chewing and swallow. "You can have as many questions as you want, babe."

"I'm thinking of maybe coming back. What do you think?"

"Sure. When? Like next summer?" I stuff a bite of mashed potatoes in my mouth.

"Actually, maybe a little sooner. Billie mentioned that I could crash with her. And Harley needs a research assistant, so I was thinking—"

"No," I answer quickly over my sick, beating heart. She can't stay. She has to leave. That's the only way this thing works. It's the only reason I've let myself get so close. Because I know she will be safe from me because she'll leave and go on to meet her real husband. A man who is reliable. Who's trustworthy. One who will never hurt her.

I run my fingers over my cheek where my beard used to be,

but they find no purchase. I have nothing left to tug at. Instead, I scratch my cheek until it's raw.

She's still talking, trying to convince me, but I can't hear it. Can't make sense of it. We had a plan. Two weeks. That was it. She can't just up and change that. It won't work.

I turn my chair back to look at the view, and set my leg up on the other, before dropping it back to the deck.

"Finn? Did you hear me?"

"Huh?" I shift in my seat again. These have to be the most uncomfortable seats ever designed.

I sneak a peek at her. Her chin rests on her palm, fingertips curled into her lips pressing into the soft skin there. She looks off into the distance and I can tell she got my message. She has to leave. It's the only way we both get through this. I only wish she didn't look so frustrated by it.

She shakes her head and picks up a slice of her pizza, letting the motions of eating a meal settle us both down.

We finish without another word. Except for both of us practically shouting our dissent when the waiter suggests dessert. I slide my card to him before he has a chance to flee and never return, leaving us in this awkward limbo perpetually.

We silently stroll along the same boardwalk I fled on earlier. Maybe I should have just left then. Might have avoided this horrible moment.

The crowd is thick and we spend more time avoiding people stopping without warning to take selfies or parents chasing their toddlers along the path. I weave my hand into Em's arm and guide her onto the sand where we can walk undisturbed.

We slow as the sand gets soft. I risk a look her way. She is watching me intently, the frustration from earlier gone now, replaced by curiosity. She bumps my hip with hers and a devilish look breezes over her.

I know that look. The one that all those years ago meant I had to get into the saltwater.

But we're not those same kids. We don't have the same relationship. She doesn't have that power over me anymore.

"Sorry, Em. I didn't bring any trunks." Even though I have

a pair back in the truck, I don't think I could handle seeing her in a bikini right now.

"Oh, please. We both know you wear black boxer briefs that cover way more than those pink Hawaiian-print trunks of yours." I follow her hand as she hooks her finger in my waistband and tugs them away from my skin to confirm.

Unable to look up at her, I mumble, "I'm not going in alone."

She giggles. "Of course not." She starts lifting her tank top.

"Whoa, Em. What are you doing? There are people around." I push at her hands to drop her top.

"You're hilarious, Finn. My bra and undies cover way more than my bathing suit." She isn't wrong. Those bikini bottoms of hers barely leave any bum to the imagination.

She continues inching her shirt over her head, revealing a red bra with barely enough material to keep her covered. She has to know she is killing me with this.

If the smile slowly ticking up her lips is any indication, she knows full well the power she's got over me.

But, we both know this is our last night, this is it. So, what's the harm in a little swim. And she's not the only one who can play this game.

I lock my eyes on her and slowly unbutton my shirt, letting it slip off my arms behind me and fall to the sand. I lift the hem of my undershirt teasing her with the tan abs I have worked my butt off for. Ones I know she loves. Her eyes are glued to my skin as I reveal more and more, inch by tiny inch.

When I slip my shirt over my head, she shakes her head. "Damn, Finny."

Saying my name like that, the one only she gets to use, has me making all sorts of bad decisions. I lower my hands to the top of my jeans and flip the buttons open, keeping my eyes on her. But I can only hold on for so long.

I nearly sprint to the water once they hit the sand. I dive in until I'm chest-deep, hoping the cool water will ease my burden. It does nothing of the sort.

Still on shore, she locks her eyes on mine and takes her time. She slides her feet backward out of her sandals, stepping onto the sand behind them. She tugs at her belt and slowly unhooks the buckle, sliding the whole belt out loop by loop. When it's free of her skirt, she drops it gingerly on the sand beside her sandals.

She rests her fingers on the top of the denim along her hips and slowly runs them toward the front. She flips open the button with a flick, and slowly lowers the zipper.

She spins ninety degrees so she is facing the restaurant we just came from, making sure I get the best view of every move she makes.

She tucks her hands inside the denim along her hips and bends at the waist as she shimmies out of the skirt revealing only a thin layer of red tropical print undies that match the bright red of her lace bra.

I have to lower my mouth below the surface of the water to hide my gaping grin.

She slowly strolls into the water, never taking her eyes off me, until she is mere inches from me.

She wraps her arms around my neck, inching closer.

The water moves behind us from a swell, bumping her up against my chest.

I lay my hands on her hips drawing her a little closer.

She has all the boldness of a woman who knows exactly what she wants and how to get it. I'm so envious of that. Oh, how I want to be able to share everything I am with her. But the last time one of us wanted to push the boundaries of our friendship we spent four long years in darkness. I'm not sure I could do that again.

She hoists herself up onto me, wrapping her legs around my waist, hauling me into her.

I know I'm falling into dangerous territory. My hand catches on her Dexcom sensor on her bum. I look at her eyes to gauge her reaction. "Does that hurt?"

She leans in and whispers in my ear, "Your hands on me, Finnegan Ruth MacGregor, always feel good."

My name, breathed out over her lips like that, is nearly unbearable. I slide my hands lower, supporting the round fullness of her bum.

She withdraws her head from my ear and her gaze falls to my mouth. If she leans in and kisses me, the thin string of restraint I have left will break and I won't be able to stop myself.

Another swell of water hits us, lifting her weight from me and then settling it back down. That motion nearly does me in. I have to look to the horizon to keep myself from taking Em right here in the warm salt water. We are far enough away from the shore that we wouldn't be seen.

The ripples on the surface of the water are reflecting the moonlight in and out of Em's amber eyes, and I know if I look back into them I will be lost forever.

She bites her lower lip and slowly lets it roll back out. My Em is a far cry from the little kid I met in college. She is all woman now. I just don't know if I'm man enough to not destroy her.

I can feel her breath on my neck right before the feel of her soft lips lights up my skin. She kisses her way from my neck to my jaw to my cheek, before pulling back and touching her forehead to mine. "So, maybe I don't leave tomorrow."

Not this again. We agreed. This is our last night. She leaves. "Em," I growl in warning.

"Come on, Finny," she purrs in my ear.

"You can't move here Em," I plead. "You have to go home tomorrow. Go on and live your life how it was meant to be"

"How it was meant to be?" She untangles herself from me and kicks up the volume. "How it was meant to be is long gone. It's long gone twice over. All I have left to do is try to pick up the pieces and make something out of the crap hand that I have been dealt. Try to find some bit of happiness, which I thought, somehow, stupidly, that I could possibly find with you. But I guess not. Cause Finn is incapable of being happy. Right? Anytime happiness comes anywhere near you, you have to destroy it. Isn't that how it is? Shut down. Throw up your walls. Make sure happiness has no chance of ever coming anywhere near you. Well congrats, Finn. You got your way. You destroyed my happiness all over again. Like it wasn't bad enough the first go around."

"We should go." I don't wait for her reaction. I turn and march onto the shore.

Chapter 29

EMERSON
PRESENT DAY

My feet touch the seafloor. Finn doesn't look at me or say another word. No explanation or clue as to why he is so against this. He just turns and marches onto shore.

I silently follow him, gathering my clothes from the sand.

When we get to his truck, he plucks a towel from the bed and tosses it to me. "Don't get the seats wet."

I wrap it around my waist and wrench my tank over my head, not caring if triangular wet spots from my soaking bra show through it immediately.

He turns on the engine and throws it in reverse, putting his arm on the back of my seat as he guides us out of the parking spot.

When he turns back, he pauses as his gaze catches mine. The hardness I saw appear on his face before he hauled me off of him dissolves into the kind, soft Finn I've come to know and love.

He sets the truck in drive and lowers his hand to my knee, rubbing soft circles with his thumb as we coast along the narrow highway beside the shore. If I thought I was confused by a blurry line before, his hand on my knee the whole ride home has completely obliterated any concept of a line even existing.

We pull into the driveway and he kills the engine, yet neither of us makes a move to go inside. His hand is still resting on my knee warming my skin and my heart.

His face tenses.

He clears his throat.

Please, talk to me, Finn.

I know he is bursting at the seams with things he wants to say. But I can't find a way to draw it out of him.

I was so fortunate when I found Timmy. He seemed to have the secret combination to open up my heart and teach me to speak. I thought I would be that person for Finn. I was patiently waiting for him to gain the strength to tell me he loved me. That he couldn't live without me.

He licks his lips.

Lowers his head onto his left hand, tilting it to look at me.

Now, I'm thinking that all those things that he wants to say are not the things that I thought he was feeling. They are not the things I want to hear.

He starts chewing on his lower lip.

Studies my face.

Why do I suddenly feel like that scared little girl again who doesn't know how to share what I'm feeling, to ask for what I want? The little girl who finally got the strength up to try to show him how I felt, to seduce him. The one who got her heart shattered when she finally realized that he would never feel the same way about her.

But that's not me. I'm not that scared little girl anymore. I know how to tell someone how I feel. To ask them for what I want. And I know how to do it well.

"Finn, we are so good together. We always have been. You were the best friend I ever had. And now I know we can be so much more. But, I can't keep riding this blurry line of what we are. I want to stay. To be with you. Really be with you. I love you, Finnegan Ruth MacGregor."

And the moment I say it, his whole face falls.

He looks at the ground.

Shifts in his seat.

And, most importantly, says nothing in return. He looks off in the cold, dark driveway behind me.

When he finally starts to speak, it sounds like he has to think about each and every word. "You... are... very... brave... for saying... what you... are feeling." He shakes his head like he knows he screwed up.

And there's no *but*. There's no, *and I'm feeling*. That's it. Just, *Thanks for sharing*.

And it's then that I know that I will never get more from Finn.

The wind picks up outside the truck and bends the line of banana plants until they are lit up by the solar lighting scattered around the yard. The broad leaves dance in and out of the light.

I'm brave for sharing? Really?

I search Finn's face for any indication he has something more to say. Anything more. But there's nothing. His dark eyes only showing the torturous dullness of disbelief.

How is this happening again? I am so completely different. And I did things so differently. But I ended up in the exact same place.

I can't blame it on my youth or my virginity. Those things have vanished long ago.

For all those years, I thought we didn't work out cause I was so closed off and never let on how I was feeling. I never showed it. I never totally showed him who I was. How could I expect him to fall in love with me if he was never able to fully see me? But for the last two weeks I have said everything I felt. And shown him all the ways I love him. With my looks. With my touch. And now with my words.

And it still isn't enough. I'm not the right girl for him. And maybe he isn't the right guy for me either. I was so completely myself and we are back in the same place we were before I figured out how to do that.

I slide my hand into the door handle and slowly move the lever. The door cracks open with a pop. I look back, one last time, hoping that Finn will give me more than he has. He draws his hand from my knee where it has been since I sat down in this truck with him.

I slide out of the car and slip into the darkness of the yard, wandering under the orchard toward the ohana.

Chapter 30

FINN
PRESENT DAY

Em's face falls.

I knew the second I said it that it was the wrong thing to say. But being that brave, being able to say exactly what she was thinking is something I have longed for my entire life. She just opened her mouth and laid it all out there. Held back nothing. I have no idea how you get to that place. To be able to put words to the swirling thoughts of misery and self-loathing instead of having my mouth sewn shut by the overwhelming hurricane of emotions overpowering my mind.

I knew it was the wrong thing to say. I should have been able to share with her what I have been feeling for her. And the reasons why it can't work between us. But when she's there asking, I can't get it out. Can't find the words to make sense of it all. The only thing I can think is that she has to leave, save herself from me. But even that, I can't convince my mouth to say.

And once again that leaves me alone. In the dark. Knowing that one more time, I have crushed her and caused the exact pain I was trying to save her from.

But at least she can walk away. She is still alive to leave.

I sit in the dark, the passenger door still wide open as she left it when she found enough sense to leave until all the lights have gone out in the main house. I'm in no shape to talk to anyone without destroying any more relationships.

I slip into my room hoping against hope that I'll find her there in my bed, full of the grace it would take to forgive me. And that I could somehow find the words. But they don't come. And she's not there anyway.

It's around three in the morning when I finally give in to the urge to be near her. And since I know there's no way she'd let me in, I choose the next best thing.

I first found the box full of all my Em memories inside of the first house I flipped out here so many years ago. Went to tear down the wall between the kitchen and living room and found the hand-carved box inside. I knew all the stuff I had kept from Em deserved a better home than some dinged-up, cardboard box.

I let my hand slide across the engraving of four Hawaiians paddling a canoe into the sunset. I slide the lock out of the clasp, lift the lid, and am floored by the sight of that smile. The one that always drags out of me a matching smile.

I wonder if I will ever be graced with her presence again. With the friendships she made on this trip, I'm sure she'll be back. I just don't know if I'll have the guts not to flee to the other side of the island when it happens.

I pick a stack of pulpboard coasters from the box and flip through them. I swiped the first one from The Campus Pour the night I realized that Em was only seventeen. I wanted something to remember one of the best nights of my life. That one is worn around the edges. I can't tell you how many nights I spent in bed, flipping it through my fingers wondering about her.

The coaster from Someplace West is pristine, though. I took it from under my beer the first time Em poison-tested my drink and wished me good luck before a gig. By then, I had started a collection of coasters from places that meant something to me.

At the bottom of the pile is the custom coaster Em made to complete the Baja Cantina she set up in my house before I wrecked us the first time. Across the middle is "MacGregor's" in bold white font, and "Mexican Food" below it in a smaller script. Above both is a red chili pepper wearing a striped sombrero on a yellow background.

All these years later, I'm merely repeating the same patterns that drove me to run the first time around. And I prepare myself for more of it. Years of not shaving and hardly speaking. Years of a dark existence without any of the joy I had been trying so hard to stock up on. Another card from Em, one year from now, announcing the death of our friendship, just like last time.

But I suppose that it's better than the card I gave her on graduation day. Or rather, gave her dad, too chicken to even face her.

We had planned on going to graduation like we did everything else. Together. But after I wrecked things days earlier, I knew I couldn't face her. I didn't answer her texts or phone calls. I was a no show to pick her up for the ceremony like we had planned. Didn't answer the door when I knew it was her knocking that morning.

I showed up late to the ceremony after debating with myself if I even wanted to risk seeing her. But graduating was something I earned and I needed to see it through.

When she crossed the stage to receive her diploma, her typical joyous smile wasn't there. Her face was clouded with weariness. A weariness I had put there.

I hung around after the ceremony. It might be the last chance I had to be in her presence, even if it was from across a soccer field. Her parents were taking heaps of pictures of every possible combination of people. The classic grad flanked by her parents. One with the grandparents and a few aunts and uncles I recognized from the many holidays I spent with Em. One with her little brother in the mix. One of just the two kids. The look of adoration on her brother's face. I knew he'd be following in her footsteps very soon.

Em was surrounded by the people she loved. With people who loved her and would only bring more joy to her life. She was capable of sustaining relationships. People didn't leave her. She didn't drive them away.

After four years of being a part of that family, that circle of love, in the end, I was where I belonged. Alone.

Again.

My parents couldn't be bothered to show up. I tried. I invited them at Em's urging. She said no parent wouldn't want a relationship with their kid, but she had no idea what I could destroy. And how I end up driving everyone away.

After torturing myself long enough, I trudged back to my van already packed with all our gear and my clothes. I hadn't found the strength to unpack it now that we wouldn't be going to Baja. In a rush earlier, I parked in the red and was rewarded with one more insult. I yanked the ticket from my windshield.

"Finn," a low voice commanded.

I knew the voice immediately. Em's dad had taken me in four years ago. Given me more care and advice in four years than my own dad had in a lifetime. It sounded like he was ready to dispense more now.

"Sir?" I put out my hand to shake.

His hesitancy was obvious. So, maybe advice wasn't headed my way. More like a sharp rebuke.

But it never came. He shook my hand and waited in silence.

I pulled my hand from his and dug something out of my back pocket. "I was hoping you could give her this." I handed him the card. It had a dolphin on the front. It flopped open because I was too stupid to snag an envelope when I bought it that morning at the grocery store.

He took the card and graciously closed it without reading the short message written inside. "I just have one question, Finn. I don't know what went down between you and my daughter. I do know she is here alone today, struggling to put on a happy face while you show up to graduation, a pretty big day in your life, and you look like hell. Like you've been up all night partying and doing Lord knows what. You can't even bother to shave. Why should I give anything to my daughter that comes from a guy like that?"

"Because, although you're probably right about me, she deserves an explanation."

When I woke up that morning, I had no intention of taking our trip. It wouldn't be the same without Em, and there was no way she'd be joining me after what I did. But, the second I sat down in my van after the ceremony, after seeing her dad, I knew I had to leave. To get as far away as I could. So I took our trip to Baja alone.

I spent nearly six months camping, surfing, and stewing. Down there, I became the man I had always been. Stopped shaving. Stopped talking. I figured it would be easier if people knew right away the kind of man I was. They wouldn't be deceived when they met me. They would know right away that I was not worthy of any sort of relationship. Maybe I should have kept it up when Em first came out to Maui. Could have saved her a heap of pain.

I put the MacGregor's Mexican Food coaster back into my Em box and slide over to my nightstand to retrieve a few more. I put the Barometer Soup coaster I swiped earlier tonight and the one from The Painted Lantern on top of the flyer I pocketed in the Open House we wandered into when Em first got here and close the lid.

When the sun finally shows its face, I'm already at the kitchen island nursing a cup of coffee and a massive headache. Em comes trudging through the door, setting a few bags just inside. Our eyes meet and she stills, studying me with hesitant expectancy.

"Let's do this thing," Indigo's booming voice blasts through the agony.

Em joins Indie and Charlie in a girly group hug.

JJ pulls Indie from the group, wrapping her in his own hug. When she tries to step away, he wraps his arms tighter. "Nope. Not gonna let you get away that easy."

Em shoulders her backpack, waiting restlessly for Indigo.

"I'll be back in three weeks, cuddle bug," Indie laughs. "You can hold out for three weeks, right?"

"If I have to." JJ gives her another hug. "But call me the second you get home."

I watch as the whole scene plays out as if I'm not even here.

Sure, I don't make any attempt at engaging, but no one has even acknowledged that I'm here. Except for Charlie who keeps looking my way, nodding at me to get in there.

"One more group hug," Charlie declares.

Em begrudgingly joins in.

When the farewells are over, Em follows Indigo toward the door. She stops just short of where I'm sitting. Both hands on her backpack strap, she studies her feet, before taking a deep breath in. Her amber eyes soften and, for a moment, the walls fall. "One more time, we're saying goodbye, and I don't get what I need from you."

"What's that?"

Her voice is resigned. "You don't need me."

I need you, Em. Of course, I need you.

You just need someone better than me.

"Okay." She hoists her bag higher. "Guess I'll see you in another ten years."

Two days later and I'm drowning myself in twenty-five-hour workdays. I forgot to go home last night. Fell asleep at my desk. Don't plan on making it home tonight either. Justin and Kate headed home hours ago. They're well accustomed to me being the last one here. Me and Baja, that is.

I stand from my desk stretching my hip flexors. After sleeping at my desk and a going for a punishing run this morning, I was stupid enough to plop back down at my desk all day. Now, I'm paying for it with a body that doesn't want to straighten without some prodding.

I make my way to the workshop attached to my office. I leased this place for that very reason. When all of the administrative work gets to be too much, or talking to people becomes too demanding, I can escape out here and make something with my hands, settle my head.

But, right now, not even ripping down a table with a hand plane is doing anything to settle my head. And if I don't stop soon, I will have taken a six-inch-thick, live-edge slab and completely annihilated it into a pile of shavings.

My phone buzzes with one more text. Ignoring them has done nothing to slow the influx. Maybe it's time to get more aggressive and tell them all to stop texting.

I scroll through a list of texts ranging from inviting me to game night to scolding me for not coming. The last is from Billie.

BILLIE:

Remember when you took over Game Night for me? You said you needed it.

BILLIE:

We need you, too, Finn. And whenever you're ready, we'll be here.

I remember. And I did need it.

Ryder invited me to my first Game Night a few years ago. I thought he was nuts, playing board games as a fully grown adult, but I was new in town and it wasn't like I had a raging social life. If anything, I had spent the previous six months avoiding all contact with other people. But after spending a few weeks at his place to build a fire pit overlooking the ocean, I could manage being around him without too much annoyance. Figured his friends might be just as laid back.

I was right. And the routine of gathering each week welded me to this new group. By the time Billie had split for The Keys and couldn't host, I had become dependent on it. So much so that I began hosting it at my place. But the thought of showing my face around my friends when I hurt Em so badly has me back in full-on avoidance mode.

That was not my plan, to hurt her. It was just supposed to be a temporary thing. A vacation diversion. Before she went back to her real life.

But I can't even do that right.

Chapter 31

EMERSON
PRESENT DAY

I spend the flight home to San Diego in a dazed exasperation, weeping like a child with my head on the tray table until I pass out. When we land, Indigo has to wake me from my stupor. We trudge through the airport as muted alarms sound all around me.

"Em. That's you. You're low," Indigo tries to get me to do something.

I was in such a daze on the plane, I forgot to lower my basal rate for the dreaded Baggage Claim Low. After sitting immobile in my seat for so long, insulin tends to pool in my muscles. When I finally get up to walk to Baggage Claim, all of it drops into my bloodstream at once, instantly bringing on a low every single time. Usually, I lower my basal rate an hour before we land to head this off.

I silence the alarm and keep walking, not caring enough to do anything about the low.

"Em. Sugar." She unzips the small pocket on the side of my backpack and removes an energy gel, shoving it into my hands. "Eat it."

I do.

"And change your pump thingy so you get less insulin

tonight. You sure as hell aren't going to become Dead in Bed on my watch."

It's probably a good idea. I tap on my pump and make the changes.

I survive the night.

Barely.

I wasn't threatened by a low, but an agonizing night that stretched forever before the dawn finally graced me with its presence.

They say everyone falls in love an average of twice and gets their heart broken twice. If that's true, I'm out of great loves and way over on heartbreaks.

You'd think it would get easier each time, grieving the loss of a relationship, but it feels like it just gets worse. Each time, it dredges up pieces of the old wound that I realize I haven't dealt with yet. And those simply serve to magnify my current misery.

With each new souvenir of my previous pains, I solidify the notion that I'm not supposed to have the typical things that other people get. Friends and marriage and kids, a normal life. I am still, and ever will be, a freak.

The light of day does nothing to lessen my heartache, except to add the guilt of not having the strength to get out of bed. At least at night, I can lay here guilt-free.

The day stretches into night which stretches back into day. The only time I leave bed is when my alarms are screaming at me that I'm once again going low and am forced to put food in my belly.

At some point in the endless series of changes from dark to light, there's a knock at my door. Ignoring it only makes it sound off again, louder this time.

I scrape my hair back into a low ponytail as I make my way to the door.

"Sonny, you in there?" Indigo's voice is laced with worry.

No sooner do I pull the door open, than she is wrapping me in a bruising hug. "I'm so glad you're okay." She steps back. "Now, answer your stupid phone."

I don't even know where my phone is. Haven't seen it since I got home. "Sorry, Indie."

I plop down on the couch as she surveys my darkened apartment. Table covered in the remains of the last however many meals I ate there. Apple juice bottles scattered over the room, thrown at the wall once I emptied them in a low daze.

Then she surveys me. Hair a tangled mess from too many days in bed. Still in the same clothes I flew home in days ago.

"Okay. Worse than I thought," she laughs kindheartedly. "Probably time to jump in the shower, don't you think?"

Unable to find the strength to resist, I comply.

The water is warm and washes some of the crust off my misery. I let it run over my body for far too long before getting to the business of washing my hair and body.

After drying off, I toss on a comfy pair of leggings and an extra-soft, baggy shirt with the chemical formula of caffeine on the front.

By the time I make it back to the living room, it is spotless and filled with a cacophony of disembodied voices.

"Oh, good. You almost look human. Now sit," Indigo commands.

I do as I'm told and Indigo holds her phone up in front of us both. I'm greeted by the loving faces I've missed so much since getting home.

"Em, how are you holding up? We were so worried," Charlie says. "Especially when you didn't answer any of our texts."

"I swear I wasn't ignoring any of you. I think I left my phone in my bag when I got home and seriously haven't even thought about it since. I promise I'll plug it in and answer every single text and call." The last thing I want to do is lose any of these amazing women I've come to call my friends.

"So, how are you?" Billie asks.

"Not great." I shrug. "It's been hard. I've been in a really dark place again."

Indigo wraps her arm around me and squeezes. "Don't worry, ladies, I'm here now to pull her out."

"Thanks. It's a million times better seeing all your beautiful faces. I'm so happy to see you guys."

"We love you, Em. And anytime you want to come back out here, you know you always have a home," Charlie reassures me.

"I, for sure, will. Soon, too. I promise. Just need to get back on my feet first. And find a new job," I joke.

Indigo hangs up.

"I'm headed out to start shooting on my next film. You gonna be okay here? Not gonna hop back in that pit?" she asks.

"Yeah. I'll be fine." She doesn't look convinced. "I promise."

"Okay, Harley's home now, and I've instructed her to check in on you every single day. And we both know she's not going to let you sit and mope."

"I'll be lucky to make it out alive of whatever she has planned for me. That one still scares me."

Indie gives me one more big hug before leaving me to my empty apartment. But after seeing my friends again, and fearing the torture Harley is planning on implementing tomorrow morning, I have the will to at least sit in the sun while I eat my lunch.

My body has been craving the Vitamin D, but that doesn't mean my head is out of the depths. I can't stop myself from running over and over that last day with Finn. What I could have done differently.

But I come up empty every time. I wouldn't change a thing. I needed to tell him everything I did. I won't hide myself anymore.

Even when I tried to hide from Finn back in college it didn't work out any better. Finn left then too.

Didn't even say goodbye that time.

We had plans for him to celebrate graduation with my family since his family wouldn't come. And we were going to dinner afterward. Before the ceremony, I couldn't find him anywhere. He wouldn't answer my texts or phone calls. I eventually had to go to the ceremony without him.

As I climbed the steps to receive my diploma, I caught a quick glimpse of him. He was there. Without me. Without a word.

It was the longest ceremony in the history of long graduation ceremonies. I went through the whole thing not knowing if I'd ever be able to fix what I'd done. If we'd ever get back to normal.

On a day that should have been pure joy, I was left a mess of confusion, misery and loneliness. What made it even worse was I had to explain to my parents and brother and aunts and uncles after the ceremony that I didn't know where he was or if he'd be joining us after the ceremony. Over and over and over, I had to admit that I had no idea what I was doing. That the only time I had ever tried to share who I was deep down, I totally messed things up.

I tried my best to keep up the happy face all through lunch, but with his empty chair staring me in the face the whole time, I could only keep it up for so long. I excused myself to get some air.

My dad found me leaning on the railing overlooking the harbor, staring out at the horizon. "Hard day for you, Hon?"

I wanted to lie to him, to reassure him that I was so happy. But I knew it was no use so I just nodded.

"I didn't know if I should give this to you now." He held out a card. "I know it may end up ruining your big day. But from the looks of it, you aren't in a celebratory mood anyway."

I flipped open the card. "You saw him? What did he say? Was he okay? Why didn't he talk to me?"

"He looked pretty bad, Em."

I ran my fingers over the shimmery blue dolphin on the front.

"I'll give you some privacy. Take your time, Hon. It is your day, after all."

With trembling hands, I flipped the card open.

Inside, in Finn's scratchy handwriting, I read, "I have to do this alone. And you're right. I suck. You're dodging a bullet, Em. I'm truly sorry. F."

If I had known then that it would be the last thing I would get from him for years, maybe I wouldn't have torn it to shreds.

Chapter 32

FINN
PRESENT DAY

*A*fter four days sleeping in the workshop, I stagger back home to take a shower. Waiting until mid-morning, I figure the house will be empty and I can clean up in peace. But I can barely make it to the front door before being smacked upside the head with awful memories. Everything in that damned house reminds me of Em now. The way she flirted with JJ during basketball to make me jealous, when she poured her heart out to me about Timmy's death being her fault, when she patched up my hand after I split it wide-open taking out my frustrations with her on a row of bamboo.

I wish she was here now to patch up my heart the same way.

I consider leaving before I even get inside. But the stench of four days in the Maui heat without a shower has me thinking otherwise.

When I make it inside, I find Charlie sitting at the kitchen island. I nod my greeting.

"Good, Finn. Come sit down," she offers.

I shake her off.

"Sit," she commands.

I approach the island, but won't give her the satisfaction of sitting. This is going to be a short conversation if I have anything to do with it.

"We love you, Finn. And we really don't want to go back to the sad and quiet and sullen Finn. Not after we got to meet the real Finn. The happy and chatty and full-of-life Finn. We want him back."

"He's gone," I growl. "We done here?"

She studies me, considering. "Do you really not know?"

"Know what?"

"You ever hear of Gabriel Garcia Marquez?"

"Is that some sort of vegan food?"

"He's the author who wrote, 'I never imagined that curiosity is another mask of love?'"

Is she seriously spitting out random words to confuse me or is my mind so numb I can't make sense of anything?

"It's a quote from him. He was saying that sometimes love might not look like love." She must sense my confusion because she keeps going. "When you fall in love it's not like there's a magical sign that illuminates in your brain flashing *You're in Love, Stupid.*"

"Okay..."

"Do you like to be around her? When something great happens to you, who do you want to tell? When you've had a crappy day, who do you imagine telling? You want to touch her all the time. You never want her to leave you."

She looks at me like I'm supposed to know what all that means.

"You're in love, stupid."

Thank you Captain Obvious.

But that's never been enough.

"Even if I am, it makes no difference," I grumble.

"She loves you, too, you know," she says gently.

I know. And I can't unhear it.

The joy and satisfaction I could hear in her voice when she told me that has been haunting me ever since. I selfishly let her get close enough to think she loves me. Just had to take all the joy I could find. Thought she could handle being close for two weeks without doing any damage to her.

"You know that right? She loves you," Charlie repeats.

And that's about all I can take of this intervention.

Or any future interventions they try to foist on me.

I lumber into my room and stuff handfuls of clothes into my duffel bag. I swipe the picture frame from my nightstand and the Em box from under my bed, tossing them on top.

Back in the kitchen I swipe a six-pack from the fridge and head out.

"House is all yours," I call over my shoulder before slamming the door shut.

With Baja tethered in the back of the truck, it only takes forty-five minutes to drive to the other side of the island. Once again, I'm in a loaded-up truck, fleeing for some other place to be, having burnt down my entire life. No more friends. No life. No Em.

At least this time I have Baja with me.

When I see the water on the other side of the island, it still doesn't feel far enough away. So, once I hit Maalaea Harbor, I head west, hoping to outrun this feeling building in my chest.

How exactly does Charlie know what Em's feeling? Have they been talking all about how I screwed things up? Clearly, I didn't do a good enough job of ending things with her if she's still pining for me.

Maybe I should have told Em about Sophia. Should have told her that first night I saw her again, the first night I met her, instead of trying to get as close as I could without letting her fall for me.

The moment I did, she would have left forever and I wouldn't have screwed up and hurt her all over again. She would have left me just like my parents did when I came whimpering home to tell them about Sophie, looking for some comfort, and instead, ended up with their wrath and what I deserved all along.

An hour later, when I hit the winding roads of the north side, the lower speed limit has me itching to speed up, so I turn around and head back.

Last time I burnt down my life, the only thing I could hold onto, the one place I found any hope was to live out Em's dreams, building a ghost of a life in hopes that she would one day move back into it and bring it alive.

I know that is not a possibility any longer. Not after what I've done. And I've done it twice now. Maybe, the first time she could forgive me, but not twice.

Unfortunately, it's the only direction I can find.

So, I guide my pickup toward the curb in front of 526 Oia'i'o Road.

Chapter 33

EMERSON
PRESENT DAY

*I*t only took me nineteen days this time to pull myself out of the mopey, soul-sucking grief of losing yet another relationship. And, sure, I'm not really over it all, but I have been able to implement the discipline to drag myself out of the pit once again.

With Harley's help of course. She followed Indie's orders and dragged my butt out of the house every day that first week for an early morning swim in the cold Del Mar waters that felt much too cold after being in the warm Maui water. Then she dropped me back home with a list of things to accomplish for the day.

After having spent all my vacation days on the Maui trip with only three days' notice to my boss, and then calling in sick when I got back, my stint as a paint waitress is now officially over. Honestly, I should have quit that job at the paint-your-own-pottery shop the first day I got it. But I needed something to pay my rent, and I was in no mental state after Timmy's death to do any real work.

But this time, I'm going to look for something real. Something permanent. A real career where I can be challenged to use my mind and discover new things. One that uses the education I worked so hard for. I just have no idea what it might be.

The thought of working in research with Harley awakened

something in me that I think I need to pursue. What it will actually end up being, I have no clue, but I head in that direction anyway. You can't steer a stationary ship.

After a week of Harley's training, I now start each morning with a surf. It's been tough but I have promised her and myself that I will get wet every single day. Some days, I can spend a couple of hours out there washing away the pain, some days it's only as long as it takes to get my hair wet. But each day I feel stronger.

And then I spend hours online trying to figure out what career is out there that I can spend the rest of my single life pursuing.

I break from my career research at The Perky Coffee Shop, which has changed its vibe since I was in school here. It has now morphed into a chill workspace with large tables and plenty of power outlets. Gone are the obnoxious signs and cutesy drink names. And they've widened their menu to include a whole host of iced tea flavors. It has become my favorite place to work.

As long as I don't have to sit at the ill-fated table where I tried to ask Finn to move to Palo Alto with me.

I take a break from deciding my future to scroll through the group chat I'm now in with my new besties. At least that's one type of relationship I can maintain.

I scroll past a dim pic of the girls in the ocean with the sun peeking up over the horizon behind them, a video of Billie and Charlie paddling toward each other on SUPs, trying to knock each other off with the pink, cushioned handles of their paddles. Also, I find a story of the sailor Harley has been working with who passed out in the pool because he held his breath for too long. It seems some people have a hard time listening to their bodies and knowing when to quit.

A text from Billie dips down from the top of my screen. But this one is not in the group chat. And that has me a little worried.

BILLIE:

Can you talk?

I click on her face and hit the call button.

She picks up on the first ring. "Em, oh good."

I close my laptop so I can focus. "What's up?"

"We need your help." She sounds distraught and now I'm completely worried.

"What's going on?"

"It's Finn. He's moved out."

"From his compound? There's no way."

"Charlie said he grabbed a bag of clothes and disappeared over a week ago. He won't answer his phone. No one has seen him."

"Sounds about right." I take an absent sip of my tea.

"He hasn't even gone to work, Em. His business partner called the landline here looking for him, saying he was worried because he hasn't heard from him in a week and he isn't answering his cell."

"That's just Finn." Distant, flinching, cowardly Finn.

"Ryder and I had to track him down. JJ had his cop friends look for his truck. He called us when they found him and we followed him. He's been staying at one of his rentals."

"He's fine, Billie. He'll just show up in your life again in a couple of years."

"Em, it's bad. We went in to talk to him. It's like a druggie lives there. The place is totally empty except for a bare mattress in the corner and food wrappers everywhere. Empty beer cans."

"Finn doesn't drink."

"Well, then, Baja has been getting wasted every night."

"Fine. But he's made it clear he wants nothing to do with me."

"Em, I have never seen Finn smile like he did when you were around. And he laughed. Like deep-down belly laughs. He never did that before you came. He isn't letting anyone near him. He has put up so many walls. You're the only one who can get through to him. Please."

"If it will help *you*, Billie, I'll do it. But it won't work."

When I was young, I thought everything was about me. Finn would withdraw and I would assume I had pushed him for something he didn't feel. That I made it awkward.

But now I realize that what other people do, how they behave and react, usually has very little to do with me and so much more to do with the battles they wage in their mind, the sense they've made of the bad things that have happened to them.

And once I took myself out of the picture, emotionally disengaged from it, I could see it for what it was, and I could respond instead of just reacting. And that alone has made my life so much easier to live.

I can see Finn's pattern—engage and flinch, and then his defenses go up. It's his thing. Always has been. I run through situation after situation from our college days and realize the story I told myself about it, the sense I made just wasn't accurate. It wasn't true.

I only wish I had learned that earlier. It would have saved me so much heartache and so much lost time. But I know it now. And I won't react to his reaction. I will respond to the reality of the situation. And, right now, the situation is that Finn's hurting and isolating himself. And he's alone.

So, no matter how hard he tries to push me away, I won't let him. If he doesn't want romance with me that's fine. But, he is my friend. And I don't let friends suffer alone.

My rental car doesn't have a GPS, so I'm left to glance at Google Maps on my phone as I try to find the address Billie gave me. I spot Finn's truck in a driveway a few houses ahead and pull my small sedan to the curb in front of the place.

It's *my* house.

Well, my *dream* house at least.

Wait. My house is one of his rentals?

Did he buy this before or after I said it was my dream home and I would one day own it?

And this is the house he's been hiding out in? Finn's not suffering. He's living the dream. If this place were mine, I wouldn't leave either.

I knock on the front door, the force of my knuckles pushing the door open, and it's a completely different house inside than I remember. When we saw it last time, it was formally staged and beautiful, but far too fancy for my taste. Now, it's completely empty which lets the woodwork shine. And it lets my imagination run even more wild.

I have never stepped into a house that felt more like home than this one. Like someone seized my dream home from my imagination and set it down in reality.

Billie did say it was one of Finn's rentals and it feels vacant, so, knowing I'm not breaking into someone's home, I make my way toward the back of the house to the open living room and kitchen overlooking the pool and ocean beyond it. Cupboards hang open and empty in the kitchen, but the appliances still shine.

What is going on? Finn drives me away and then buys my home and hides out in it?

My hands fly to my head as I spin around trying to make sense of the riot battling in my head. I can't figure out if I want to hit him or hug him.

Until my gaze settles on the living room which looks like the nauseating aftermath of a frat party. A bare mattress in the far corner of the room floats in an ocean of food wrappers and beer cans. A few dirty shirts lay crumpled next to a pair of work boots covered in multiple layers of different construction materials.

Next to the mattress is Baja's bed, thankfully free from any of the repellent clutter. If I didn't recognize his dog bed, I would swear some drugged-out hobo was squatting in my dream home.

If Finn really hasn't left this place in a week, he's in here somewhere. It's time to get this over with. I walk back to the garage and swing the door open. Empty. Backing out, I open the door to my office. Okay, so not actually *my* office, but...

The entire far wall of the office is under construction. Around a bay window with a bench seat below, two open columns run from the floor to the ceiling. No shelves yet, or face plates, but I can see where the bookshelves are going. And they're beautiful. Lucky girl who gets this room.

As I pull the door closed again, I freeze, my hand still on the doorknob.

Because Finnegan Ruth MacGregor is perched on an upturned five-gallon bucket in the corner of the room, staring at me, silently wiping his hands on a shop rag. "What are *you* doing here?" he sneers.

"What? What am *I* doing here? What are *you* doing here?" I look around us, "In *this* house?" Tears gather in my eyes as I point out the door to the wreckage he has been living in. "Like this?"

I finally let my gaze settle on Finn. His beard is growing back, making the darkness beneath his eyes even more pronounced. The misery that radiates off of him has me reconsidering my ability to do anything for him.

The sound of "A Piece of You" sneaks into my consciousness. I played it on repeat when I first heard it. It was the only thing that could make any sense of the whole Finn debacle the first time around. I search the room for the source to make sure I haven't conjured it up out of thin air. My gaze settles on a small speaker in the far corner of the room.

I listen for a moment as I realize that it's Finn's voice I hear, not Amos Whitlock who recorded it years ago.

I glance back to Finn for an explanation, but he won't meet my eyes. He simply keeps rubbing his hands with that filthy rag.

Knowing I can always out-wait Finn, I silently linger. He'll come around. He always does. And if not, I'll just drag his sorry butt out to the pool. It may not be cold water, but any water is better than nothing.

He finally looks up at me and shakes his head before standing and flipping his makeshift seat over and slamming it on the floor.

"You don't like how I'm living, you're free to leave," he snarls and lumbers toward the door.

I slam the door behind me and stand my ground in front of it. I'm doing this. I have to ask the hard questions no matter how much I don't want to hear the answers. If he's going to leave me again, I have to know why this time. I refuse to be left wondering again for years. "You're not running away Finn. Not this time."

Chapter 34

FINN
PRESENT DAY

ove, Em," I growl, inching toward her as she backs up into the door.

"No," she says, standing her ground.

It was finished. I sent her back home to Del Mar so she could move on and find the man she deserves. The one who can love her like she deserves. And give her the life she wants without screwing it all up.

I finished it and now *she's* the one screwing it up again.

She spreads her arms across the door as if it could be enough to stop me from jerking it open.

I move forward. She wouldn't actually try to stop me from leaving. I grasp the doorknob, gauging how much force it would take to open the barrier to my escape without doing any harm to Em.

She lays her hand on mine, gently. She's not fighting me for control or trying to stop me. Her touch is tender and amazingly sure.

My gaze drops to the point of contact as my anger ebbs and I give in to the magnetic draw that Em has always possessed.

She lifts her other hand to my chest, her gaze roaming over my face and searching my eyes. Something in her touch soothes me and draws me closer. My fingers ache to reach out and touch her.

Her look is so galvanizing it sends a tremor through me. Belief and love and hope pour out of her. But it's all false. Her belief and hope are but a vapor. She has no idea what kind of reckless beast she is believing in.

"Finny." She rises on her toes, closing the distance between us, but the touch of her hand is suddenly unbearable.

"Dammit, Em." I spin around and stomp to the far end of the room which is not nearly far enough away. I swear if the window was any bigger I'd be climbing out of it right now.

I have to make her understand, make her go. She deserves that. "You are supposed to be gone."

The shock of my words hit her full force. "Supposed to?" she spits out. "According to who? You?"

"You went home. Now, you just need to leave me alone. You need to move on, Em."

Propelled by fury, she steps towards me. "I'm not going anywhere until you explain yourself."

I grind my hands back and forth over my short hair, before flinging them outwards and shrugging. "What do you want me to say?"

"I want you to tell me why we had a perfect two weeks and without any warning you send me away like I mean nothing to you. How you can kiss me like you did and still tell me that you don't want something more. Why you think you can tell me that I can't stay here, like you own the whole damned island or something. I want you to tell me why every time we get close you flinch. That's what I want you to say."

There it is again. She's said it before. Flinching. And for some reason that word stirs in me a deep rage. Maybe because it feels too close to the truth. Maybe because I hate that she has had to endure it enough times that she has a nickname for my destructive actions. Either way, I have no explanation for it. She's asking for the Whys that I have no idea how to explain.

"I don't *flinch*," I say, the word laced with disgust.

She gives me a sidelong glance of utter disbelief. "You do it all the time. Any time we cross some imaginary line that only you know the location of, you run." She shakes her head in frustration. "You did it before graduation, too. I tried to kiss you and you freaked out and bailed. You vanished, Finn. Without a word. Left me alone on graduation day, a day when I was supposed to be celebrating and happy, you left me pretending not to cry through the whole ceremony and then I had to make up excuses to my family when they asked where you were. You didn't even say goodbye, Finn."

She takes a step toward me. "Did you know that I dropped out of Stanford three days into my program because of you? The only thing I have ever quit in my life, because I couldn't pull myself together enough to step outside my apartment without bawling. I had the opportunity of a lifetime and I threw it away because my best friend in the world couldn't figure out how to tell me that I was expendable to him. So, he took the coward's way out and disappeared."

That hits like an ax to the rotted wood of my heart. I knew how leaving Em completely destroyed me, but I had somehow convinced myself that she would bounce back easily. I shouldn't be that hard to get over.

A demoralizing wave washes over me as I consider the pain I caused her.

"So, why, Finn? I deserve to know. Why do you always flinch?" Her accusing voice stabs the air.

"You *deserve* someone perfect," I thunder. "And I can't be that for you."

My angry retort hardens her features.

"Why not?" she demands.

"That's not me. Why don't you get that? It's been eight years and you still don't get that."

Her expression is ferocious. "No. I don't get it, Finn. I have never gotten it. You left without ever explaining any of it. Did you leave because I wanted more? Did you leave because I wasn't enough for you? Because I was that easily replaced? Why?"

She stares unwaveringly, expecting me to be able to come up with an answer that will make her feel better. I don't have one.

"You owe me that, Finn."

"I don't owe you anything!"

The outcry unleashes something fierce in her. She draws in a big breath to scream back at me, but it doesn't come. Instead, she deflates, nearly collapsing onto the bench seat below the window. She sits and doesn't answer back. She doesn't yell. Doesn't scream. Her face is full of strength, shining with a steadfast and serene peace that is so out of place.

She looks to the spot next to her and waits, challenging me.

I resist as long as I can, but I'm drawn to her side. I stagger toward her and sit beside her. "I can't promise never to hurt you," I admit, hoping that she understands all of what that means.

"No one can, Finn. Love is risk. I can pretty much guarantee that we'll both hurt each other. The only thing I can ask is that you'll always tell me the truth."

I lean my arms onto my knees trying like hell to keep my world from crashing in on me. "I know you think you know me, Em. But you don't. If you knew the truth, you'd have been out of here years ago."

She lays her hand on my arm, tilting her head, curiosity written all over her trusting face. "Then tell me. I want to know all of you, Finny."

Fine. I'll pull out the big guns. I'll just tell her the truth about what I did to Sophia. Then I can guarantee that Em will never want to see me again and she can move on and find a real man to love until her dying days.

My failures that day were enough to drive Sophia away. And her parents.

It was enough to drive away my own parents.

If that's what it takes to get Em to leave and find her happiness, I'll tell her.

And so I do.

A few moments into my story, I look up, searching for the moment she fully understands and bolts. It didn't take much more than a few sentences for my mom. My dad held out for a few more details, but he still bailed.

But Em's still looking at me with such compassion. I lower my head into my hands, suddenly not wanting to see the moment when the truth will drive away that look of belief and love from her face, and I lay it all out for her in excruciating detail.

She lays her hand on my head, running it through my hair softly. When I'm done telling the story, she just sits there.

Sits there and doesn't leave.

She laces her fingers into mine, her face brimming with compassion, shining with calm understanding.

Why isn't she screaming and throwing things or running off?

I lean my head against the window behind me. I want to ask if she heard me. If she understands I was the reason Sophia's dead. That I was too busy drinking and ignoring her to listen. That my reckless behavior cost her her life, but I don't have it in me to say it.

"So, you've been holding this in since Nashville?" she asks.

"Yeah," I mutter. "It's why I left. Why I came to UCSD."

She nods her head slowly, taking it all in. Maybe her anger is slowly brewing and will spill over soon.

"You've never told anyone?" she presses.

I scrub my free hand over my short hair. "Told my parents and they kicked me out. It's why they haven't talked to me since."

"Hmm," she nods and considers. Probably considering doing the same thing. It's a viable option for her. But one I finally wish she won't take.

Her face is a series of emotions—I can see her going through them one after the next— but I can't make sense of any of them. Anger, disappointment, disgust. Those I could recognize, but I don't see any of those.

Could there be a way that she now knows what kind of monster I am and still doesn't leave? Could she still believe in me? Love me?

I scan her face for any sign that my confession was too much for her. That it was enough to drive her away, but the only thing I see is concern.

Em can tell I have nothing left in me. That was more than I've ever said to anyone, so she doesn't ask more of me. Instead, she sits with me until the guilt and pain start to wash away.

She gives my hand a squeeze. "You okay?" she asks sweetly.

I give her a limp smile. "I'm fine."

"I know you are, Finny, but I've got you anyway."

The amount of comfort that brings to me is unreal and I just hope it gave her a fraction of that solace every time I said the same thing to her.

Her smile vanishes, wiped away by confusion.

And then she is standing. She runs her hand along the bookshelf behind her, considering. "I have just one more question."

Not sure I have any more words left in me, I still acquiesce. "Go for it."

"Did you actually buy this house?"

Ha. That's what she wants to know? I tell her my darkest secret and she isn't running for the hills or begging for some explanation to make it okay. She wants to know about the house. So, I tell her. At this moment, I'd give her anything she asked for. "I had to make sure it would be ready for you the moment you decided you wanted it."

"Really?"

"I've been living out your dreams for years. Why stop now?"

Her face scrunches up in confusion.

With the truth of Sophia's story no longer pinning my tongue, everything else comes rushing out. "You remember the bookshelves with the ladder in The Library Coffeehouse?"

She steps back to take in the frames where those bookshelves will go any day now.

I stand and point to the far corner of the room where the brass rail for the ladder is lying.

"I told you that I'd have a set just like it when I grew up," she recalls wistfully.

"Living in a tent on Maui, growing an orchard, bartering with our neighbors?"

"You agreed only if you could grow bananas." She looks at me with amused wonder.

I smile, thinking back on how that one decision finally gave me a direction in life, made it possible to begin moving forward.

I'm really starting to enjoy this memory game.

"You remember my duplex in La Jolla? How we were walking back from a surf nearby our freshman year and you said you had to see inside them one day to see how they possibly fit a whole house inside a building so small?"

She nods slowly as if the pieces are starting to fit together to build an actual picture.

I shrug, owning the conclusion she's starting to come to. "I've been living out your dreams ever since I met you."

"But didn't you have any dreams of your own?"

"Besides growing bananas, you mean?" I joke, trying to lighten the weight of what I've just dropped on her.

"Yeah. Besides bananas." Delight flickers in her eyes when they meet mine.

"Just one. But I couldn't let myself even dream it."

"What was it?"

I push my hands deep into my pockets. "That first day you wandered into my show in PB in that neon yellow tank top that showed off your tan arms, I knew. The look of disappointment on your face when I said I was going to play a Buffett cover, and the grin that spread over your beautiful lips when you realized I wasn't going to play one of his notoriously bad bar songs. Watching you mouth every word to that song made me want to write songs that you would one day learn every word of."

"That's a great dream, Finn."

She has no idea that wasn't my dream. "From that day on, the only dream I had, besides the bananas," I concede.

"Of course," she agrees.

"Was to love you and make sure you had everything you always wanted."

Her brows draw together in an agonizingly confused expression. "There's no way." She starts to pace. "There's no way," she repeats.

I lean back against the bookshelf and give her the space to process it.

She pauses and faces me. "From the first day you met me?"

I nod.

She makes it to the far wall before spinning to face me again. "Even when you told me over and over that we could only be friends?"

I nod again.

She resumes her pacing, looking for her next rebuttal. "Even when you dated those other girls right in front of my face?"

"Then, too," I admit, with not a little guilt brewing.

Her pacing slows and her voice softens. "Even when you disappeared to Baja and left me alone and crying?"

"Especially then."

She chews on her bottom lip. "Why didn't you ever tell me?"

Not that I didn't come close to telling her too many times to count. "Because if I told you how I actually felt it would be like promising you a relationship I couldn't fulfill."

She seems to like that answer. "And now?" she asks hopefully.

I've always loved her. That's never been in question. I always thought that once she knew what kind of a man I was, she'd run like all the rest of them. But she knows. She knows and she's not running. And what's more, she doesn't seem to love me any less.

Now that she knows, maybe it's time I let *her* decide if I'm good enough for her. She said that love is risk. At least now she knows the risk she's taking.

"Now?" I close the distance between us.

She inhales sharply.

"Now, maybe I start living out *my* dreams." I lift my hand, stopping before I touch her face, trying to overcome years of built-in hesitancy as an invisible web of attraction builds between us. It is too easy to get lost in the way she is looking at me.

My hand skims her face, her skin soft under my fingers. I rub my thumb over her cheek as her smile grows wider. I don't want to rush this moment.

I slide my fingertips into her hair and she leans her cheek into my hand, as completely spellbound by this moment as I am. This is so much better than the thousands of times I have imagined this.

Her face screams kiss me. The idea of her eagerness encouraging me, I kiss her, lingering, savoring every moment of it. The touch of her lips sends a shock wave through my entire body.

I deepen the kiss, her lips more tantalizing than I care to admit. She wraps her hands in my shirt drawing me closer. The implication sends waves of excitement through me.

Our first kiss was a kiss of passion, years of holding back everything in me that wanted to do that. This kiss is rational. This is a kiss of promise. A promise that I plan on spending every day of the rest of my life fulfilling.

Raising my mouth from hers, I gaze into her eyes and wrap my arms tighter around her waist, having no desire to back out of her embrace.

She settles back into the feel of my arms around her. "What took you so long, Finny?"

I'm suddenly overwhelmed by regret that I let so many years go by without doing that. Without pursuing her. So many years assuming that she couldn't handle the risk of loving me back. That I wouldn't be the right man for her.

She must see the weight of that thought on my face because she says, "Don't make me throw you in the water, Frowny Finn."

Getting in the pool with her right now sounds like Heaven. I pull her to me and kiss her again. When I can finally extricate myself from her lips, I hold her hand and walk her toward the backyard.

It's not long before I'm hit with a thought. "First, I want to show you something."

Instead of the backyard, I draw her into the kitchen and stand triumphantly in front of the oven. "So, I wasn't sure if turquoise is the same thing as aqua. Viking only had it in turquoise, but the sales guy assured me it's the same thing. And no other company around makes it in any color even close. But, if it's not right, I'll get one custom-made."

Her face scrunches up like I'm speaking a foreign language. So I let the oven speak for itself. Pulling the door open, my gaze locks on her eyes, and I swear they get misty.

She looks back and forth between me and the oven. "You didn't."

"You know I go all out for the girl I love."

Her smile grows wider, brows raised, daring me to say it again.

"I love you, Em. Always have."

She pushes me up against the island and kisses me, the touch of her lips a delicious sensation. Her hands slip under my shirt and dance along my abs. She pulls back and says, "Still perfect."

I study her eyes, waiting to hear her say the words I cringed at the last time I heard them from her. She can tell what I'm waiting for and takes her time getting there, loving the torture she is exacting.

"I really love…" She moves her hands to my chest, "that oven."

"Oh, yeah?" I tickle her until she is a wriggling heap in my arms and she gives. She spins back around in my arms. "Okay, okay. I love you, too, Finn."

I kiss her again. As I pull away, she sways towards me, like she never wants to stop.

"Who needs to be thrown in the cold water now?" I say. Then I demand she gets in our new pool. Or, maybe, push her into our new pool is more accurate.

After she has exacted her revenge on me by wrapping her arms around me and pushing me underwater, then punishing me with slow, drugging kisses, we hang off the infinity edge taking in the neverending view of the Pacific.

Filled with an amazing sense of completeness, my heart bursting with love and acceptance, I realize that I have every dream I never knew I dreamed. Living in Maui. Having a terrific network of incredible friends. Writing and recording my own music again.

And, for the first time ever, I get to be fully myself with Em. No more hiding or flinching. Just me and Em forever.

Chapter 35

EMERSON
THREE MONTHS LATER

I always thought I would never get more from Finn, that he would always be holding back. But ever since he spilled his guts about Sophie, he has been a non-stop chatter box and I am here for it.

There's nothing completely shocking that he shares, but the gritty details of his past, his childhood, his dreams for our future have filled in the gaps that I've always wondered about. And hearing stories of our shared history from his point of view is making me love him more and more each day.

Finn let me move into my dream home while he moved back to his compound temporarily. He figured I'd do a better job of nesting in and decorating the place anyways.

He comes over every chance he has to get our food forest started. He says most trees will need a few years before they are producing and he wants to get a head start on it.

The hammock overlooking the water is already hung up and a whole row of banana plants along the east side of the property are starting to take root. We're going to have so many bananas, we're going to be making banana bread for all our friends every day until we're ninety.

Since Billie has been overwhelmed planning her and Ryder's

wedding, she's had to relegate her Game Night hostess duties to me. Charlie has been puking her guts out well past her first trimester, so I offered to host Game Night while she busies herself with building a new human and trying to balance the roller coaster blood sugars that come with ever changing hormone levels.

I've decided on a little game of guys versus girls friendship trivia. See who's been paying more attention around here.

Last week, I handed out a survey of personal questions and then used the most hilarious or revealing ones for the game. I think reading through these surveys has been the absolute best part of prepping for this whole night.

I also love that as host, I didn't have to answer any of these questions. Especially the job title question. Unemployed isn't all that impressive. Though that won't be for long. Harley has agreed to let me run her next study while she is back in Coronado trying to make a deadline for the write up on her last study.

I may have even stalked everyone on Facebook and printed out some horrible junior high photos when I could find them to put up around the backyard on huge stands. That is if I could find them. Harley is like a ghost online.

I've broken the game into three rounds. For the first round, each team will match trivia to a member of the opposite team. I reveal each one on the board and the team has to pick who it's referring to and put a magnet with that person's name on it under the trivia fact.

The hardest part was trying to figure out which of these amazing answers to include in each round. Except for when I read Harley's answer to the category, worst childhood memory. That one was easy to skip. With an answer like, "THAT'S CLASSIFIED!!!," I knew I'd pass on that one.

"You guys ready?" I ask, trying to wrangle the herd.

I pull back the top sheet of poster board to reveal the answers—Insane Izzy, The Rationalizer, Spielberg, Little Miss Pigtails—and the boys make quick work of it. They divide up the girl's magnets, Ryder taking Billie, Greyson taking Charlie, JJ taking Indigo and Finn being left with Harley. Hopefully with the process of elimination he won't miss too many.

"Let's take a look." I put on my best Game Show Host voice to reveal the answers. "Insane Izzy is Billie. Charlie, The Rationalizer. Indigo is Spielberg, and Harley, do you want to explain Little Miss Pigtails?"

"That's okay," she says sharply.

"Alright then. Five points for the guys, including the bonus point for getting all four correct. Now, for the girls this time. If each guy could only eat food that starts with one letter, what letter would it be? Your options are B, G, L, and M."

"What?" Charlie asks.

"How are we possibly supposed to know this?" Billie complains. "They get nicknames half of which were given to us by the boys and we get a completely cryptic question?"

"Okay, fine. How about I tell you what examples they gave for each. But I won't give you G. You're gonna have to give me the G reason for the bonus point."

They seem to be pacified by this. I don't really want a revolt on my first Game Night as host. "B is for bars, burritos, beer and bacon."

"That's got to be JJ. That man can eat bacon like it's going out of style." Indigo hops up and slaps JJ's name plate under B.

"M is for meat. And Maybe Butter."

"Butter starts with a B," Charlie protests.

"Maybe butter starts with an M. Don't shoot the messenger. I'm just reading what I got from your answer sheets."

"Meat and butter is definitely Finn." Harley staggers to the front and lays his name under M.

"L is for large fries, large protein shake, large pizza."

"Grey," the girls shout in unison.

"Which leaves G. Ladies, what does G stand for for the bonus point?" I prompt.

The girls huddle up and discuss before breaking and shouting, "Gluten-free."

"Why yes, the correct answer for Ryder is gluten-free. Gluten-free pizza, gluten-free beer, and gluten-free snacks is the answer he gave."

"Yes. Please, Ryder, stick with the gluten-free," Finn teases gently. "No one wants to witness what happens when you decide to go gluten bomb again."

"Okay. Match the life-philosophy Jimmy Buffet quotes to their owners." I pull back the next sheet of poster paper and watch as the girls discuss. As they do, I catch Finn's eye.

He mouths, "You're doing great," and gives me a thumbs up. I may have been a bit nervous about stepping into this role. Finn told me I couldn't do much worse than he did when he tried to take over, and, for some reason, it helped.

Billie is certain about Ryder's quote. "The ocean is my only medication." But they are debating "If the phone doesn't ring, it's me," and "Live a lie and you will live to regret it. That's what living is to me." Charlie pegs that one as Greyson's, leaving the other one to Finn. No one is debating even for a second which one is JJ's—"Wrinkles will only go where the smiles have been."

Greyson jokes, "He should have gone with 'If we couldn't laugh we would all go insane.'"

"Or 'I'm growing older, but not up,'" Finn adds.

"I've got a Caribbean Soul, I can barely control," Ryder suggests.

"Yeah, yeah. I get it. I'm an out of control child. Ha ha."

We finish up a few more questions before we get to round two, the speed round. Both teams are tied at fourteen points each.

"This one's a game of whodunit. Whichever team answers each question correctly first gets the point. The answer can be anyone," I explain. "But if it's you, you lose thirty-seven points for giving it away. Are you ready?"

A crop of yeah's and ready's ring out.

"Okay. Question one. Who— "

"Anyone!!" JJ shouts.

"What?" Finn demands.

"She said the answer could be 'anyone'" he explains.

Everyone moans at his lame joke. Indigo playfully smacks him in the shoulder.

"Let's try this again. Who's worst habit is nibbling the salt off of pretzel sticks before eating them but only on long car trips?"

The girls look at each other hoping they can guess. The boys do the same. "Ryder?" Greyson guesses.

"Wrong. Girls, a guess."

"JJ?" Indigo tries.

"The correct answer is Harley," I say.

"Huh. Never would have known it," Charlie says.

No one is surprised about not knowing a Harley question. It seems that all of the stumpers have been Harley's answers tonight. The truth is, I've learned more about Harley through this questionnaire than I ever have directly from her.

"Question two. Who's least favorite noise is endless small talk?"

"Finn!" both teams shout together.

"We got that first," JJ pleads. "We did."

"Great. Then JJ, you were wrong first. The correct answer is Charlie. Finn's least favorite sound is a mosquito buzzing."

"The score is still tied at fourteen. Question three. Whose imaginary friend was a mermaid named Daryl with the power to summon gentle sea breezes or fireflies to comfort them?"

"Don't you mean merman?" Greyson asks.

I just shrug trying not to give away the answer.

"Indigo?" Charlie asks. "Daryl, like Daryl Hannah from Splash? That feels like an Indigo thing."

"And the girls pull ahead with fifteen. Very nice."

"I saw Splash when I was eight and fell in love with movies right then and there," Indie fills us in.

"Last question before the bonus round. Who collects beer coasters?"

Greyson nearly spits out a mouthful of beer trying to get the answer out first. "Finn. I saw him grab one just last night."

"Correct. Now for the bonus round. Ten points for the first team to find one and bring it back. Go."

Everyone jumps up and scrambles like some giant hide-and-seek game. It shouldn't take too long to find one since I've hidden a few dozen around the house earlier.

JJ comes out first, but Harley chases him down, tripping him in the process. I hope it was accidental but with her seriousness, who knows? She's followed closely behind by Ryder and Greyson each carrying their own coasters. The girls fill in behind them with their own.

"Looks like the girls pulled ahead. Final question of the night. One hundred points to the team that can figure out the story behind the coasters you now all hold in your hands. Finn, you clearly can't help."

I catch Finn's eye. He is grinning from ear to ear. He makes his way to stand behind me and wraps his arms around me. I turn over my shoulder to give him a quick kiss before watching for anyone to make sense of the custom coasters I had made.

The MacGregor's is written across the middle in white font on a red background just below a surfing taco. Beneath both is the date June 24.

While they're huddled in teams, I reach into my pocket and pull out the ring I've been hiding all night and slide it onto my ring finger.

The girls all break from their huddle and sprint to wrap me in a group hug.

JJ shouts, "They're cheating."

"No, JJ. They're congratulating her," Greyson tries to explain.

"Congratulating her for what?"

Ryder holds up the coaster and points to it. "It's a Save the Date, JJ."

"Save the what?"

Finn takes pity on him and just comes out with it. "We're getting married, JJ."

"I guess that makes me the last man standing. Indie, Harley, either of you want to put me out of my misery and become my wife?"

They look at each other and say together, "Pass."

JJ puts his hand on his heart as if he was truly in pain and says, "So harsh. How will I ever recover?"

Finn wraps his arms around me even tighter and I am finally home. Here, in Finn's arms, in my dream home with my dream guy, surrounded with dream friends.

Maybe I am not the total freak I have always thought. Maybe

I do get to have those same milestones that everyone else gets. I just had to get to them through a different, more turbulent route.

In the end, the way I got here only makes it that much more sweet.

THE END

When your best friend becomes the biggest 'what if' of your life.

Charlie Sands has one rule: don't fall for Greyson Steele. Ever. For the past twelve years, their friendship has been her safe haven—witty banter, midnight runs, and unspoken rules that keep her heart in check. But when a summer of career sabotage, meddling roommates, and a few too many margaritas throws them together in new and uncomfortable ways, Charlie's not sure she can play it cool anymore.

Greyson has rules of his own, and at the top of the list? Protect Charlie. From the workplace bros who undermine her brilliance, from every surf dude who doesn't deserve her attention, and maybe, just maybe, from him. But the more time he spends in her orbit, the harder it gets to ignore the truth: he might be breaking his own rule.

Set against the sun-kissed beaches of Southern California, California Promises is a witty, heartwarming closed-door romance filled with razor-sharp dialogue, irresistible chemistry, and the kind of friendship that dares to become something more.

Pick up or download your copy today!
ErinSpineto.com
Sea Peptide Publishing

Nothing says romance like salty air, stolen glances... and awkward self-defense lessons.

Billie Styles lives life at full speed—surfing waves, chasing sharks, and sketching rainbow street art across Maui. But even adventure-packed days and laughter-filled nights can't stop her past from catching up. Stuck in Lahaina on a day she'd rather forget, Billie finds herself aboard Ryder Jax's fishing boat, where his easy charm and saltwater wisdom make the ocean feel like home again.

From self-defense lessons to sunset swims, Ryder's steady presence keeps pulling Billie closer, no matter how hard she fights it. In a world full of laughter, adventure, and one unforgettable Hawaiian summer, Billie's biggest risk isn't facing sharks—it's letting her heart finally take the plunge.

Set against the lush backdrop of Maui, Anything, Anytime, Anywhere is a swoon-worthy closed-door romance brimming with heart, healing, and the courage to start over. So, pour yourself a cool drink, put up your feet, and start your journey with Billie and Ryder.

Pick up or download your copy today!
ErinSpineto.com
SEA PEPTIDE PUBLISHING

High seas, low blood sugars, and a journey that redefines resilience.

When Erin Spineto was diagnosed with type 1 diabetes, she refused to let it define her life—or her dreams. Armed with determination, a trusty insulin pump, and a rebellious streak, she set out to do something extraordinary: sail solo through the Florida Keys.

Islands and Insulin is a witty, heartwarming memoir of one woman's journey to reclaim her adventurous spirit while managing a chronic illness. From juggling blood sugar calculations on a sailboat to discovering the true meaning of resilience, Erin's story is a blend of humor, raw honesty, and pure inspiration.

Whether you've ever felt boxed in by life's challenges or simply love tales of personal triumph, Islands and Insulin will leave you laughing, crying, and ready to tackle whatever life throws your way—one wave at a time.

Pick up or download your copy today!
ErinSpineto.com
SEA PEPTIDE PUBLISHING

About The Author

*E*rin Spineto started her writing journey in 2011 with Islands and Insulin, her memoir of sailing solo 100 miles down the Florida Keys with type 1 diabetes back in a time when doctors were foolish enough to recommend against this kind of wild adventure with diabetes.

She followed it up a few years later with Adventure On, a nonfiction book on using adventure to increase motivation to take care of chronic conditions like diabetes. Since then she has moved on to fiction and is currently working on Warrior Women, a four-book angsty RomCom series full of female surfers who happen to have diabetes and other autoimmune issues.

Erin's journey with autoimmune conditions started in 1996 with type 1 diabetes. She added hyperthyroidism to the mix in 2007, and has rounded out her collection with a little Anti-Synthetase Syndrome, which she thinks is so appropriately abbreviated ASS. Not letting anything slow her down, Erin is also a long-distance endurance adventurer and autoimmune advocate who uses stories to encourage others with chronic illness to go big.

Erin started surfing at age five when she stood up on her boogie board and realized waves were so much more fun to ride standing up. Since then she has had a love affair with empty beaches, warm water, and a post-surf lunch of fish tacos and Diet Dr Pepper (though she's had to give that up to fight the ASS) eaten on a patio in the sun with her own real life hero, Tony, and their two surfing teenagers.

You can learn more at SeaPeptide.com.